The Diamond Caper

A Crystal O'Mally Mystery – Book 1

By Leah Pugh

Mystic Mustangs Publishing

Acknowledgments

Thank You, God, for giving me the creative imagination to write this novel. Will Your wonders never cease?

Mom and Dad, thank you for allowing me stay up late and work on my mystery... even when I needed to work on history.

A warm thank you to my sister, Grace, for drawing such an awesome cover for the back of the book and the diamond on Crystal's notepad on the front cover. I really adore the look.

Thank you, Stephanie Mathis, for sending a synopsis of my book to Mystic Mustangs Publishing.

Thank you to both, Ms. Linda, for teaching me proper placement for the comma and Ms. Candace, for helping me with manuscript formatting... even though my major is English Lit.

Thank you to everyone who helped make my dream a reality. It really means a lot to me.

Prologue

"Are you there, Morgan?"

"I'm here, Boss." Morgan's eyes glittered eerily in the moonlight as he turned to face the man behind him.

There was an agitated pause. "Well? It's been all of five months, and I'm just now hearing from you? A man can't wait forever you know!"

"Hold your horses." Morgan lifted his pointed chin and smiled arrogantly. "I got it."

"You mean you've got it with you?" Boss' voice went up at least two octaves with excitement.

"No, I mean I got everything under control."

"You sang the same tune four months ago," Boss snarled. "And, you still don't have it with you."

"I seriously have things under control, this time." Morgan's tone changed to a gentler one, not wanting to arouse Boss' anger further. "I can get it to you within the next two weeks."

A skeptical look found its way onto Boss' face. "Are you sure?"

"Positive."

Boss' face relaxed. "Good job, man."

Morgan suddenly smirked. "I have some other news I know will catch your interest." He paused dramatically, before continuing. "I've found Crest."

"What?" The word exploded from the other man's mouth.

"Hush!" Morgan peered anxiously around the ally in case someone had heard them. "Yeah, I found the dude in this little poke of a town. It took me a really long time before I recognized him. He's changed quite a bit since we last saw him. I'm surprised he decided to settle down in the very place you wanted to send him, years ago. He was so against the idea, then. I wonder what made him change his mind?"

Boss stroked his chin thoughtfully, before smiling meanly. "We can use him for our cause."

Morgan laughed softly. "You bet we can!"

"Are you sure you'll be able to pull this off without anyone spoiling our plans?"

"Pfft!" Morgan rolled his eyes in disgust. "C'mon, the people in this town aren't *that* determined to get their stuff back when someone takes it from them."

Chapter I

Gone!

"Give me my book back before I pummel you!" I pinned my eight-year-old sister to the floor. Actually, she's more of a pain in the caboose, than a sister. She squirmed as I tried to grab my book out of her chubby hands. I'd been wrestling with her for nearly five minutes, trying to get my beloved novel back, and I was more than ready to turn her into a throw rug. "If you don't want a flat nose, you'd better let go of my book," I warned her.

"Play dolls with me and I'll give you your stupid book back," Emerald retorted, twisting to the left to evade my grasp.

Emerald, we call her Emma for short, is obsessed with dolls. All she ever does anymore is play with the darn things. Sometimes I wish she *were* a doll. That way, I wouldn't have to put up with her babyish antics and childish hissy fits. I sat up a little and dropped all of my ninety-eight pounds on her stomach as hard as I could.

"Pu-oh," she groaned, as the air whooshed out of her body.

Ha-ha! Triumphant at last! I managed to get my book out of her clutches, and tore like a maniac for the tree house outside.

I knew Emma would be on her feet in an instant, more than ready to grab my book from me. I reached the rope ladder and scrambled up it faster than a monkey climbing a tree. Just as I finished pulling the rope ladder up, Emma arrived at the base of the tree. She reminded me of a wolf cornering its prey. Her rusty red hair looked like a rooster's comb from where I was perched. Her emerald green eyes, which were the source of her name, snapped angrily up at me. "Crystal Elizabeth O'Mally, let me up there right now, or else I'll get you in trouble!" she shrilled.

Lord have mercy. She has the biggest set of lungs ever known to mankind, and could put the wildest and noisiest banshee in all of Ireland to shame. I poked my head out of the window. "Baloney. Like I'm going to fall for it." I pulled my head in, plopped on the floor, and opened my book.

I'd been reading a good mystery novel when Emma had so rudely interrupted me, five minutes ago. Without taking my eyes off the page, I fumbled around for the bowl of candy I kept in the tree house for just such an occasion. I found some and munched on the soft chocolate, as the detective and his chief assistant started to discuss the information they'd just been given. "Quit discussing and just go investigate!" I cried, spitting chocolate on the page.

"Yow! What the heck?" Something hard walloped me right across the noggin. I flipped to the left and saw Emma standing at the window with a long, stout stick in her hand. "Why'd you hit me?" I almost asked how she got up here without the ladder, but then I remembered how well she could climb... and this tree was a piece of cake.

"Let me in," she ordered.

"No. Let me finish reading."

"You're always reading and never playing with me."

"Not true. I play baseball and Clue with you. I'm not always reading."

"But we always play what *you* want to play and never what *I* want to play," she whined.

What my sister said was partially true. I avoided playing with those dolls as much as I could... especially after the humiliation I received at my last birthday party.

Emma had been pleading with me to play her stupid imaginary games with her. I had agreed to play dolls with her, on one condition... if she got me a fashion doll for my birthday. And, it couldn't be just any fashion doll. No, it had to look *just* like my favorite female detective from the mystery novels I was always reading.

Well, at my birthday party a few weeks later, I had all my friends there, and I got the biggest humiliation ever! I was unwrapping the present from Emma, when I noticed a doll's face underneath the wrapping. Before I could stop her, Emma reached over and yanked a big chunk of wrapping paper off my present.

My face heated up so fast, I was surprised the doll didn't melt. I could hear my friends trying to hide their giggles. A fashion doll made up to look like my hero stared back at me with unblinking eyes. The doll had obviously been taken out of the package and put back in. Her straw blond hair was cut in the 1920's bob. She was wearing a flapper outfit and she even had a tiny magnifying glass taped to her hand.

What fifteen-year-old gets a fashion doll for her birthday? Unfortunately, I was unlucky enough to get one. Emma crowed right in front of my guests, and reminded me of my agreement to play dolls with her when I got one who looked like my hero. *Where was a toilet plunger when you needed one?*

"Can't you let me read in peace? Puh-leeze," I begged.

"You play with me or I'll tell Mama I saw you talking to Officer Snout, yesterday," Emma challenged.

My heart jumped into my throat. The last thing on this earth that needed to happen was for Mom to know I'd disobeyed her.

Going to the police station without permission from the parents was not only frowned upon by my mother, it was usually followed with a swift and unforgettable punishment. I tried to make it look like Emma's threat didn't affect me, as I shot back, "Oh yeah? Then, I'll tell her how you took ten cookies out of the cookie jar and ate them in your room." Another no-no in the house.

The threat helped me to get the upper hand. Emma's eyes took on the puppy look and she tried to look angelic. "Could you please just play with me, Crystal? I don't like playing by myself."

I quietly blew out a frustrated breath, knowing the only way I was going to get any peace was if I promised to play with her. "Fine, I'll play with you." You'd of thought I just handed her a lottery ticket and told her she'd won, with how her face brightened up like a 100-watt light bulb.

"Really and for truly?" she squealed.

"Really and for truly." I sighed.

"Pinky promise." She crooked her little finger.

I groaned. If there was anything more childish in this world than playing with dolls, it was pinky promises. I crooked my pinky with her and gave it a half-hearted wiggle. "Pinky promise."

"Thank you, Crystal! I'll love you forever and ever," she vowed, shimmying down the tree.

"Until the next time I refuse to play dolls with you," I muttered under my breath, watching her ponytail bob up and down as she ran for the house.

The Diamond Caper

* * * *

"Hey, Crystal, how's it going?" Detective Stan Snout gave me a toothy grin.

"Ah, nothing much." I shifted my backpack from one arm to the next. "Any new mind boggling cases come up, yet?"

"Let me see." He began flipping through a stack of papers sitting on his desk.

I nibbled on my fingernail while waiting for him to find something. *Oh please, find something worthwhile. Please, please, please,* I silently begged. *Please God.* I wanted to be a detective so bad, it almost hurt. I adored Carolyn Keene's mystery stories, and figured if her main character could start being a detective at eighteen, then I could start three years younger.

So far, there'd been nothing really big happening in the tiny town of Alamo, Texas. The only thing this town's known for is the eighteen-carat diamond sitting on display in the Alamo museum in town. It's the biggest diamond for miles around, and people come from as far away as Houston to see it. You'd think with at least a hundred or more tourists coming in and out of Alamo, there'd be plenty of crimes to keep trainees like me busy. *Not!*

"Mrs. Peters lost her cat, and Tony's Auto Repair Store is offering a fifty-dollar reward for finding the vandal who scribbled all over the front window of his shop. Nothing else." Officer Snout pushed the stack aside.

My shoulders slumped in dejection. Was anything exciting *ever* going to happen in this sleepy little town? *No way.*

As if he read my thoughts, Officer Snout gave me an encouraging wink with one of his odd green eyes. I thought of sandwich pickles whenever I looked at those eyes of his. "Don't worry, hon, you'll get your chance one day."

I bit back an urge to snort in disgust. Officer Snout was trying to be helpful and I was grateful for it. He and his wife Terra, who worked for my dad, had lived in Alamo for about seven years. They had managed to establish themselves as well-dignified town members in the short time they'd been here.

"Why, I can remember the very first time I was a detective. I was in a small, one-horse town in Georgia." He shook his head. "I was there for almost three months, before I got my first case… and then, it happened."

I wasn't ready for one of Officer Snout's three-hour tales. He could talk the ear off a blue-nosed mule in no time. I tried to appear interested as I studied the diplomas behind his head. I noticed one of the diplomas bore the name, 'Harvard University'. I silently vowed to save up my money and go there when I was older. Unable to stand the story any longer, I politely thanked Officer Snout for his help and turned to leave. I wasn't watching where I was going and bumped nose first into Todd Russell, the police station janitor.

"Oh, excuse me." He stepped back.

I rubbed my smarting nose and skirted around the man. His olive green eyes, sandy hair, and missing side tooth, made me edgy. *Okay, so maybe it wasn't the missing tooth which made me edgy.* There was something weird about him, and it made me want to stay as far away from him as possible. Maybe it was the fact he mostly kept to himself, and no one knew anything about him, except for two facts… one, he was married, and two, he worked at the police station. "Good day, Mr. Russell."

"Good afternoon, Miss O'Mally." He held the door open for me. "Tell your dad I said thank you for the sapphire. I gave it to my wife as a birthday present."

Both Officer Snout and Mr. Russell had wanted this rare Aurora sapphire stone for their wives. Officer Snout had noticed it the day Dad first put it on display in the store. Mr. Russell not only noticed it about a day later, but he was the one who came in with the money first and purchased it. Officer Snout did come to buy it a day after Mr. Russell bought it, and the detective discovered much to his dismay, it had been sold. He was pretty sore about it for a while, because Terra had fallen in love with it the first day she saw it, however, Mr. Russell got to it first. Being a sport, Officer Snout put the past behind him, and was polite to Mr. Russell, once more.

"Yes, sir, I will." I scooted passed him and hurried down the hall.

Once outside, I adjusted my backpack to where it was more comfortable on my back before heading down the asphalt to my dad's store. Cars zoomed passed me as I jogged down the sidewalk and opened the door. A bell jingled musically above me as I entered the shop. Once inside I stopped, closed my eyes, and inhaled deeply. I loved how my dad's jewelry store smelled of lemons from the freshly polished wood.

"Top of the afternoon, Crystal," Dad called to me from behind his position at the counter. "How's me little detective?"

"Hey, Dad." I grinned as I went to join him behind the counter. Dad is positive I'm going to make the greatest detective in the world. If only I'm given a chance to prove myself, maybe my dream could finally come true. "I'm still waiting for something to come my way."

"Just keep lookin', lass," he said in his slight Irish accent, and winked at me.

Granda was from Ireland, and Dad had never really lost his accent even though he was born in America. I liked his lilting accent. "Need any help today?"

"Would you like to help Terra arrange the rin' display?"

I let my pack thump onto the oak floor, and moved to the center of the room where Terra was putting up a new ring display. "Hiya, Terra."

She smiled at me, pushing her coke bottle glasses further up the bridge of her pug nose. "Good afternoon, Miss Crystal. Would you like to start helping me out by putting these amethyst rings in order?"

"Yes, ma'am." I began putting the rings in their proper slots according to their size. Dad had been a jeweler for as long as I could remember.

"So, you want to be a detective instead of a jewelry store owner like your dad, eh?" Terra asked, looking at me through her thick lenses.

"Yeah. I mean, no offense, I like jewelry and everything. I just find solving mysteries more entertaining, as well as more up my alley."

"Maybe you can solve the mystery of Todd Russell."

I was instantly on the alert. My notepad was in my backpack, but being a good detective, I always carried a mental notepad around with me. "Why? What's wrong with him?"

"Oh, I don't know… and you didn't hear this from me." Her tone turned low and I had to bend down a little to hear what she was saying. "Now, don't quote me on this, but Stan told me Russell was in jail once for thievery. He said Russell stole over ten thousand dollars from a men's clothing store, and also robbed a woman of all her jewelry."

"Wait, wouldn't he have gone to like federal prison or something? Wouldn't he have been locked away for a really, really long time? Like eons? Or would he get life?"

"No, you get life if you murder someone. Stan told me the store turned softhearted on him, as did the lady victim, because Russell claimed he stole the money to help pay his wife's medical bills. They didn't press for the justice they deserved."

"What's wrong with his wife?"

Terra shrugged. "I don't know. The few times I've seen her, she's looked as healthy as the next horse."

"Looks can be deceiving. I would like to meet her someday. Perhaps, we can pay her a visit."

"I see your mouths movin', but why aren't your fingers doin' the same?" Dad called from across the room.

"Sorry, Dad." I resumed my work, my mind working a million times faster than my fingers. *Mr. Russell, jailed for embezzlement?* Or thievery, but embezzlement sounded more detective like, as well as grown up. *And his wife?* I'd only seen her a handful of times in the single year the Russells had lived in Alamo. She did look a little sick to me, but any good detective knew a person could use makeup to make them look however they wanted.

"How about some candy?" Terra reached into her pocket and pulled out two small packs of crunchy chocolate. She snuck a look at my dad whose back was to us, and then handed one of the packs to me.

I have braces and need to watch what kind of candy I can eat, however, I know crunchy chocolates are on the 'okie-dokie' list. I finished slipping a ring into its proper slot, and then eagerly snatched the candy. "Thanks, Terra. You're awesome!"

She grinned sheepishly. "Just being me."

"And *you*, are awesome." I popped some of the pill-sized goodness into my mouth. "Oh, yeah. Dad?" I called to him. "Mr. Russell says thanks for the sapphire. You know, the one he bought for his wife a few months ago."

"He's already thanked me at least a million times." Dad chuckled.

"You mean the sapphire your dad was selling, a while back?" Terra asked.

I nodded, my mouth full of chocolate.

"It was very lovely, and I must admit to being a little bummed not getting it. If Mrs. Russell's happy, then I'm glad she got it... though, I do wish Stan would just let it go."

"What do you mean?"

"I mean he's still throwing a fit about it, seven months later. Saying how I should have gotten it, and not some woman no one knows anything about." She shook her head. "I wish he'd just forgive and forget."

Why was Officer Snout still holding it against Mr. Russell for beating him to the sapphire? It didn't make sense. I saw him shake the janitor's hand and wish him luck with his wife's present. The detective was even wearing a smile on his face when he did it. However, I did notice a look of skepticism on Mr. Russell's face as he reluctantly thanked Officer Snout for his compliments. *What had been up with that?* I'd wondered then, and I still wondered now.

The door opened and the bell jingled merrily. A cowboy stepped in wearing a denim jacket, blue jeans, black boots and a white cowboy hat. He removed his sunglasses and looked around. Dad went over to help him while Terra and I finished working on the display.

Much to my surprise, the man didn't buy anything. He just seemed to be asking Dad a lot of questions. Dad, in turn, did a lot of pointing out the window, as if he was giving the man directions. The man tipped his hat to Dad and left.

"Who was he and what'd he want?" I looked at Dad.

"He said his name was Joshua Lesler, and he was lookin' for some land to buy. Apparently he's a rancher and wants to build a ranch out here," Dad replied.

"Why'd he come to you and ask where the land is? You don't sell land."

"He's new in town and obviously got a little lost."

Odd, a newcomer would come to the jewelry store and ask directions. Usually they go somewhere else, I thought. My mind was in a whirl two hours later, as I watched Dad lock the store.

A warm March wind blew across the open plain and I lifted my face to let the wind brush over me. My brick red curls bounced around my face like slinkies, and I tried in vain to brush them behind my ear. I watched the white, neon lights shaped in the words 'Brian's Treasures' blink, and then go off.

"Ready to go home, lass?" Dad pocketed the keys to the

shop.

"See you tomorrow, girl." Terra gave me a loving squeeze, then nodded in farewell to Dad.

"Dad, what do you know about Mr. Russell?" I blurted out as soon as she was gone.

"Very little, I'm afraid. It seems no one knows a whole lot about him."

"Why do you think he takes great pains to keep himself such a loner?" Hermit sounded like a more apt description for the man. I could almost see him eating stale bread, drinking water out of a medieval silver goblet, and doing whatever else hermits do.

"It all has to do with choice, Crystal. God didn't make people to be lonely. They, as human bein's, choose to do it." Dad stopped in front of the Santa Anna Museum. "I want to speak to Mr. Wington, before we go home. See if he still wants me to polish the diamond. Speakin' of jewels…" He looked at me. "A certain 'jewel's' birthday is comin' up, very soon." He lovingly tweaked my ear. "What do you want for your birthday, honey?"

My birthday's on April 30th. I had no idea what I wanted, at the moment. "I'll think about it and let you know," I promised.

"All right. You have a few weeks to decide."

I followed Dad through the glass double doors and into a hallway containing things pertaining to the Alamo… the fort, not the town. Such as a six by eight portrait of Davy Crocket, a sword Santa Anna had supposedly used in the infamous Alamo battle, and an old-fashioned rifle resting on the wall.

My footsteps echoed weirdly on the spit and polish marble

floor in which I could see my reflection. I nodded to the security guards, who smiled back at me. Since it was five minutes to closing time, there weren't a lot of people there.

While Dad went straight to the door marked 'Alexander Wington, Manager', I went to stand behind the thick, red velvet rope and stare at the diamond imprisoned in the glass case. It was the size of a small boulder and had never been under a jeweler's laser. At first glance, the precious stone looked just like any other misshapen, glittery rock shaped object... almost like a larger version of the crystal rocks people buy at lawn and garden places. The only way people knew it was the famous Alamo diamond, was because of the sign right next to the display case.

According to legend, the artifact had been dug up about fifty-five years ago, by some old man who was trying to bring prospecting back into style... complete with the tobacco spitting and panning. He wasn't very successful, until one day he was trying to dig a garden next to his house and unearthed the diamond... so the legend goes. If the story really was true, why didn't they name the museum after the guy and have his picture next to the diamond, with a sign reading, 'This is the dude who found this hunk of money in his backyard'?

An odd feeling crept over me, like I could sense someone was watching me. Turning one hundred and eighty degrees, I scanned the room. There were only two other people in here with me. One was a tall man wearing ranch hand clothes, and the other was a woman wearing tight fitting shorts with a baggy, brown leather jacket. If they were the only ones in here with me, why was I feeling like a vampire was hiding in the shadows waiting to get me?

Wait! I thought I saw something move toward the artificial tree, just beyond the marble pillar at the back of the room. Squinting, I began walking toward the tree. *Yes! I did see something... or was it someone?* I made out the form of a man crouching and staring back at me, but when I blinked, he was gone. Puzzled, I ran the remaining ten feet and pushed the tree away from the wall. There was no one there. *I'm sure I saw something there. My eyes must have been playing tricks on me.*

Shaking my head and feeling disgusted with myself for letting my imagination get the best of me, I walked back to the diamond display. As I moved a little closer to the case, I noticed three teenagers standing on the other side of the glass, staring at the diamond. They were also nudging one another and pointing to the rock.

A boy with shaggy, black hair reached out and started to touch the glass. His buddy, who was wearing a crystal earring in his left ear, caught sight of me. He elbowed his friend, and jerked his head in my direction. Shaggy Hair stared at me all startled like for a few seconds, before giving me a flirtatious grin. "Don't worry. I was only going to touch the glass," he informed me.

"Uh-huh. Well, just make sure you brought your own glass cleaner with you, 'cause the guards would have made you clean your prints off," I replied.

The boy let out a noise and I couldn't tell if it was a laugh or a bark. "Oh, really, little girl?"

I automatically stood up as straight as I could. I'm five foot four and hate being called 'little girl'. The third person in the group, a girl who was shorter than me and wearing spiked, orange hair, looked me over. "You're the O'Mally girl, aren't you? The one whose dad owns the jewelry store in town?" Her voice was low and rough.

"Yes, I am," I said proudly.

She smirked. "Do you still think if I get my nose pierced, my brains are going to fall out?"

I immediately felt my face heat up with embarrassment. There was only one person in the universe who would say those kinds of things... *Emma*.

The teens hooted and hollered at me. I could see one of the museum employees coming toward us, to either tell the punks to pipe down or throw them out on their backsides. I personally preferred door number two.

I forced myself to smile. "Well, it really all depends."

"On what?"

"If you've even got anything in there, to begin with."

This time it was *her* face that turned a bright red, and her two friends laughed at her. The employee came over just then, and asked them politely to leave. The girl turned livid eyes on me. I wrinkled my nose when I saw her eyes were rimmed with too much mascara. "Just wait, I'll get you! You'll be sorry, fence face," she hissed.

I bit my tongue to stop myself from calling her a nasty name. I'm really sensitive about my braces. I made myself grin, trying to make it look like her comment didn't bother me, at all.

The guards started turning off the lights and dimming others, as a warning to lingering sightseers it was closing time. Dad came out of the office with Mr.Wington behind him. The man reminded me of a walking pork barrel. He's short, kind of fat, and has as much hair on his head as the lid of a barrel. In other words, he's bald.

"Crystal, nice to see you." He shook my hand. "I was just telling your father to come tomorrow morning, thirty minutes before the museum opens, and take the diamond to the store and clean it." He turned to Dad and lowered his voice, but since the room was empty, it still carried a little. "I'll have a security guard go with you when you take it to your store. He won't be wearing his uniform, so as not to cause suspicion."

"All righty, then. It'll be just fine, it will." Dad nodded.

I saw movement out of the corner of my eye, and saw Orange Hair still standing in the doorway. We made eye contact and she stuck her tongue out at me. *Oh, grow up!* I rolled my eyes, in disgust. A guard motioned for her to move along, and she obeyed.

Out of the corner of my eye, I saw something slinking toward the exit. I turned my head as far as it would go, and made out the outline of a man in the dim light over the entryway. He looked like he had shoulder length hair and a weird looking hat on his head. He turned and looked at me, but I couldn't be sure, for in the next instant he was gone. I decided against telling anyone what I'd seen, because I didn't want them to think I was going crazy or anything. I didn't think about the teenagers either, as Dad and I walked home.

As soon as we entered the house, we were hit by a torpedo. Really, it was Emma, but she threw herself at Dad with just about as much force as a torpedo. "Bring anything home for me?" she chirped, nuzzling his cheek.

"Not tonight, me little star." He set her on the floor, just as

Mom came to greet us.

"I don't see my diamond with you," she teased him, standing on tiptoe to kiss him. Mom's all of about five foot two, red hair, soft nutmeg eyes and tan skin.

Dad's hair is almost straw blond, and he has moss green eyes and fair skin. "She'll be comin' tomorrow, she will. Mr.Wington will have me brin' it to the shop. I'll clean it there, and then take it back."

"Dad, may I go with you tomorrow before school?" I asked.

"Me, too," Emma piped up. "It wouldn't be fair if just Crystal went, would it, Daddy?"

I groaned. *Please say no, Mom and Dad. Please say no.* They're obviously not mind readers, because they said yes. I wrinkled my nose at my little sister and she merely tossed her hair over her shoulder. "How soon 'til supper?" I changed the subject.

"In about a half an hour," Mom replied.

"Good, then Crystal can play with me. Remember, you promised." Emma planted her hands on her hips and stared up at me.

"Maybe later." I started to move passed her.

"Mom will find out," Emma started to say.

"I have to put my things in my room, and then I'll meet you in yours. Deal?" I cut her off.

"Deal." She gave me a haughty, triumphant smile before waltzing off to her room.

"I'll find out about what?" Mom turned to me.

"Oh, nothing of importance." I gave her a quick peck on the

cheek before bolting to my room. I dropped my pack in the closet, picked up my fashion doll... *excuse me, the embarrassing piece of plastic...* and went to Emma's room. *Sheesh!* I thought, as I lowered myself onto the ugly brown carpet. *The things I do just to keep my sister's mouth shut.*

* * * *

"Don't be gettin' too far ahead now, Emma," Dad called after her as she skipped down the sidewalk.

"We should have brought Mayo's leash with us," I said. Mayo was our little Irish terrier. She was two when we got her, and lived with us for seven years before a car hit her. She'd earned her name because she was the exact color of mayonnaise. I still kept her leash in my room for sentimental reasons. Now, I think I've found another use for it... tying it around Emma's neck so we can keep her close by.

"Crystal, are you bein' nice?" Dad reproved me.

"No, sir," I muttered. "But it's true."

"Oh, come now, girl. We're all overly active at one age or another. Emma's overly active stage just so happens to be right now, it does."

"Unfortunately." We stopped at a crosswalk, waiting for our turn to cross the street.

"Well, good morning, Brian."

I looked over my shoulder to see Mr. Russell standing behind us. He was carrying a rather large black bag he kept close to his side.

"Good morning, sir," I said politely, edging away from him a little.

"How you doin', Todd?" Dad shook Mr. Russell's hand.

"I see you've brought your beautiful girls with you." Mr. Russell smiled at us.

For once, Emma was totally still. She stared up at him with her big eyes, and stuck close to Dad. She didn't greet him in her usual cheery way. Instead, she stared at him like a child would stare at a dog, trying to make up their mind whether or not the animal's going to bite them. "Hello," she whispered.

"Quite the shy one." He reached out as if to ruffle Emma's hair and she quickly drew back. A hurt look came over his face, and he let his hand fall to his side.

The light gave us the okay to cross. Emma held tightly onto Dad's hand as we crossed the street. I couldn't help but feel a little jumpy with Mr. Russell only three feet behind me. Once we reached the opposite sidewalk, he bid us good day and disappeared into the morning fog in the direction of the police station.

"Emerald Grace O'Mally." Dad frowned at her. "You weren't nice to Mr. Russell."

"He's a bad guy, Daddy," she said. "He stole lots and lots of money. He was probably gonna' steal me, too!"

"Who told you he's a thief?"

"Mrs. Tellers."

I snorted a laugh and had to turn it into a cough. Mrs. Tellers was the town gossip. She did a way better job of informing people on the happenings around Alamo, than the local newspaper. Dad obviously knew I was trying not to laugh, and shot me 'The Look'. I ducked my head and stared at the pavement.

"Listen, Emma, don't go around talkin' bad about people unless you know it to be true." Dad got on eye level with her. "How would you like it if someone started sayin' thin's about you and they weren't true?"

She stared at her sparkly pink tennis shoes, and muttered, "I 'pose I wouldn't like it."

"I'm sure Mr. Russell doesn't like bein' talked bad about, either."

"Yes, sir."

"Good girl." He ruffled her hair and stood up to his full six feet. "I'm goin' inside to speak with Mr. Wington. Wait here and don't go wanderin' off into the car park."

"Yes, sir." We chorused.

Dad mounted the stone steps two at a time and knocked on the door, since it was before museum hours. The door opened and he disappeared inside. There wasn't much to do except sit on the steps and wait. Emma sat down and rested her chin on her hand, while I sat down and let my arms rest on my knees.

A few people were out at seven thirty in the morning, including Mr. Graceland, the grocer, Papaw Greg, the newspaper editor, (everyone in town calls him Papaw), Miss Gopher, owner of the local Gopher's Hole, (a popular after school hangout for the kids), Ms. Prool, the bank teller, and a few of our school-mates.

Another person we saw was Officer Snout. "Well, well, well. Will I have to write you up for being tardy?" he teased us, as he came over.

"No, sir. School doesn't start for 'nother hour," Emma informed him.

"*Half* an hour," I corrected her. I turned to the detective. "School starts at eight o' clock sharp."

"Are you ladies waiting for the bus to arrive?"

"No, we're waiting for Daddy to come out. He went inside to get the diamond," Emma announced.

"He's not stealing it, is he?"

"Daddy never steals!" Emma cried indignantly. "He's being trusted with it 'cause he's gonna' clean it."

"I forgot he's the town jeweler. Tell him I said to make sure he doesn't break it, or else he'll have to pay for it."

I thought I saw a funny look come across Officer Snout's face… like a look of annoyance, and yet, fear at the same time… but the next instant, he was smiling. *What was it with my eyes, lately?*

Emma's eyes grew big as saucers. "Gosh, I'll be sure to tell him, Officer Snout."

"Reminds me of the time I was in Nashville with Terra." His eyes took on a faraway look.

"I hope you remembered to bring along enough snacks to last awhile," Emma grumbled quietly, as Officer Snout plunged into a story of days gone by.

I silently agreed with her. It didn't take much to get the man started on his tales. Ten minutes later, he finished his story and our ears were hurting.

"You ladies have a nice day." He tipped his hat to his us and was getting ready to leave, when Dad came out with one of the security guards next to him. Officer Snout seemed to eye the slip of paper Dad was carrying.

Did I just see a gleam of interest in the detective's eyes? I was most likely seeing things again, for Officer Snout smiled graciously at Dad and the guard, before hurrying down the street toward the office.

"Daddy, Officer Snout says not to break the diamond," Emma reported, jumping up and grabbing Dad's hand.

"Why did he say that?" Dad grinned down at her.

"'Cause, he said if you break it, you're gonna' have to pay to get a whole new one." Emma was totally serious.

I bit my lip to keep from laughing, though I couldn't stop the grin. Dad chuckled and the guard snickered.

Emma wasn't fazed. "You know what Mama always says. You break it, you buy it."

"True. I promise to be careful." Dad turned to the guard. "Are you thinkin' we've given the others enough time to get the box in me car?"

"Most likely." The guard nodded.

"Wait, if we walked here, how come your car's here, too, Daddy?" Emma looked hopelessly confused.

"Someone came by earlier and drove it here," Dad explained.

"Why?"

"To avoid suspicion."

"Why?"

"You'll understand when you're older," I impatiently interjected. My little sister gave me an annoyed look and I simply ignored it.

Dad had to look away to keep from laughing aloud again. When he'd composed himself, he turned to us. "Girls, would you mind walkin' to school alone? I have to help the men transport the diamond to the shop, and I don't want you two to be late for school."

I didn't want to miss out on seeing the diamond taken to the shop and was about to object, when Emma did it for me. "Aw, please Daddy, please." She grabbed his hand again and swung it back and forth. "Pretty please." She went so far as to give him puppy eyes.

"Not now. If you'd be wantin' to come to the shop after school, it'll be there," Dad promised.

With such a prospect awaiting me, I didn't want to be late for school. I could see Emma was forming another argument. I grabbed her hand and began pulling her down the sidewalk. "See you later, Dad."

"Let me go, Crystal." Emma jerked her hand loose. "I wanna' go with Daddy and see the diamond unveiled."

"You will get to see it unveiled," I told her, still hurrying down the street. "But, if we miss school, your teacher will make sure you don't get to see it at all."

"How can she?" Emma demanded, still standing where I'd left her. "She's not my mother."

"No, but she *can* send you to detention and send a note to Mom and Dad."

If you thought the Road Runner on cartoons runs fast, Emma would have beat him in a race hands down with how much speed she put on in order to catch up to me. It seemed like I just blinked and she was next to me, her mouth running a mile a minute... babbling on about how she was going to have Dad take a picture of her holding the diamond, then she was going to send a picture to Granda. I chuckled as I thought of Emma trying to lift the diamond. It probably weighed more than she did.

As we paused at the crosswalk directly across from school, I was looking both ways when I suddenly felt Emma press up against me. I looked down at her and saw her staring at something, or someone, coming our way from the direction of the museum. It turned out to be Mr. Russell, still carrying his black bag. I noticed the look of agitation on his face. "He's come to get me," she whispered.

"Hey, remember what Dad said about being nice," I reminded her.

"Hi," Mr. Russell said softly as he stood next to us. "Ready for school?"

"Just about," I answered.

"What's in your bag, Mr. Russell?" Emma reached out to touch it.

"Don't!" Mr. Russell quickly put the bag out of my sister's reach, his shout startling both of us. In all the time we'd known him, we'd never heard him shout. Emma looked ready to cry as she stared up at him. He seemed to be fighting back some emotion, as he dug into his pocket and pulled out a small sucker. "Here, I'm sorry for startling you. Want some candy?

Want to call it a truce?"

At first, Emma looked like she wasn't going to accept his peace offering. After eyeing him for a few seconds, she slowly reached up and took the sucker out of his hand. "Thank you," she whispered. She unwrapped it and stuffed the blue sucker into her mouth. I shook my head. Her mouth and lips were going to be as blue as if she'd just stepped out a freezer.

"Where's your dad?" asked Mr. Russell

"He's helping move the diamond to his shop," Emma blurted out.

"Emerald!" I jabbed her with my elbow. "Would you be quiet?"

I saw Orange Hair had appeared out of the fog and came to stand beside us. She was wearing an extra heavy dose of mascara, making her eyelashes long like a spider's legs. She was pretending to ignore me, yet I knew she'd overheard the comment.

Emma's announcement seemed to interest Mr. Russell greatly, and he seemed to calm down for a second. "Did he purchase it or something?"

"He's just cleaning it." I saw we were clear to cross. Not wanting to be impolite, I said, "Have a great day, Mr. Russell."

"You, too." He nodded and crossed in the opposite direction, clutching his bag close to his side. A second later, he broke into a run and disappeared into the fog.

"I wonder what he's got in there?"

"Maybe a dead body," Emma whispered dramatically.

"One more mean comment out of you and I'm telling Dad." She stuck her tongue out at me and I sighed in exasperation.

As we jogged up the concrete steps, I saw Orange Hair glaring at me from the bicycle rack. I simply tossed my hair over my shoulder and ignored her. I dropped Emma off at her class, made sure my cell phone was on mute, performed my usual school routine, and ran to my class just as the first bell rang.

Seven hours later, Emma and I were flying down the sidewalk toward Dad's shop. It was a race. I won, obviously, since I have much longer legs than she does. We arrived at the shop out of breath and overly excited.

"I hope Daddy remembered to bring the digital camera," Emma said, smoothing her wrinkled shirt and smiling up at me.

I found myself smiling back. Her excitement was catching. I pushed the door and to my surprise, it was locked. "Huh, strange." I looked at the hours, 'Open from 9-5'. It was only three o' clock. *What was going on?*

We hurried around to the rear of the store, hoping the back door was open. We were totally unprepared for what greeted us. The back door was hanging on two of its three hinges, and it looked like it'd been hit by an angry bull.

Stunned, Emma and I quietly stepped inside the sagging door. Four or five police officers, including Officer Snout, were standing in the room. Dad's face was tense and white, and Terra's eyes were so big, I was surprised they were still in her head.

"What's going on?" Emma whispered to me.

"I have no idea." I did have a hunch, though. Something wasn't right, and that's all I knew.

Dad came over to us, jaw clenched tight. The look on his face sent my heart into my green and blue striped gym shoes. "Dad, what's wrong?"

"I've been robbed," he said, in a strained voice. "The diamond's gone!"

Chapter II

Confusing Clues

Gone! How could that have been accomplished? Dad had a state of the art burglary system. There was no way even a mouse could have made off with a scrap of cheese.

"Did you break the diamond, Daddy?" Emma asked fearfully.

Dad gave her a forced smile. "No, dear. Daddy didn't break it. He just doesn't know where he put it, is all."

"Oh, okay. Want me to help you look for it?"

"Maybe later."

I could almost hear a light bulb go off above my head, as an idea hit me. *Here it was! My chance to prove I have what it takes to be a first class detective.* First, I needed to get Emma out of the way. I turned to her. "Hey, would you mind running home and getting the doll house set up?"

She looked at me skeptically. "Why?"

"I'll be playing with you, when I get home."

"Really?" she squealed, throwing her arms around my waist. "Oh, you don't know how happy that makes me, Crystal."

I grinned, feeling guilty for bribing her to get her out of my way. "Yeah. Just make sure everything's ready."

"I will! I will!" She zoomed out the door.

I unzipped my backpack and dug around for my notebook. I yanked it out, opened it to a blank page, and pulled out my mechanical pencil. *Hmm... who to interview first?* I decided to start with Terra, since Officer Snout was busy talking with Dad.

"Oh, Crystal! Whatever they say, it isn't true," she blurted out as I approached her.

"Who say what?" I asked calmly.

"The police think I helped the criminal." Her huge gray eyes filled with tears. "Why are the workers always considered the bad person?"

I couldn't think of a comforting response as I nervously cleared my throat. "Uh, I have a few questions to ask you." I studied her pale features. "Or would you prefer me to wait until you've calmed down a bit?"

She gave me a watery smile. "I've been answering questions almost all day. A few more won't hurt."

"Thanks. At what time did you notice the diamond missing?"

"It was at quarter after two."

That'd be right around the time Dad or Terra, would be in the back having their lunch. Not exactly a perfect time to steal the diamond, because someone was always in the front of the store and could press the silent alarm button if whomever was in the back yelled for help.

"A UPS truck pulled up, and it seemed like another routine delivery. I just opened the door to bring the deliveries in, and the man hit me on the back of the head."

I felt my eyes widen in shock. "How hard did he hit you? What'd your attacker look like?"

She took my hand and placed it on the back of her head. It felt like she had a bump the size of a boulder. I guess the crook had nothing to lose by attacking a woman. *Wuss!* "Were you able to get a good look at him before he conked you out?"

"Yes. He wore a traditional brown UPS outfit including the brown hat, though what stuck out to me, was his build. He reminded me of a bouncer with his thick shoulders, wide neck and bulldog features. His voice sounded really deep, almost like your dad's voice, only way deeper." She took her voice down several octaves to demonstrate. "Uh, let's see. As far as facial features were concerned, he wore sunglasses, but I noticed his nostrils were rather large and his nose was somewhat squashed."

I peppered her with all of the questions I could think of, such as, 'Who was the last person to see the diamond? Were you here as the box was being delivered from the museum? Did you actually see the diamond?'… things like that.

I wrote down everything she said, even the 'ums'. I could worry about editing, later on. I had to ask her once or twice, to please slow down. When she asked why, I answered, "I can't write as fast as you can talk."

"But, like I said, I thought it was merely another routine 'go and get the packages' type delivery," she concluded two minutes later, folding her small hands in her lap. "I had no idea this *particular* UPS man was delivering lumps. He hit me for no real reason."

"Well, apparently there was a reason. He needed to rob the store and he couldn't do it with you conscious, now could he?" I remarked.

"Good point."

"Thanks for taking the time to answer my questions."

"No problem." She smiled softly. I gave her a reassuring hug before walking over to Dad.

He grinned when he saw the notebook in my hand. "All right, Detective O'Mally. I'm ready." He sat down on a stool and winked at me, some of the tension leaving his face. I giggled, feeling myself blush.

Before I could begin my questionnaire, Officer Snout came over. "Excuse me, Crystal, but I need to complete this investigation. I'd appreciate it if you stepped aside, so I can finish questioning your father."

My shoulders slumped in dejection. *No fair!* I opened my mouth to object, just as Dad spoke up. "It's all right, Stan." He placed a proud hand on my shoulder. "Crystal's trainin' to become a detective, and she has to start somewhere."

Officer Snout's jaw tightened, revealing his displeasure. "How nice, but this is no school picnic. It's a serious matter, and we don't have time for childish games. It'll waste precious time and the trail will grow cold. The newspaper will get a hold of the story, and then things will really get sticky. When people find out the diamond was stolen from your store, they won't want to buy from you, anymore. Think of how it'll affect your standing as a jeweler in the community, Brian."

"People have trusted me for the past twenty years, they have," Dad said defensively. "They'll know it wasn't me fault."

"Okay." Officer Snout threw his hands up in surrender. "Only trying to warn you and just being neighborly, here." He licked his finger and flipped to a page in his notebook, gazing at me over the top of the metal spiral. "All right, Crystal. You can stay."

My heart soared. I was so thrilled he said yes. I tampered down the overwhelming urge to throw my arms around Officer Snout's neck and squeeze him as hard as I could.

"However," he continued, "what goes on in this room is *strictly* confidential. *Nothing* is to go outside of this room. Is that clear?"

I nodded, feeling important and honored to be included in the group of detectives. Terra gave me thumbs up and Dad lovingly patted me on the back.

After the questioning, I drifted out front to check on the security cameras. They were totally shut down. The little TV's were all blank. Puzzled, I went outside and checked the fuse box. There, I found evidence of tampering. The main switch to the security cameras had been turned off, and one of the wires had been severed. Whoever did this was no criminal in training… they meant business.

Three hours later, I was sitting at the desk in my room sorting through my notes, trying to think things through. I was still thrilled to be allowed on the detective force, however, I wanted to figure this out on my own, and with no help from the police or anything. I smiled dreamily, as I imagined how everything would turn out. I could see it… *me foiling the thief's plot, stalling until the police arrived, my name blazing across national headlines…*

"Crystal?"

I didn't like the coaxing, cooing sound of my sister's voice. I turned around in my swivel seat and looked at Emma standing in the doorway, her arms full of dolls. Without being invited into my room, she came in and stood beside my desk. "Ready?"

"Just about, Emmy. I need to finish working on something."

Using the tip of her finger, she pulled one of the sheets toward her. 'Last seen at 2:15pm, Monday, April 1st, 2002' "What was last seen today?"

"Nothing that concerns you." It was all I could do to keep the edge off my voice. The last thing I needed was a little pest rifling through my things.

"What am I missing out on?" Her voice raised a notch.

"Nothing important."

"It *must be* important, 'cause you're keeping it from me." She crossed her arms as best she could, squishing her dolls in the process. "Otherwise, you wouldn't be trying so hard to hide it. Lemme see!" She grabbed the sheet.

"No!" I tried to grab it back and to my horror, it started to tear as both of us tugged on it, neither side willing to let go. "Emerald Grace, let go right now before I call Mom."

"I want to see." She tugged harder, dropping some of her dolls on the carpet.

A thought hit me. I quickly let go of the paper and she stumbled backwards, crashing into my oak dresser. Mindless of it, she eagerly looked at the paper. "Is it a mystery?" she asked, in an excited whisper. I pretended to be fascinated with my Algebra and ignore her.

She came closer and poked my elbow with her finger. "Psst... Crystal? Is this the beginning of something exciting?" I merely looked at her, and raised my eyebrows in mock suspense. Her face lit up, and she stepped even closer. I could smell the chicken tots she'd had as an after school snack on her breath. "Is it?" Her breathing became quick and heavy.

I suddenly burst out laughing, causing a look of shock to spread across her face. "April Fool!" I leaned forward placing my hands on my desk, and laughed until I thought I was going to start crying.

"Crystal Elizabeth O'Mally! You played a nasty trick on me. Take your stupid paper." She threw it at me and it fluttered to the floor. "I'm telling.Mama," she howled, running out of the room. "Mama, Crystal's bein' mean."

Her little antics made me laugh all the more. After having a good two-minute laugh, I finally tried to concentrate on the task of sorting the notes. However, every time I looked at the wrinkled note and thought of how I'd fooled Emma big time, I'd start to chuckle all over again.

"Crystal." Mom stood in the doorway, hands on hips.

Uh-oh, not a good sign. "Yes, ma'am?" I shoved the notes under my math book as inconspicuously as possible. "Is something the matter?"

She came to stand beside my chair. "Emma says you were being mean to her."

"Mom, it's April Fool's Day. People play tricks on other people," I started to argue, but then I saw a glint of humor in her eyes. "Aw, Mom, you're funning me." I grinned.

"April Fool to you, too." She reached over and playfully yanked one of my slinky curls. "I think your little trick this year was better than last year's prank."

"Hey, snap & pops under the toilet seat was a hilarious idea."

"For you, maybe. For others, such as your sister, not so much." Mom perched on the edge of my desk. "Dad called and told me everything. Naturally, he's quite upset."

"I am, too. Who would be low enough to do something mean like steal from Dad?" I almost reached for my notes, but remembered I was supposed to be doing homework. "Do the police have any leads?"

"None whatsoever. The security cameras were tampered with. This job was obviously done by an expert."

The earlier conversation I'd had with Terra concerning Mr. Russell, immediately came rushing to mind. He'd been imprisoned once before for stealing. *So, what would make him think twice about stealing, again?*

"Well, I'll leave you to finish your math." Mom stood up. Before leaving, she looked at me and said in a serious voice, "Crystal, pray for Daddy."

I frowned, feeling a sliver of fear sneak in. "Why? He didn't have anything to do with the robbery, did he?"

"Oh, no. Not at all. It's just he's very worried. Pray he'll have peace through the entire ordeal, and the criminal will be found very soon."

I nodded, though I couldn't help but feel God wouldn't be concerned with something as petty as a diamond robbery. I mean, c'mon. He's the God of the *universe*. He probably has much better things to do, than listen to some little girl in a one-horse town.

As soon as Mom had turned to go, I pulled out my notes and reviewed them once more. *How was I supposed to make progress with no suspects?* Another thing nagging me was Mom's calm demeanor about the whole thing. *Why wasn't she upset? Her husband had just been robbed. Wouldn't the horrible news make her sad? Even scared?* "Mom," I called softly.

"Yes?" She turned around.

"Why are you so calm about this whole thing?"

Her mask instantly fell away, and I saw fear and anguish on her face. Her lower lip trembled and her voice quaked as she spoke. "I have to be strong for my girls. If you and Emma see me falling apart, then you two will fall apart, as well."

I got up and went over to give Mom a big, loving hug. She squeezed my back as tight as she could, before letting go and looking up into my eyes. "I'm sorry for upsetting you," I whispered.

"You asked, and I answered." The mask slipped back into place just as quickly as it had fallen off. "Just remember, pray. God will turn things around. You'll see."

Huffing in frustration I stomped back to my chair, dropped down onto it, and rested my forehead on my arms as I tried to remember the events of the day... Going with Dad to the museum, meeting Mr. Russell, then Officer Snout, Mr. Russell, again, and finally Orange Hair... *Wait, why did Mr. Russell appear twice? Why wasn't he at the police station, yet? Our school's in the direction of the police station, but since we ran into him earlier, shouldn't he have been at work already?* And, when I replayed our meeting him at the cross-walk, he did look really antsy when I saw him the second time.

An important question I'd completely forgotten to ask Terra came to mind. I pulled my cell phone out of my pocket, hastily dialed Terra's number, and nibbled my thumbnail anxiously. She answered on the second ring.

"Hey, girl. What's up?" she chirped into the phone.

I grinned with relief. "Nothing much. Hey, I forgot to ask you an important question earlier."

"Shoot."

"Who were some of the people you saw before the diamond went missing?"

She was silent on the other end, and I could almost hear the wheels in her head turning. "There were a few people. Mr. Russell…"

I totally zoned out as soon as she said Mr. Russell's name. In a way, he *was* at the scene of the crime. *But why was he at the store, instead of the police station?* Terra's next sentence brought me back down to earth.

"…and then, this teenage girl with pumpkin colored hair."

"Wait, was she wearing a lot of mascara?"

"Oh, yeah, *baby*! I thought she was a walking tube of mascara when I first saw her."

I whole-heartedly agreed with Terra's description as I jotted down this newest piece of information. "Did Mr. Russell buy anything?"

"Yes, he ordered a gold chain for his wife. We didn't have it in stock, so I had to special order it from Houston."

I thanked her, folded my phone shut, and dropped it in my

drawer. I absently rolled the pencil across my lips, as I thought about this newest angle to the case. I recalled only too clearly, how Orange Hair had threatened to get even with me for humiliating her in front of her friends, yesterday. *What better way to do it than by stealing the diamond?*

Wait a minute, something didn't ring true. Mom had said this looked like a professional job, and Orange Hair was probably an amateur at everything she touched. I couldn't see her trying to smuggle a fifty-pound box out of the storeroom. *But, what if she had Shaggy Hair or Pierced Boy do it for her?* They seemed muscular enough.

And the robbery had taken place ten minutes after school lets out. *Would she have had enough time to get her cohorts together, run down to the store, and steal the diamond before Emma and I got there?* Eh, maybe... then again, maybe not. *Another thing, what would a girl like her be doing in something as upscale as Brian's Treasures?* I couldn't see her wearing any of the sparkly diamonds and lovely opals Dad sold.

"Crissy." Emma gently tugged at my earlobe. "I'm sorry for getting you in trouble. Is that why you're not going to play with me?"

"Huh?" I snapped out of my revere. "What's wrong?"

"You were talking with Mama, and then you didn't come into my room to play with me like you promised. Did she ground you? If so, I can talk to her. Maybe she can un-ground you. Just long enough to play with me, at least."

It was then I remembered the bribe, and gave my sister a half-hearted grin. "No, I'm not grounded." I shoved my Algebra book aside and stood to my feet, stretching my long arms. "I have a little bit of time to play."

I think the fact I was able to finally pursue my dream, made me so agreeable to play the dumbest game on the planet with Emma. As I made the dolls go on an imaginary trip to Europe, I couldn't wait until Dad came home to tell him the newest development on the case.

* * * *

"That *is* interestin'." Dad propped his long legs up on the coffee table. "You certainly have been busy, me girl. The police don't even have any leads."

I cocked an eyebrow. "Dad, how can that be? I mean, how could I have figured something out before the police even had the slightest hint?"

"Because you ran into at least a handful of people today, and their world is sometimes limited to the station. Plus, there were some events that happened yesterday, allowing you to create a list of suspects. I'm proud of you, Crystal."

My head swelled at Dad's praise and I squared my shoulders. I licked my thumb and forefinger, just as I'd seen Officer Snout do earlier, and flipped through my notes.

"There's been a lot of petty mischief goin' on around town lately, such as vandalism, and the police think this is just another prank."

I frowned stubbornly. "I don't think so, Dad. I saw the security cameras had been tampered with. I highly doubt a teenager would know what to do, to properly tamper with security cameras. And then, there's sneaking the diamond out. I'm guessing it weighs at least fifty pounds or more, and trying to lug it out without being detected is quite an accomplishment.

I can't picture anyone but a high class thief doing this kind of job."

I could very easily envision Mr. Russell as the culprit... dressing up as a UPS man and hitting my best friend on the head, without giving his vile deed a second thought. "Oh, by the way, Terra told me she'd been paid a visit by a mock UPS man before the diamond was stolen. Were you able to see him at all?"

"No, I wasn't. I didn't know anythin' was wrong, until I heard a big crash and I went runnin' into the back room to see what had happened. Terra was lyin' on the floor unconscious, and the truck was already halfway down the road. So, it was too late to do anythin' except make sure my employee was okay."

"Drat!" I snapped my fingers in disappointment.

Dad was staring absently at the ceiling before lowering his gaze and looking at me. "Part of me is wishin' this whole ordeal *is* either a teen prank or a nightmare."

"But Dad, this is a top notch job, something I can't see a teenager doing. They'd have to have been planning this since they were in diapers. The wires connected to the power box were cut. If this were a teen prank, then they'd have one heck of a bill on their hands for destroying the back door *and* your security cameras. Also, the description I have of the phony UPS man, definitely doesn't sound like a teenager." *I didn't want this to be a petty affair. I wanted some action!*

As if he read my mind, Dad said, "You really want the diamond to be stolen, so you're able to recover it, don't you?"

"No offense, but yes, sir. I would like some excitement around here."

"Are you callin' our fair town boring?" He pretended to be insulted.

I grinned. "Except for the cattle stampede on Main Street, which happened when I was five years old, the town's been pretty slow."

"Watch what you wish for," he warned me.

"Grandma O'Mally used to say the same thing."

"Out of the mouths of two or three witnesses, a thin' is established." His green eyes turned serious. "I've told your mother about your detective work."

I couldn't help but groan aloud. "Aw, Dad. Now why'd you go and do that? You know she's going to object and not let me do it."

"I know, but I was able to convince her to let you stay on the case under the condition you don't make any fool-hardy decisions. And, when you know beyond a shadow of a doubt, you're headin' into trouble you can't handle yourself, get help. Promise me you'll do that?"

I didn't want to promise him anything. I wanted to prove to the world I could take on the tough guys by myself, without any help... but I knew if I didn't agree, I'd be stuck playing with dolls until college. "Yes, sir."

"That's me girl." Dad looked tired as he let his feet slide to the carpet. "All right, missy. It's bedtime for you, it is."

I glanced at the clock just as the little bells chimed ten o' clock. I still had dumb Algebra to finish before going to bed, so I could turn it in tomorrow. I stood up, kissed Dad good night, and went to my room to finish the hated work. As I worked on sines and cosines, my mind was on the case. Somehow, I managed to finish all fifteen problems, and had just closed the book, when someone knocked lightly on my door. "Come in."

Mom came in, wearing a worried expression. I knew at once she wanted to talk about the case, or at least to try and talk me *out* of taking it. She didn't say anything at first, and I could tell by looking into her eyes, she was struggling with some inner emotion. "Promise me, you'll be careful," she finally whispered.

Why was everyone making such a huge fuss over my safety? I mean, I'm almost sixteen for crying out loud! I can take care of myself. Instead of saying that, like I wanted to, I stood to my feet and gave Mom a big hug and a loving kiss on her cheek. "Don't worry, Mom. I can handle it."

"Another concern I have, is Emma finding out about the case." Mom looked straight into my eyes. "You know what's going to happen when, and if, she does find out what's going on."

"She'll throw a fit until I let her help me," I muttered in disgust.

Whenever that girl wanted her way, she'd squawk louder than a hen until she was either reprimanded or given her way. Mom and Dad normally reprimanded her for being such a baby. I often just gave Emma her way, just to shut her up and let me live in peace. "Again, don't worry about it, Mom. I'm doing everything in my power to keep her in the dark, and so far, it's working."

Mom sighed. "For how long? She *is* nosy."

"That's the first time I've ever heard you admit she's nosy. Curious, yes, but to say she's nosy? Never."

Mom chuckled. "Curious and nosy often run hand in hand, my dear." She reached up, and patted my cheek. "Promise me one more thing. You'll never forget to ask for God's guidance when you're unsure of something."

I can do this on my own, without any help, I thought. Aloud I said, "Okay."

"That's my big girl." Mom beamed proudly at me. "Accepting other people's help shows you're mature. And to show I'm mature as well, I'm going to let you get your beauty sleep." She gave me a loving hug before stepping out of the room.

Ten minutes later, I was lying in bed on my back. The room was dark and I was staring at the ceiling as I went over every possible angle of the case. Mr. Russell kept coming to mind constantly, and he wouldn't vacate my brain. I closed my eyes and replayed today's events. I remembered how he clutched the black bag very close to his person, and didn't seem to want anyone to touch it. It didn't look big enough to hold a diamond, but then again, a professional thief would know what size bag to carry so he wouldn't look conspicuous. And, he *did* act kind of edgy when Emma had wanted to touch his precious bag. And to top it off, he was one of those seen at the scene of the crime... but then again, so was Orange Hair. It was all so frustrating! I didn't think I was ever going to be able to fall asleep.

"Get up!"

I shot up in bed as something punched me in the stomach. Emma was sitting on me, all eighty pounds of her. She's kind of stout for an eight-year-old. Mom and Dad are trying to get her to exercise more, instead of spending so much time locked away in her room. "We're gonna' be late for school, if you don't get your lazy bum out of bed," she announced, still sitting on me.

I waited a minute before replying, so I could get air back into my lungs. "I can't get dressed with you sitting on me," I rasped out. "So, if you could please be so kind as to let me get up and get dressed, I'd be much obliged."

"Two minutes." She slid off me and skipped out of the room, her braids bouncing with every hop she took.

I rubbed my stomach, thankful it hadn't come up when she'd made like a bomb and thunked on me. A glance at the clock told me it was seven-thirty in the morning. *What the heck? I never sleep in that late, unless it's summer break or the weekends. Why hadn't the alarm awakened me?*

As I was pulling my navy blue shirt over my head, I remembered how I'd been so preoccupied with the case the night before, I'd completely forgotten to set the alarm. Feeling disgruntled the mystery had me this baffled, I nearly tore my jeans in half pulling them on. I simply ran a brush once through my hair and pulled it back in a ponytail, before running from the room.

"Is the house on fire?" Mom stopped stirring her coffee to stare at me as I came tearing into the room.

"It will be soon with how fast you're tearing around the house," said Emma. "You'll leave a blazing trail, just like they do in 'Looney Tunes'."

"Very funny," I grumbled, pouring myself a bowl of granola and almost dumping the entire carton of milk into my bowl. I bowed my head, rushed through the prayer, and then stuffed my mouth full of soggy granola.

"It seems your manners stayed in bed," Dad teased.

I shrugged my shoulders and mumbled around the soggy mess in my mouth. "I'm gonna' be lade if I dun hurry."

The phone rang and Dad got up to answer it. I didn't pay any attention to the conversation, until I heard the word, "Stan," and instantly knew whom Dad was talking to. I pretended to be interested in my cereal, all the while trying to hear what was being said. I couldn't really make out very much of the conversation, other than a handful of words, such as, "Diamond... arrest... suspect..." and, "...be right there." I brought the bowl to my lips and drained the rest of the milk, just as Dad walked back into the room.

"Well, me lasses, it's time you headed off to school or else you'll be late," he said.

"I'm already ready," Emma bragged. "Crystal slept in, and she would've missed school 'tirely, if it hadn't of been for me."

With how she said that, you'd of thought she'd saved me from a killer whale. I mentally rolled my eyes as I put my dirty dishes in the sink. Without bothering to brush my teeth, I grabbed my backpack and flung it over my shoulder.

As I stood on tiptoe to give Dad a hug, he whispered, "That was Officer Snout on the phone. He said they've arrested a likely suspect, or three."

My shoulders slumped so low, my backpack nearly hit the linoleum floor. *No fair!* I didn't even get a chance to do some first class sleuthing.

I was getting ready to complain, when he added, "Would you like to go down to the police station with me after school, to take a look at the suspect?"

I think I nearly bit Dad's ear off, as I leaned close and

whispered, "You bet."

During the walk to school, I dragged my feet and ignored Emma's chatter. The criminal was caught, and as any good detective knows, it means the case is over. I couldn't help but hope and pray the one caught was innocent. I had already gathered some clues... and I wasn't *about* to let them go to waste.

Chapter III

Fedora Guy

At first, all I saw was just a blob of black sitting on the wooden bench. Then, I made out a face with mascara and dark red lipstick on it. I peered closer to the glass and saw a thatch of bright orange hair underneath the black hoodie. *I should've known it'd be Orange Hair.* She glared at me with hate-filled eyes... probably, because she was embarrassed to be on the wrong side of the glass. Shaggy Hair and Pierced Boy sat on either side of her, both boys looking dejected.

The barrel-chested officer who'd shown us the culprits, looked at Dad. "Do any of these kids look familiar to you?"

Dad studied the trio very closely. "The girl with the hoodie, but the other two I don't recognize. Why are they in there?"

"They were caught putting graffiti on old man Greg's office window. He started chasing them with his cane, hollerin' at the top of his lungs." The officer's large chest shook as he laughed at something. "For an old goat, Papaw Greg sure can run fast. His hollering alerted the baker next door, and the baker, in turn, called us. I questioned these kids for at least an hour, trying to trick them into confessing stealing the diamond. Unfortunately, they heatedly insist they had nothing to do with any stupid diamond."

"May I please talk to them?" I asked quietly.

"Well, I dunno." The officer scratched his balding head. "What do you think, Brian? Think I should let her go into the shark tank?"

"For just a few minutes. From one child to the next, she

might be able to get information out of them that we, as adults, wouldn't be able to get."

"Sounds like a plan. Right this way, little missy." The officer spun around on his heel and marched toward an open doorway.

I ignored the annoying name of 'little' as I followed him down the hall. I passed Mr. Russell, who was busy mopping the floor. "Good afternoon, Mr. Russell," I said politely.

"Miss Crystal." He nodded at me, but kept his eyes on the floor.

He's certainly acting guilty, I thought, as I passed Officer Snout at his desk. The detective nodded politely to me, not taking his attention away from whatever he was typing on the keyboard. I purposefully slowed down my pace, so I could get a peek at whatever was on the screen. An image of a bright, sparkling diamond popped up on the monitor. Apparently, he was Googling something about diamonds. He looked over his shoulder and caught me staring at the screen. I quickly ducked my head and hurried on.

"Here we are." The officer suddenly stopped in front of a brown door. I had to quickly put on the brakes before my nose rammed into his back. He pulled a small ring of keys out of his right pocket, and after flipping through about six of them, stuck a silver key into the lock. "The piranhas are right in there. Watch out, they're a feisty bunch." Barrel Chest chuckled, as if he'd told the silliest joke ever.

"Yes, sir." I slipped inside the dimly lit room and saw the three suspects, sitting dejectedly at a table. Shaggy Hair was smoking a cigarette. I think he failed to realize this is a smoke-free environment.

Pierced Boy saw me first. "It wasn't us," he blurted out, startling the others so badly, Shaggy Hair nearly swallowed his lit cigarette. "You've gotta believe us, sister. We didn't take no diamond. I don't care *what* that guy says. We didn't do anything."

"Shut up," Orange Hair snapped. "She won't believe you."

"My name's Crystal," I said civilly, taking a seat in a chair across the table from them. "May I have your names?"

"Minx," Pierced Boy said instantly.

My eyebrows raised at the name. *Minx? What kind of mother would give her poor baby such a ridiculous name? Nah, it's most likely a nickname. He was a catch, though... Whoa! Where did that come from?* I studied the pierced boy sitting across from me. He had a little black goatee, a straight nose, and a crooked grin. *Wait... why am I suddenly paying attention to a vandal's facial features?* I wondered in disgust, as I forced my mind back on business. "I'd like your real name, please."

"That *is* my real name."

"Not a nickname?"

"Nope. I don't go by nicknames." He looked completely serious.

"Um, okay. How about you, two?" I looked pointedly at the others. "Might I have your names?"

They didn't seem to want to give out any information, so Minx gladly offered it. "Celine and Cory. They're cousins."

"Nice to meet you." Then, my mind went blank. *What should I say next?* I began to nibble my bottom lip as I frantically probed my mind, desperately trying to think of something else to say.

"We don't know anything about no diamond," Minx continued to insist.

"Uh, okay. Why are the three of you in here?"

"We were just trying to have some fun." This came from Cory. He dropped his cigarette butt on the floor and squashed it with his black sneaker. "If there's anyone you want to ask about the stupid diamond, it's the dude we saw hanging around the back door of your dad's shop."

I was in the process of writing down their names, just as Cory made his comment. I quickly looked up. "What guy? Who? Where?"

"We were looking around town, deciding which place we should paint up," Minx answered, when Cory refused to say anything else. "We saw this guy with a strange looking hat pulled low over his eyes, like the kind of hat gangsters wear in those old black and white films."

"A fedora?" I guessed. *A fedora! That was what the person in the museum was wearing, when I saw them the night before the diamond was stolen. No wonder he looked so weird. His hat was cocked over one part of his face.*

"Yeah." Minx placed his elbows on the table and leaned forward, his tar black eyes pleading with me to believe him.

"What was the guy doing?" I prodded.

"What guy?"

"The one you said was snooping around the back door. Fedora guy."

"Oh, yeah. It looked like he was messing with something on the back of the building. He seemed to be mighty nervous, and kept glancing over his shoulder every two seconds. A few moments later, a lady appeared out of nowhere and he hurried over to her."

"What did the lady look like?"

"Too far away to see any facial features, but I did notice she had medium build and blond hair." He paused for a second. "And she was wearing glasses."

I nearly dropped my pencil as reality set in. *Terra!* She was of medium build, had blond hair and wore glasses. *Oh, please let Terra be innocent. She's my best friend.* "Did… did they do anything that looked suspicious?" I asked urgently.

"Kept their heads close together for a little bit, before the lady went inside and the guy left. Hey, got any gum? I need something to chew." Minx finally paused for a breath.

I gave him a big grin, showing off my metal braces. "Sorry, I can't chew gum."

"Tobacco? Cigarette? Anything? Girl, I'm all stressed out and my mouth's gotta be doin' something."

"You've been flapping it for the past ten minutes," Celine snarled.

I dug around in my pocket and came up with a piece of soft candy a classmate had given me earlier. I didn't want to give it up, but I had to keep Minx happy or else he might turn as sullen as the other two. "Here you are. Hope you like chocolate." As I handed it to him, I half hoped he'd say he despised chocolate.

"Thanks, girl." He snatched it, tore the wrapper off, and

popped the candy into his mouth. "Guess you aren't so bad, after all."

"She'll only tell everything to the police," Celine grumbled.

"Maybe she can help us get off the hook," Minx insisted.

"She'll distort everything, and we'll wind up in the slammer overnight," she warned him.

I heard a tapping noise and looked behind me. Through the small window in the door, I could see Barrel Chest motioning for me to come out. I stood up and pocketed my notebook. *What should I say? Have a nice life? Hope you're innocent?* "Uh, thanks for being cooperative, guys. I really do appreciate it."

"No prob, girl. Just try and make good for us out there, 'kay?" Minx pleaded.

"I'll do my best. Bye." My mind was in a tumult as I left the interrogation room. I loved Terra and hoped she had nothing to do with this dirty and despicable deed.

"I see they let you live," the officer commented, as he held the door open for me.

I looked up and quickly read the nametag on his shirt. Barrel Chest's real name was Olav. "They did, Officer Olav. Thanks for letting me in there."

"Were you able to get any new information on the diamond mystery?"

I opened my mouth, ready to tell a lie, but I caught sight of Officer Snout watching me intently. He looked like he was waiting impatiently for me to say something. "Kind of... sort of... not really. Not too much to go on. Just a description of a guy they saw hanging around the shop, not long before the diamond was stolen."

"What did this person look like?" Officer Snout demanded.

"All Minx could tell me was the guy was wearing a fedora. Nothing else. He was too far away to get a close enough look." I didn't tell them the part about the blond woman. I desperately wanted to solve this myself.

Officer Snout nodded his thanks as he jotted down my information on a piece of paper.

"I think the only thing those kids are guilty of is vandalism."

"All right. We won't hold too much against them," said Officer Olav.

Considering it my good deed for the decade, I said good night and jogged down the hall. Dad was waiting for me in the lobby. His face was again tight. "I should have known it wouldn't take long," he said quietly.

"What? What's wrong?" I felt fear start to creep up my spine.

He held out a newspaper for an answer. I took it, glanced at the blazing headline, and then dropped the paper as if I'd been burned. The gigantic bold words seemed to taunt the two of us, as it screamed...

'Local Jeweler Responsible For Famous Alamo Diamond Disappearance'

The article went on to describe how Dad was so careless as to let the diamond get stolen. The article also had the audacity to suggest Dad might have had a hand in helping it disappear. It listed not only Dad's name, but Mom's name, mine, and

Emma's, as well. *Why were the kids being brought into this?*

"It's a lie!" I cried, tears stinging my eyes. *Who would be as blatant as to let such untrue trash be written about us?* I saw it was a Houston paper. I felt a little bit of relief knowing Papaw Greg didn't write it. Deep down inside, I knew he wouldn't let anything so nasty leave his press room. I looked up at Dad through blurred eyes. *Why was I crying? From embarrassment? Probably.* When I'd envisioned my name in the newspaper, I didn't think it would be attached to such a vile, low down criminal act as this. "This means only one thing."

"It wasn't a teen prank," Dad finished for me. "There have been plenty of pranks around here, and none of them have made the Houston paper." He cleared his throat. "Crystal, I didn't want to tell you this at first, but the police have ruled out the possibility of this bein' a prank."

"What made them change their minds?"

"There have been more robberies around town in the past twenty-four hours, *all* of them involvin' jewelry. I lost fifteen hundred dollars' worth of jewelry, last night. The thief used a different method of operation this time. He waited until the shop was closed before makin' his strike. I'd just gotten the cameras fixed last night, and the thief shut them down, again." Dad put his arm around me and drew me close. "Don't worry, sweetheart. We'll get through this."

I nodded, too close to tears to speak. Something told me if I did try to talk, I'd start bawling worse than Emma ever did. With my head practically hanging between my knees, I followed Dad out of the station and to the car. I kept my eyes on the floor the entire ride.

Dad was quiet, which is unusual. Usually he's singing old Irish songs like, 'She Moved Thru' the Fair', 'Last Rose of Summer', and songs like that.

As always, Emma was there to greet us when we got home. I could tell she instantly sensed something wasn't right. "What's wrong, Daddy?" she asked, following him to the kitchen.

"Daddy needs to have a talk with Mama," he replied in a weary voice. "How about you and Crystal go watch cartoons?"

Instead of rushing off to turn on the tube like I expected her to do, Emma blocked Dad's way. "Daddy, I already apologized to Joey Staton for putting cheese dip in his hair at lunch this afternoon."

A smile tugged at the corners of Dad's lips. "And why on earth did you do somethin' like that?"

"He kept calling me tomato head, and wouldn't quit. I called him cheese head, since his hair's yellow, and to prove he had a cheese head, I splotted some cheese dip in his hair."

"We'll talk about it later, sweetie, okay? I need to talk to Mama about somethin' else. Grown up stuff."

Emma immediately looked relieved. "Okay." She hugged Dad's knees, and then ran for the den. I slowly followed her, not really enthused about anything. She turned on a 'Bugs Bunny' episode, and settled on the couch to watch it.

I plopped down next to her, my eyes on the floor. It was then I remembered I'd forgotten to call Terra. "Hey, I need to go to my room for a second, Em. Be right back." I stood up, digging around in my front pocket for my cell phone.

"Want me to pause it for you, Crissy?" she asked, her finger poised above the pause button on the remote. "I know how much you like Bugs."

Despite my current predicament, I couldn't help but smile. Emma could be a cutie when she chose to be. "Naw, it's all right. We have it on DVD, so I can watch it again whenever I want to."

"All right, just hurry back." She turned her attention to the screen.

I ran to my room and shut the door behind me, feverishly dialing Terra's phone number. "Please pick it up. C'mon, pick it up!" I panted into the phone. To my utmost dismay, it rang seven times before going to voice mail.

"Hey, whoever you are, it's me, Terra. Leave a message, and if I think it's important enough to return, I'll do it. Have a great day!" BEEP.

I nearly folded my phone shut, but decided to leave her a message, hoping she'd call back as soon as possible. "Terra, it's me, Crystal. I was wondering if you could call me back directly after you get this message. I need your help on something concerning the diamond mystery. Thanks, bye." I pressed the 'END' button, pocketed my phone, and trudged back out to the den. I sullenly sat down on the floor and watched fifteen minutes of cartoons with my little sister. During one episode, Yosemite Sam was exclaiming in disgust about the person who'd 'Gotten footy-prints all over his desert'.

Wait a second! What was an important aspect of being a detective? Looking for fingerprints and footprints, of course! I vowed to start looking for both finger and footprints tomorrow, as soon as I had the chance. My mind was in space for the rest of the evening.

Dinner was visibly strained for everyone, including Emma. She tried her utmost best to be cheerful, but as Mom and Dad responded with four or five word sentences, she gave up and concentrated on eating her lasagna.

Later that night, as I got ready for bed, I was seriously ticked. Terra hadn't returned my call, and when I'd tried to call her again it went straight to voice-mail, which meant her phone was off.

"Crystal." Emma stood in my doorway, clutching her stuffed teddy bear instead of dolls. I knew Emma was scared about something, because the only time she went walking around the house with her old bear, was when she was scared.

"Come on in." I sat on my bed and patted the empty space next to me.

Emma slowly entered the room like she expected me to change my mind and throw her out. She sat down next to me clutching the bear so tightly, I was sure if he could speak he'd be protesting... while at the same time, gasping for air. "Are Mama and Daddy gonna' divorce?" she blurted out, tears filling her eyes.

"What makes you say that, Emmy?"

"They just seem mad at each other a lot, lately. And, I'm scared if they stay mad at each other, then they'll divorce. Who will I live with if that happens? Will I get to see you ever again? Will I ever see my dollies again?"

I felt my heart fill with pity for my baby sister, who did an A+ job of making my life miserable when she chose to. I put my arm around her shoulder and pulled her close. She snuggled up to me like our dog Mayo used to do during thunderstorms.

"No, Mom and Dad aren't going to divorce."

"Then why are they always so mad?"

Ooh, boy. How to put this in simple terms without lying and totally spilling everything? "Dad's just worried about something at work, is all."

"Is it 'cause the diamond's gone?"

My eyes widened. "How'd you know about that?" I demanded.

"I heard a guy say it."

"Who? Where? Why?"

"This afternoon at school. I was waiting for you to come and join me outside, and there was a guy talking on his cell phone. He was wearing a hat like Granda used to wear and it was pulled really low over his face, to where I could barely see it. I heard him say, 'Yeah, the diamond's gone, and nobody knows where it went,' in this really deep voice and he gave this funny laugh. He must have seen me staring at him, 'cause he turned around and walked toward the police station."

"What did he look like?"

"He was really skinny. And he was wearing a light blue shirt, like what Dad wears to church on Sunday, blue pants and the brown hat. He had really long hair, like a girl." Emma wrinkled her nose. "It was white, like an old lady's."

That was the best description I'd been given so far. "Guy's sometimes have long hair like a girl. He must have been really close for you to get such a good look at him."

"At first he was walking toward me, then he saw me staring

at him and changed directions." Emma looked me full in the face. "Are you gonna' act like a dektive now?"

"It's *detective*, and maybe." I didn't want to tell her I was already working on the case.

"And can I please be your sidekick?" She clasped her hands in front of her and wiggled her bottom. I couldn't help but laugh. "Please? Oh please, Crystal? I promise I'll be the bestest sidekick you *ever* had."

"I don't know, Ems. What if I ever get in some pretty rough spots?"

"Then, I'll be there to yank you out of 'em!"

"Emerald…" I looked into her eyes, and what I saw, cut me off in the middle of my objection. What I saw in her eyes reflected what I'd been feeling the past few days… the pleading and the wanting to be accepted in the detective community. No doubt, I gave Officer Snout puppy eyes when he was about to turn me down, because of my age. I sighed, unable to say no to Emma. "Oh, all right. You can be my sidekick."

"Oh, thank you, Crystal, ever so much!" She wrapped her arms around me and gave me her tightest squeeze. I pitied her poor teddy bear and what he must go through whenever she holds him. "You won't be sorry!" She released me, her face still beaming excitedly.

"Just promise me this. You'll never get into dangerous situations and you'll obey me, and give me no back talking."

"I promise."

"Your job will be to keep an eye out for fedora guy. If you see him again, mentally record what he's wearing, or if you happen to have pen and paper on you, write it down."

"What if he's shirtless?" Emma wrinkled her nose. "What if his chest is all hairy like an ape?"

"Then, tell me that, too. It's all part of you being my sidekick."

"Isn't it bedtime?" Mom's voice startled both of us. She was standing in the doorway.

"Yes, ma'am. I'm sleeping with Crystal." Emma looked at me, her face reading, 'Right?'.

"Uh, yeah. She's sleeping with me tonight."

Mom smiled, even though her face told me she knew this was a last minute decision and it wasn't my idea. "I'm glad you girls are spending sister time together."

"Mmm-hmm." Emma rested her head on my shoulder and smiled angelically at Mom.

"It's lights out, you two." Mom came in, kissed both of us good night, and then left.

As we snuggled under the covers, I remembered to set my alarm and turned the light off. I was dozing when Emma's voice startled me. "Crystal?"

"Hmm? What?"

"Can I use your magnifying glass, please?"

"Why? What for?"

"To look for clues, of course." She sounded insulted.

It sounded like she was going to make this a lengthy conversation and I was exhausted, so I replied, "We'll see in the morning. Let's play a game and the prize will be the magnifying glass."

"A game?" she was instantly interested. "How do we play it? What's it called?"

"Who can get to sleep, first. The object of the game is to see who can fall asleep first. Whoever wins gets to use the glass."

"You're on!" She flipped onto her side.

I buried my face in my pillow so she wouldn't hear my giggles. It was hilarious the way she fell so easily for the game. I was still smiling as I drifted off into a deep sleep.

I dreamt I was chasing this guy wearing a fedora, and I'd almost caught him, when suddenly the fedora grew to an enormous size and started chasing *me*. It chased me up and down Main Street and all the way to the lake, five miles out of town. Then, just as quickly as it'd grown, it shrunk… and in its place, was Terra. She was grinning smugly at me as she elevated the diamond. How she managed to hold a rock that big, I don't know. *Maybe, she's really Wonder Woman in disguise.*

"Give it to me, Terra." I held my hand out.

"You want it? Go and get it!" And with that, she hurled it into the lake.

I woke up yelling, "NO!" Beside me, Emma stirred and groggily, opened her eyes, mumbled something incoherent, and went back to sleep. I raked a shaky hand through my hair, my heart pounding like I'd just run a marathon.

I decided to have my devotional time, even though my alarm hadn't gone off yet. I flipped onto my side as I turned on my flashlight, pulled my Bible off my nightstand, and opened it.

It fell open to Proverbs. As I was reading Chapter three, verses five and six stuck out.

'Trust in the Lord with all your heart and lean not on your own understanding; in all your ways acknowledge Him and He shall direct your paths.'

I'd heard this scripture since I was knee-high to a fire ant, however, this time it was almost like God was asking if He could be my partner in this. I glanced over my shoulder at my current partner, who was busy slobbering on her pillow. *Do I take a more experienced Partner… or one who's still finding out she needs to wear matching socks to school?* A fear lingered at the back of my mind. *What if I called on God, and He didn't respond in time?* I didn't want to run that risk, and decided to get back with Him. I closed my Bible, set it on my nightstand, and gently kicked my sister. "It's time to get up, Emmy."

"Did the alarm clock already go off?" she mumbled.

"In a way, yes." I reached over, and turned off the alarm. Even though it was five minutes until it was set to go off, I decided to get up and start my day.

I rushed Emma through her daily routine of getting up in the morning. I did it so much, she finally turned to me, planted her hands on her hips, and retorted, "You're not my mom!"

"Yeah, but I do own a certain magnifying glass you want to use and I can say whether or not you can use it," I shot back. I didn't mean to be irritable. It's just I wanted to leave the house a few minutes early, so I could stop by the Snouts' house and talk to Terra. I'd turned my phone on about five minutes ago, and saw she hadn't returned my call. I bit my lower lip, trying to tap down my irritation. Fifteen minutes later, we'd gobbled up breakfast and flown out the door.

"Where we goin'?" Emma wanted to know, running as fast as she could to keep up with my long strides.

"To the Snouts'."

"Did you remember to bring the magnifying glass?" she panted.

I winced. It was in the bottom of my backpack. I was hoping she'd forgotten about it, because I wanted to use it for my own personal use later... however, a deal was a deal. "Yes, I do have it. You can get it later, when we do more detective work after school. And I don't want to be late, so no more putting cheese dip in Joey Staton's hair. Got it?"

"Got it," she promised.

Two minutes later, we jogged up the Snouts' driveway. They lived on Sesame Street, the last house down. Whenever I visited Terra, I always expect to see Elmo, Cookie Monster, or at least Big Bird. It seemed odd they lived so far back at the end of the street. The nearest neighbor was five minutes away, and their house was shielded by trees on all sides.

I rapped on their door, hoping I wasn't disturbing breakfast. The door opened. Terra stood in the doorway, a cup of coffee in her hand. Her hair hung down her back in two braids and her glasses were partway down her nose. She seemed annoyed about something, but managed to put on a smile as she playfully ruffled Emma's hair.

"Hi, Terra. Uh, is this a bad time?" I licked my dry lips.

"No, not at all. Come right in." She held the door open a little wider and we stepped inside. "I know you only have a few minutes before school starts, but I do have some glazed doughnuts I need help polishing off." She turned and hollered toward the kitchen, "Stan, honey? The O'Mally girls are here."

Officer Snout appeared in the doorway to the kitchen, and he also looked upset about something… only unlike his wife, he didn't try to smile. "Forgive me, I'm afraid I can't stay. I have some work waiting for me at the office. Tell your dad I said hello." He picked up his briefcase, kissed his wife on the cheek, and hurried out the door.

I couldn't help but notice Terra's sorrowful expression as she watched him leave. "We can come back some other time," I said softly.

Terra shook her head. "No, not at all. Now, how can I be of service?"

Emma had taken Terra's offer and helped herself to a glazed doughnut. Bits of doughnut surrounded her mouth and she chewed with her mouth open a little. "We're solving a mystery," she announced.

"Yes, Stan told me." Terra looked worried as she turned to me. "No offense, but aren't you a little young to be a detective? It's rather dangerous work, if I'm not mistaken."

"But we're *smart*, and we're gonna' catch those bad guys," Emma insisted, wiping her mouth with the back of her hand.

"I see." Terra gave me a knowing smile and wiggled her fair eyebrows.

I felt myself blushing. I hadn't counted on the fact Emma would be telling everyone about our detective work. I forced a nervous smile. "Did you get the message I left on your phone, last night?"

"No I didn't. See, Stan had forgotten to recharge his phone and asked to borrow mine, so I let him. I think he still has it. Well you're here, and you can give me the message in person." She clasped her hands behind her back.

I hadn't wanted to ask it in front of Emma. I hesitated and glanced at the girl. Terra must have understood my awkwardness, because she sent Emma upstairs with some birdseed to feed Cocoa, her parakeet. Emma spilled a little bit of the seed on the hardwood floor as she ran upstairs, calling loudly for Cocoa as she ran.

"I went to the police station, yesterday. They'd caught three teens committing vandalism. One of them, Minx, said he…" Here, I stopped. Terra was my best friend, and I was about to put that friendship in jeopardy by asking questions. I swallowed hard. "He said he saw someone matching your description talking to someone wearing a fedora. And fedora guy was tampering with something outside the building." I didn't miss the look of fear crossing her features.

She placed a hand over her heart and sat down in a chair. I sat down next to her. We locked eyes for a few seconds, before she broke the contact and looked out the window. An uncomfortable silence stretched between us, like someone stretching a rubber band. I knew sooner or later, it was going to snap. It was Terra who finally broke the silence. "I did speak to someone matching that description."

My heart broke. *Not Terra. Not my best friend.* Tears swam in my eyes and I blinked furiously, hoping they'd stay away until I could have a good cry at home.

She looked down at her hands. "What else did Minx say?"

"The person matching your description went inside the store, and the man wearing the fedora left." A few tears escaped and slid down my cheeks. I reached up and roughly brushed them away with the back of my sleeve. This detective business wasn't turning out to be as fun as I'd thought it would be… not when you lose friends.

"I wasn't doing anything wrong," Terra whispered. She stood up, signaling the end of our conversation. I reluctantly stood to my feet and hefted my backpack over my shoulder.

Emma came thundering into the room, spilling more birdseed. "I got Cocoa to perch on my finger!" she cried, her face shining with elation. "It was funny to feel his claws on my finger."

"He didn't scratch you, did he?" Terra pasted on a smile.

"No, he was very careful."

"Would you like me to drive you to school?" Terra asked. "It's ten to eight, and I don't want you girls to be late for class."

"No, it's all right. We can walk," Emma said politely, putting the box on the table. "Thank you, anyway."

"All right. Well, you girls be good now. And good luck with your case."

"Thanks, Terra." Emma gave her a big hug.

"Let's go, Emmy." My feet moved automatically toward the door, since my mind seemed frozen like a block of ice. "Thanks for spending some time with us, Terra." I put my hand on the brass knob. I looked out the glass in the doorway and stopped. I saw a man wearing a brown fedora, black striped pants, and a black button down shirt, was standing on the other side of the door.

Terra must have seen him too, for I saw her face pale. "Here, go out the back door. It's quicker than walking across the front yard. Come this way." She practically herded us through the den, just as the doorbell rang. "Goodness, guests in and out all morning. Whatever brings the special and sudden attention?"

"It just means you're loved," Emma replied.

"Could be. See you girls later." She shut the door and I heard her running across the linoleum, hollering for fedora guy to wait.

I gritted my teeth, spun around on my heel, and marched across the yard to the road. If Terra wanted to play games, fine. I'll play it her way. If she wanted to be mysterious, then I'd be mysterious right back. I swore to get to the bottom of the mystery if it was the last thing I did... *Which involved finding out just who Mr.Fedora Guy was!*

Chapter IV
A Janitor's Confession

"I need more dust. Quick!"

"Here!" Emma swiped some dust on her finger and held it out to me.

"Thanks." I gently dabbed some on the end of my brush, and gingerly dusted the peephole on the back door. "Tape."

"Tape," she repeated, digging in her pouch and handing it to me.

I cut off a good-sized piece. and very slowly placed it over the fingerprint. After waiting for a few seconds, I removed the tape. *A perfect print!* I grinned, feeling proud of myself.

I looked at Emma and saw her grinning, too. "Way to go, Crystal!"

"There's only one problem. We don't know whose finger print this is. We'll have to get Dad's fingerprints, as well as Terra's, but we've got to do it in such a subtle way they don't guess what we're doing."

"What's subtle?" Emma's brow furrowed.

"In a very quiet way."

"Oh, okay."

I handed Emma a paintbrush. "Here's your very own brush and…" I dug in the pack. "And, your very own magnifying glass. Be very careful."

Emma reverently accepted my gift, her eyes as large as the lens. "Gosh, Crystal. Thanks a lot."

"You're welcome. Just take care of it. Now, let's get those fingerprints."

We went inside the shop. Dad was waiting on a customer, as was Terra. I watched Dad show the lady a diamond bracelet. She pointed to something else in another display case. He put the bracelet back on the velvet display and led the woman toward the ring display.

I snuck over, quietly lifted the glass, and took out the bracelet. Dad was going to get mad at me for getting the bracelet dirty, but this was an emergency. I quickly dabbed some dust on the stone, waited a few seconds, and then put a strip of tape over it. Ten seconds later, the bracelet was back in the display case and I was watching Emma wait for her chance to get Terra's fingerprint.

"Hi."

I turned around, and saw Pierced Boy standing directly behind me. "Hi yourself." I'd completely forgotten his name.

"I'm Minx," he stammered out. "You... you're Crystal, right?"

Minx. How could I have forgotten such a crazy name? "Yep, that's my name. Don't wear it out."

"Do you work here?"

"No, I'm the owner's daughter."

"Oh, I... I knew that. It's just, I thought since you were Mr. O'Mally's daughter, maybe you worked here, too."

I was impatient to get some more fingerprints. Stammering Tongue Minx was interfering with my detective work, and I needed him to move on. "If you'll excuse me, I need to get cracking on some important work."

"You mean for the big history test coming up, tomorrow? History's my strong point." He somehow managed a partial grin. "Need any help?"

"Oh, no. Thank you, anyway. I have everything under control. Have a nice day." I skirted around him and hurried to the back room.

It seemed Terra had sold something, and was trying to tape a little card to the bag. She was having trouble removing the tape from her finger. Without batting an eye, Emma simply reached up and took the tape off her forefinger, smiled all cute like at Terra, and headed toward the back room.

The little squirt was learning fast. I'd scolded her the day we left Terra's, telling her our detective work was supposed to be a secret. She'd apologized over and over again, until I finally managed to convince her it was all right. I was proud of my little sister as I followed her to the back room. "Nice."

"Was that subble?" Emma wanted to know.

"*Subtle*. And yes, very subtle."

"Let's compare prints." She danced with impatience as I pulled the tape out of my pocket and we compared the prints.

Neither Dad's nor Terra's matched the one on the peephole. I groaned. "A dead end."

Emma's shoulders slumped. "Now what?"

I didn't know what to do. I sat back on my heels, trying to think of what my storybook hero would do when she hit a dead end. *She'd go over the mystery from another angle.* "Let's just look for more fingerprints."

"No-duh, Crystal."

"It's the only thing I could think of, right now."

"When you think of something else, let me know."

"Cut it out and get to work."

After rolling her eyes at me, Emma began dusting the entire room… and I *mean* dusting. She found a big pile of dust in the corner, and used it to make everything she touched covered with dust. I was in the far corner of the room dusting a table, when Emma called my name. "Crissy! Crissy c'mere, quick! I found something!"

I flew across the room. She was kneeling in front of a large, open wooden crate. The lid lay next to it, and burlap spilled over the sides of the box. This was no doubt the crate the diamond took its final trip in, before it was stolen. "What'd you find?"

"This." She pointed to a piece of paper wedged between the burlap and the wooden crate. I started to reach for it, but Emma grabbed my wrist. "Wait! You'll get fingerprints on it."

She was smarter than I'd given her credit for. I got up and put on one of Dad's special cloth gloves, the ones he used to handle Swarovski crystals. I pulled out the paper and studied the crude writing. It appeared to be a list of names.

I recognized a few of the names, because they were townspeople. Even the name 'O'Mally' was on the list. However, there was one name I didn't recognize… and it was written in capital letters. 'SAMUEL CREST' I frowned, puzzled. *Who was this Samuel Crest? An accomplice, perhaps?* I flipped the paper over and saw the Snout address on the back. Further down, toward the end of the paper, was a message. I held it up to the light and squinted, trying to read the small script.

'If you can get Crest's jewel, as well as O'Mally's, then...'

The rest of the message had been torn off. Now, we had a missing paper to hunt for. *Perfect!* I looked the paper over again, and saw the name 'Todd Russell' written at the top of the page in extremely small handwriting.

"Why's our name on there?" Emma whispered. "And who's Samuel Crest?"

"I have no idea. May I have my magnifying glass?" Emma plunked it down in my hand and I scrutinized the paper, looking for any more writing. *There!* I saw something in the upper left hand corner. It was another name. 'Stellen' "Stellen?"

"What kind of a name is Stellen?" Emma gave me a puzzled frown.

"I don't know, might be some kind of a last name, or something." I neatly folded the paper and stuck it into my pocket. "If we can always find this many clues in one day, why, we'll solve the mystery in no time flat."

* * * *

"That's the twelfth report this week," Officer Olav groaned, setting the phone down on the receiver. "I can't understand it. How can one man move so fast, the police can't catch him?"

"Unless it's a ghost," Officer Snout said, sarcastically.

"Then, I think we need the Ghost Busters." Officer Klipper took a deep drink of his coffee.

"Miss Gopher just called in and said her sterling silver necklace, the one from her granny, is missing. Our thief must have a thing for jewelry." Officer Olav shook his head. "Maybe I should super-glue my wedding band to my finger. What do you say?" He fingered the gold band on his third finger.

Officer Snout let out a bark of laughter. "Maybe we should start selling super-glue to everyone who's lost their jewelry. Seems everyone's getting down right lazy with their things lately, and it's getting on my nerves."

As I studied the irritated detective, it looked like something other than the stolen jewelry was getting on his nerves.

"A little excitement every once and while, never hurt a body," Officer Klipper objected in his slow, Southern drawl. "Todd came in yesterday, so riled up I thought he was going to have a heart attack, or something. Was hollering and saying his wife's sapphire had been stolen."

"But, this is *too* much excitement." Officer Snout scowled. He'd been exceedingly irritated of late, and was sometimes hard to be around with his mood swings. "These locals are getting too careless with their stuff. It's like they're suckers for this thief to come in and get the drop on them."

"Which is why we're here, man," Officer Olav said. "We're here to save the day."

Officer Klipper laughed heartily, but I sighed, not seeing anything humorous in Officer Olav's comment. It'd been two weeks since the diamond had been stolen, and Dad's business had dropped drastically. Yeah, the locals still came in and bought from him, but hardly any of the tourists did. Ever since the awful article in the Houston Blaze, very few tourists came in, anymore.

Dad became more and more quiet, and Mom took to

praying at all hours of the day. Terra had grown more distant from me, which stung. I often thought about asking God to let me have my friend back, but pride kept me from opening my mouth. Emma was the only one who remained cheerful through it all. Every day she looked diligently for new clues, but so far came up dry.

Mr. Russell walked into the room wearing a pained expression on his face. He nodded a greeting to us, however, I couldn't help but notice how he and Officer Snout seemed to lock eyes for a few seconds before the former hurried down the hall. I decided to get down to business and followed him to the janitor's closet. His cell phone rang and I ducked behind a curtain to listen in on the conversation.

"Carol?" He sounded anxious as he answered his phone. "Is everything all right, sweetheart? What'd the doctor say?"

I watched him closely as he stared out the window at two robins as they pecked each other. His eyes kept darting from the window to the entryway, as if he wasn't supposed to be on the phone and was worried he'd get caught and wind up in trouble. "You did make it home safe, right? Thank goodness. What are you going to do now?" I couldn't hear what Carol said, but it must have been funny, because he grinned and chuckled. "Well same to you, sweetie. Take care, all right? I love you, too. Uh-huh. Bye-bye." He pocketed the phone and proceeded to remove his cleaning items from the closet.

"Mr. Russell," I called, as he bent down to grab a bucket.

He straightened up quickly, as if I'd caught him committing the blackest sin. He seemed terrified until he saw me standing five feet away from him. He gave me a strained smile. "Hi, Crystal. How are you?"

"Fine." I didn't know where to begin. "How are you doing?"

"Oh, you know. Hanging in there. The good Lord will see me through it all," he said, as if I knew what he was going through.

"What's going on, Mr. Russell?" I asked in a low voice.

"What do you mean?"

"I mean, I found your name on a list in the crate the stolen diamond used to rest in."

His face blanched and I thought he was going to pass out on me. He leaned against the wall, staring at me with a shocked expression on his face. "Are... are you accusing me of stealing the diamond?"

"I didn't say such a thing." I licked my dry lips. Something told me I should have approached this from a different angle. "I'm just wondering if you know anyone wearing a fedora."

"Why should it concern you?"

"Because, someone wearing a fedora was seen around the scene of the crime not long before the diamond went missing. And then, I found a piece of paper with your name on it in the empty diamond crate." I didn't tell him the list had a few other names on it besides his.

"May I see the paper, please?"

I had it in my back pocket, but wanted to see if I could trick him into somehow confessing. "I'll make a deal with you."

He eyed me as if I were a cobra ready to strike. "What kind of a deal?"

"You answer my question, and if I think your answer is valid enough, I might let you see the paper."

He sighed and shook his head. "What is the younger generation coming to?"

I chuckled. "We're becoming more and more curious."

"Well, if you *must* know, Miss O'Mally, I *do* own a brown fedora... but it went missing not long before the great diamond robbery."

I whipped my notebook out of my back pocket and started writing down what he said.

"I caught a glimpse of my thief. He was of medium build, had salt and pepper hair, white button down shirt and gray slacks."

"That's quite a description," I commented.

"He was only standing in my lighted closet when I caught him, so it was kind of hard *not* to see him."

"How about facial features?"

"A scar running across his lower jaw... looked kind of recent, all pink and shiny. He had a nose like an eagle, long and hooked at the end. And then, his eyes were an odd color. Looked like a mixture between blue and brown."

Sounds more weird than odd, I thought, but merely nodded as I jotted the description down. "Did he speak?"

"Other than to say, 'Bye', and go tearing out the window? No. His voice sounded low and gravelly, but anyone can disguise their voice. Satisfied? Now may I see the paper?" He held out his hand.

Fair was fair... though, I did hate fair. I reluctantly handed the slip to him and nibbled on the pencil as I watched his eyes scan the paper.

He studied the paper from every angle, and then inhaled sharply all of a sudden. "Where did you say you found this?"

"In the wooden crate where the diamond was."

"He's found me," Mr. Russell whispered to no one in particular. "Stellen's *found* me. I can't believe it!"

"You know who Stellen is?" I took a step forward. "Mr. Russell? Mr. Russell?" His eyes were closed and he didn't appear to be breathing. Scared, I took his arm and led him over to the nearest bench, and then flew to the water fountain letting my backpack hit the ground next to the closet. I sloshed a good portion of water out of the paper cup and onto on the floor as I ran back to him. "Mr. Russell? Can you hear me?" I was terrified, thinking he was going to have a heart attack. "I have some water for you." He didn't seem to hear me.

Oh, boy! What should I do? I recalled learning in science class in order to revive a heat stroke victim, one needs to gently dab their face and wrists with water. Well, Mr. Russell wasn't a heat stroke victim, but I decided to give it a try, anyway. I didn't have a handkerchief on me so I tore to the bathroom, grabbed some paper towels, and ran back to the bench. "Hang in there, Mr. Russell." I dipped the towel in the water and dabbed his forehead, neck, and wrists. After a few scary moments, he moaned and opened his eyes.

"I have to go home," he whispered hoarsely.

"But, you don't look well enough to make it to the door," I objected.

"I need to go home to Carol. I have to protect her from Stellen." He rose unsteadily to his feet.

"Mr. Russell, please listen to me. Rest for a few minutes and get your breath. You don't look like you can make it all the way home by yourself."

"Carol needs me."

His mind was obviously so stuck on Carol, that no one could change it. I decided to accompany him and find out who this Carol person was. I held onto his arm and supported him as he ran to the exit. Officer Snout was still sitting at the table with the other officers. They all stopped what they were doing and stared at us.

"Is everything okay?" Officer Klipper asked.

"I need to get home to Carol," Mr. Russell said, eyes fixed on the exit.

"I think old man Russell worked one day too many," Officer Snout commented, taking a sip of his soda.

"Hey, be nice!" I muttered, but didn't say it too loud. My mind was too focused on making sure Mr. Russell made it home all right, to say anything to Officer Snout. I held onto Mr. Russell's arm the entire five minutes it took us to walk to his house.

He practically ran the last hundred yards, and I ran beside him, still holding on. "Carol! Carol, are you all right?" he cried, bursting into the house.

A middle-aged woman sat in a kitchen chair, reading a magazine. She jumped when Mr. Russell made his grand entrance. She was bald, her face pale and drawn, and her eyes were slightly dull. "Honey, what's wrong?"

"I had to make sure you were safe." He crossed the room in one huge stride and grabbed Carol in his arms.

I felt awkward and started to scoot toward the door, but Carol asked, "Who's your friend?"

It was now Mr. Russell seemed to notice me. He blushed and stammered, "Carol, this is Crystal O'Mally. Brian O'Mally's oldest daughter. The gentleman who sold us the sapphire I gave you for your birthday."

Her face lit up with recognition. "I thought you looked familiar. Pleased to meet you, Crystal. I'm Carol, the wife of this big lug." I didn't miss the loving glance she gave her husband.

"Nice to meet you, Mrs. Russell." I studied her. It was plain to see she'd been battling cancer. I couldn't tell if she was still fighting, or if she'd won.

"Please, have a seat." She motioned to a seat across from her chair. "Sweetheart, be a good host and get our guest something to drink."

"Oh, you really don't have to," I started to object.

"Do you like chocolate milk?" Mr. Russell interrupted me.

I love chocolate milk. I nodded as I took my assigned seat. "Thank you." I felt all the more awkward, so I studied the lime green tile floor. I nervously jiggled my leg back and forth, wishing I was anywhere, but here.

"So, what brings you to our humble dwelling, Miss O'Mally?" Mrs. Russell asked, pushing her magazine to the far end of the table.

"Your husband," I answered, trying to be funny.

"Oh, I already guessed as much, with how he hauled you in as if you were a catfish or something." She chuckled. "But, I was just wondering if there was any other reason you had, in particular."

Mr. Russell had retrieved my milk by now. He placed the glass in front of me, and I stared at the milk as it threatened to slosh over the rim of the glass, if I wasn't careful. He certainly was generous with portions. He dipped a straw into the milk and I nodded my thanks, still trying to think of something to say.

It was Mr. Russell who saved me. He sat down next to his wife and without a word, handed the slip of paper to her. She looked curiously at him, but accepted the paper. He held onto her thin shoulders while she read it, as if he was afraid she was going to faint. She inhaled sharply and turned to stare at her husband. "Where did you find this piece of paper?"

"Crystal found it." He nodded in my direction. "When I saw Stellen's name, I ran like the flames of hell were after me in order to make sure you were safe." He tightened his grip on her, a look of fear coming over his features.

I wanted so desperately to ask who in the world this Stellen person was, but decided not to, since I wasn't exactly included in the conversation. I concentrated on finishing my milk, knowing full well it would spoil my supper.

"Where did you find this, Crystal?" Mrs. Russell turned to me.

I gulped my mouthful of milk, praying I didn't have a brown mustache on my upper lip. "My little sister Emma found it, actually. In the crate where the diamond was kept, before it was stolen."

"I didn't think Stellen would be able to find us," she whispered, shaking her head. "After all these years. Why now, God?"

"Stellen ain't stupid, Carol. And, when he sets his mind to something, he don't give up."

"Why is he coming after us, after all these years?"

"I don't know."

"Um, excuse me. Should I leave?" I asked.

"You don't have to leave. Honey, I think Crystal deserves an explanation." Mrs. Russell leaned back in her chair and sighed wearily.

"Wait." I pulled out my digital recorder. Really it's Dad's, but I'm sure he wouldn't mind me borrowing it, for now. And then, out came my notebook. "Okay, you may proceed."

"Well I'll be hanged. What's that contraption for?" Mr. Russell looked surprised.

"To record your testimony."

"I take it you either read mystery novels or you watch a lot of mystery shows. Am I right, young lady?"

I chuckled softly. "Yes, sir, I do. And, when I graduate from college, I want to be the best girl detective ever."

"Like a female detective from a Carolyn Keene novel?" Mrs. Russell asked.

"Yes, ma'am. Carolyn Keene's my hero." I smiled sheepishly. "I want to be just like one of her characters, when I grow up."

Mrs. Russell laughed. "I wish you all the luck in the world."

"Pardon me for butting in, ladies, but I got me a story to tell," Mr. Russell interrupted.

I quickly turned the recorder on and nodded at him to please proceed.

"Craig Stellen was a powerful rancher in Northeast Texas," Mr. Russell began.

I smothered a groan, hoping this tale wouldn't be like one of Officer Snout's Paul Bunyan sized yarns he was forever spinning.

"I worked for Stellen as a ranch hand. I was pretty good with the cattle and almost any other task given to me. I rose quickly through the ranks to where I was in line for consideration to receive the foreman's job, when the current foreman retired.

"Well, one night, Stellen invites me into his office, saying he has a well-paying job he'd like me to perform. I didn't like the way he said 'well paying' and asked for more information. He gave this odd little laugh, and said it was a fairly simple task. All's I'd have to do is go undercover to a small town, pose as a detective, and earn the trust of the community. After a few years, I'd receive a visit from another ranch hand who would give me further instructions."

I couldn't hide the frown spreading across my face. *What kind of a nutty rancher would give those kinds of instructions to his hired help?* I didn't interrupt, not wanting to get my own voice in the recording, and nodded for Mr. Russell to continue.

"He said there was a rare diamond in this tiny town, and he'd like to add the diamond to his collection. One important thing you must understand about Stellen, is he loves money and jewels. He had his whole library stocked plum full with all the most precious stones I'd ever laid my eyes on in my life. He always took to wearing diamond rings on his fingers and he always had a mother of pearl wristwatch. He didn't take no cheap or artificial stuff, as far as precious stones are concerned.

"Anyway, I couldn't believe my ears. I staunchly refused to help Stellen in such a rotten, yella'-bellied deed. I turned to go, but Stellen didn't even break a sweat as he told me I'd regret it for the rest of my life, if I didn't help him. I blew him off and stormed out of the room."

Here, Mr. Russell's voice grew sad. "Danged if he didn't stay true to his word. The following week, a bigwig oil owner's wife lost one of her most valuable diamond necklaces. Somehow, the police found their way out to the Stellen ranch and started searching all the hands and their belongings. Dang it if they didn't find the piece of jewelry, stashed under my bunk.

"No matter how many times I said I didn't take it, and with all the hands speaking up for me, it was Stellen's testimony that sent me to jail. He even claimed I'd sneak off whenever I was supposed to be working and I'd spend my nights at the call house. Stellen's pack of lies earned me ten years in jail... ten years, I can never get back." Mr. Russell covered his eyes with his hand and broke down crying. His wife, tears streaming down her own cheeks, placed a trembling hand on his shoulder and tried to console him.

As for me, I was crying so hard I couldn't see. Terra had

partially told the truth when she said Mr. Russell had served a term, but she'd been wrong on what he'd been imprisoned for. I wiped my eyes with the back of my jacket sleeve.

"So, you understand why I had to make sure Carol was safe," Mr. Russell said a few minutes later, after he managed to compose himself somewhat.

I felt terrible for unearthing feelings they were no doubt trying so hard to forget. "I'm sorry for upsetting you."

"No, it's all right." Mrs. Russell wiped her eyes with a napkin. "Since Stellen knows where we are, I don't know what to do." She looked at her husband, as if requesting permission to tell me something else. He seemed to nod and she turned back to me, her face looking more pale and drawn than when I'd first walked in. "I had cancer last year, and was just given a clean bill of health two weeks ago," she said softly. "The reason why I've never really gotten out much, is because I didn't want to make all the ladies jealous of my gorgeous up do." She stroked the blond fuzz on her head, smiling sadly.

I returned the smile as best I could, deciding I'd heard enough information to keep me busy for a while.

"Show her a picture of Stellen," Mrs. Russell suggested.

"Good idea." Mr. Russell got up and left. He was only gone for a minute before returning with a photograph, which he handed to me. "I had this taken with Stellen and a few other cow hands. We'd just bought us some new calves and were taking pictures of us branding them." He managed to crack a smile. "We were guys and being silly." He pointed to a man in the right hand corner. "This one's Stellen."

I studied the photograph. Three or four men were pinning

down a brown calf that looked quite uncomfortable. The poor calf's mouth was open in a silent bawl. Stellen was the handsome type. He had shoulder length grayish blond hair, striking sky blue eyes, and a youthful smile along with a dimple on his chin. I easily picked out Mr. Russell by his missing side tooth. *Was he born with the tooth missing?*

The third man facing the camera looked really familiar. He had strange green eyes, a little scar at the corner of his left eye, and pearl white teeth nearly hidden beneath a dark beard. The fourth guy had shoulder length bleached hair. He wasn't fully looking at the camera, so I couldn't get a good look at his face. Yet, I couldn't help but notice one of his nostrils was slightly enlarged. I handed the picture back to Mr. Russell, turned the recorder off, and stood to my feet.

"Do you remember the morning I was carrying my black bag?" Mr. Russell asked, suddenly.

I was taken aback for a second. "Yes, sir. I do."

"I guess I should explain why I yelled at your sister when she wanted to touch it." He sighed and ran a hand through his hair. "I had some of Carol's medicine in there, and I've never really wanted people to know about her cancer. I just never knew who to trust, and always worried there might be some Stellen spy out there who'd find out about my wife, and blow our cover. I was scared Stellen would take my wife and use her to blackmail me into doing his dirty work ." He stopped and took a deep breath to steady himself. "The good Lord has kept us safe, all these years.

"Amen." Mrs. Russell gave Mr. Russell's arm a gentle squeeze.

I took a small, side step toward the door. "Thanks for the milk, it was delicious. And thank you for showing me the photograph."

"I'm glad you liked it. Honey, why don't you drive Crystal home?"

"No, it's all right. I can walk. Thank you, anyway"

"But, it's getting dark outside," she objected.

"I need to stop off at the station and get my backpack. I'll be home within fifteen minutes," I promised her.

She seemed ready to argue with me, but fortunately didn't. "Very well."

"Call us when you get there." Mr. Russell grabbed a piece of yellow paper and jotted down their phone number, before handing it to me. "Good luck with your detective work." He also handed me the piece of paper containing the name 'Stellen'.

"Thanks." I pocketed the recorder and two pieces of paper.

As I turned to go, Mrs. Russell laid a gentle hand on my arm. "Just be careful," she said softly.

"I will." *Hang on... I was making a promise to a woman I'd met only thirty minutes ago. Was I going off my rocker, or what? Yeah, I was most likely going off my rocker.* "Nice to have met you."

"You, too."

I jogged to the station, the recorder hitting my leg every time my foot hit the sidewalk. Mr. Russell told me a pretty touching story, and he made it sound very believable... *but, anyone can make up heartbreaking tales.* I needed to judge what I'd just heard very carefully. I decided to see if anyone at the police station knew anything about Mr. Russell's background.

"Hey, Crystal. Couldn't get enough of us?" Officer Klipper winked at me as I entered the foyer.

I chuckled. "Naw, not at all. It's me backpack, I come for."

"Would you just listen to her? Talking all Irish, she is." He tried to mimic the Irish accent. "Well, your backpack be near the janitor's closet, it be."

"Thanks. Oh, and do you know anything about Todd Russell's background?"

Officer Klipper scratched his bald spot. "Personally, I don't know much about the guy, but Officer Snout might. He was the one who did the background check on Russell after he first applied here. So, if you want any information, you'd have to ask Officer Snout... who is unfortunately talking with some other officers, at the moment."

"I'll ask him some other time, then. Thanks, Officer Klipper." As I ran down the hall to get my backpack, the recorder had worked its way to the top of my pocket. Before I could grab the gadget, it hit the tile floor and skittered away. "No!" I dove after it. I didn't want to lose Dad's one hundred and fifty dollar piece of equipment, nor did I want to break it... the reason being, I didn't have the money to replace it.

I absently put the recorder on a windowsill and hurried to the janitor's closet. Sure enough, my pack was where I'd dropped it. As I hefted it onto my shoulder, I noticed it seemed a little heavier than before. Probably, because I'd been without it for the past hour.

I left the building and was five minutes down the road, before I realized I'd forgotten the stupid recorder. "Gee whiz!

When will I ever start keeping better track of things?" I berated myself, as I flew back to the station. I didn't want anyone to see me as I slinked in the front door. The receptionist was busy on the phone and there were no officers around. I snuck down the hallway, hoping and praying the recorder was still there. To my immense relief, no one had touched it.

I noticed it was still on. *Odd.* I knew I'd clicked the off button before leaving the Russells' house. Not thinking about it, I turned it off and clutched it in my hand as I stole out of the building and hurried home. The lump in my pack kept hitting my back, until I grew annoyed and decided to see what was making it so heavy. A shoebox had been stuffed in there. Curious, I managed to wiggle it out and opened it. A 28oz. soda bottle was inside the box.

I lifted the bottle out. There wasn't any soda in there, but there *was* some kind of liquid in there. *Wait... was it me, or was this bottle swelling?* I held it up to the light and to my horror, recognized the bottle as a works bomb. I flung it into the street as far as I could, and then dashed down the sidewalk. I got about fifteen yards, before I heard this loud **BOOM!** Instantly, I knew the bomb had blown up. Frightened, I ran like a rabbit with a hound on its tail, all the way home.

"So, where were you?" Emma perched on the edge of my bed. "You were gone forever and ever. Mama was getting really worried."

"I know." I didn't mean to snap, it's just I was trying to process the story I'd heard earlier this afternoon... but my mind kept wandering back to the bomb. Freakiest thing I'd ever experienced in my entire life! *The thugs must know I'm onto them, or else they wouldn't have done that,* I reasoned with myself.

I was still surprised at myself for actually calling the Russells and letting them know I'd made it home safely. Mrs. Russell had sounded genuinely relieved when I'd called her. She and her husband weren't acting at all like I'd envisioned they would. They were actually nice and caring. Even Mr. Russell didn't seem as creepy as he used to. *What was with me, lately?*

"What'd else you learn?" Emma lay flat on her stomach, crowding me to the far edge of the bed. "'Cause I have something 'portant to tell you."

"First, you tell me your bit of important news." I pushed the geography book under my pillow and gave Emma my complete attention.

She reached into her shirt. *Yeah, you heard me right.* She reached *into* her shirt, and pulled out a small handheld notebook. "I figured if you could carry one around, then I could, too." She cleared her throat importantly, as she opened to the first page. Her handwriting was big and in block letters. "Well, I saw fedora man again today. This time, I gots to talk to him."

"You went and talked to a stranger?" I was both appalled and surprised at the same time. Appalled Emma would be so bold as to approach a complete stranger, especially when she knew better, and surprised she'd managed to get so close to him.

"Yeah."

"Emerald Grace. You know better than to talk to strangers."

"You say hi to Mr. Russell. And no one in town is stranger than him!"

"You know what I mean." I huffed out an annoyed sigh. "What did you ask fedora guy?"

"If he wanted a piece of hard candy."

"What kind of a question is that to ask a grown-up?"

"I don't know. I thought since I liked hard candy, he might like it, too. Anyway, he stared at me all funny like for a few seconds, and then frowned. He told me to leave him alone and started to walk passed me, but I ran 'long side him and told him the flavor was blueberry, my favorite. I even held it up to him. He snatched it up, studied it, and then gave it back. He almost smacked into the street sign as he ran away." She snickered at the memory.

"What did he look like underneath the fedora?"

"I wrote it down." She eagerly flipped to the next page. "Every little detail, even his stinky breath."

"What?"

"I wrote it all down." She shoved the notebook in my hands. "Read it for yourself."

'Long hair pulled back in pony tail, like a girl's.

But his hair is white like an old man's.

What's with that?

Is this an old man diskized as a girl?

And why does his breath stink?

It smells like he ate rotten tomatoes for lunch!'

I chuckled when I read how she misspelled disguised. "Good work, Emma." I lovingly ruffled her hair.

She beamed proudly. "Thanks, Crystal. It means a lot coming from you."

"Hey!" An idea suddenly came to mind. "Do you still have the piece of candy you gave him?"

"Why? Do you want it? If you want it, you can't have it for two reasons. One, 'cause I want to eat it and I'm not going to give it up, and two, 'cause you have braces."

"And three, I want to see if there are any fingerprints on the wrapper. Do you still have it?"

"I have it right here!" I half expected her to reach inside her shirt and pull it out, but luckily it was in her pants pocket. After a little bit of a struggle, she managed to pull it out.

I bit back a groan hoping she hadn't ruined any of the fingerprints, should there be any on there. I got up, grabbed my brush and some dust, and very gingerly dusted the cellophane wrapper. Nothing happened. "It's not going to stick to the wrapper," I moaned. "I don't have professional fingerprint stuff. I wish I did."

"Let's go to the supermarket and get some," Emma suggested.

"It's not something you can just go to the store, and get a small container of the stuff." I raked an agitated hand through my hair.

"Can we make some of our own?"

"I *wish*... but, no."

Emma bit her lip as she heavily pondered something. She snapped her fingers and went tearing out of the room so fast, I was surprised she didn't run into the doorjamb. She came rushing back just as fast, holding some of Mom's makeup containers. "Will this work?"

"They will, but Emmy, these are Mom's. What's she going to say if she catches us using them?"

She went to the door, looked out, and then came back. "She and Daddy are watching TV. Now's the time to use them," she whispered.

"I am *so* getting grounded for this," I muttered to myself. "Okay, close the door. Quick!"

She closed it and was back by my side in an instant. Crouching underneath my desk lamp, I brushed some pink blush onto the candy wrapper, and then placed some tape over it. I counted to five, and then very carefully peeled the tape off. Much to my elation, a pink fingerprint was visible. "Do you have the other fingerprints?" I whispered.

"They're in a book in my room," she whispered back. Without my having to ask, she quietly went to get it. She came back with one of Dad's leather bound accounting books, empty of course. No doubt she'd helped herself to it. A slip of paper was taped to the front with the title, 'Personal Detektive Items of Crystal and Emma'. She opened it and slid the book toward me. The fingerprints were taped to a white sheet of paper.

I compared the fingerprint to the mysterious one we found on the peephole at the store, and to our surprise and delight, it matched perfectly.

"It matches!" Emma breathed excitedly.

I wrinkled my nose at the heavy scent of onions on her breath. She'd obviously helped herself to more than one blooming onion at dinner tonight. "It does, but there's only one problem. We have the guy's fingerprint, but we don't know his name."

"Want me to ask?"

"No, it's okay." The last thing I needed was for Emma to get kidnapped. I don't know if I could handle that one. "I'll find out somehow."

"How?" Emma wanted to know. "Are you going to go up and ask him?"

"No, we've got to be subtle about this, like when we were getting Dad and Terra's fingerprints. We've got to get fedora guy's name, without him even knowing about it." I made it sound easier than it really was going to be. "We'll do it somehow, don't worry." I sounded more confident than I felt.

Chapter V

And So The List Grows

I rested my cheeks in my hands and stared at the worn countertop in front of me. It was after school the following day, and Emma and I had gone to the Gopher's Hole to grab either an ice cream sundae or a soda. I didn't really want to get either one, but Emma had been in the mood for a sundae, and I didn't see any harm in giving her a treat since she'd been such a good help, lately. I only hoped she wouldn't order anything too sugary, or else we'd have to make a pit stop by the playground and let her burn it all off, before we went home.

Behind me, the Andrew Sisters sang 'In Apple Blossom Time' on the old-fashioned jukebox. Gopher's Hole was fixed up to resemble a 1940's drug store… and it looked like one, with old-fashioned red leather stools at the bar, the black and red striped seats at the booths, and the type of attire the employees wore. Not exactly like a Steak & Shake, but dating a decade before the 1950's.

"What'll it be, ladies?" the boy behind the counter asked.

"What do you have?" Emma asked.

I just continued to stare at the counter, as if it fascinated me to no end.

"We have triple fudge sundaes, mint chocolate chip sundaes and banana strawberry sundaes," the boy answered.

"I'll have a triple fudge ice cream sundae, please," Emma requested. "With extra nuts."

Lord, have mercy! Now, I knew we were definitely going to have to hit the playground before we went home, so Emma could work up an appetite for supper and burn off all the extra sugar.

"What do you want, Crissy?" Emma turned to me.

"I don't know. I'm not really in the mood for anything," I muttered. I was still a little frustrated with how we only had four things of clues to work with... a janitor's confession, a photograph, a piece of paper with half a message, and some fingerprints... not exactly the end result, which is the capturing of the suspect.

"Aw, c'mon," Emma pleaded. "You've got to eat something."

She made it sound like I'd been so depressed for the past few weeks, I'd been starving myself. I grinned, despite my glum attitude.

The boy must have thought I was on a diet or something, because he offered, "We do have low calorie ice cream."

"Well..." I finally looked up, tired of talking to the countertop and having someone else respond, only to lock eyes with Minx. "Minx! What are you doing here?" Stupid question to ask. He was only wearing an employee's outfit, and he'd only been trying to take our orders.

"I work here," he answered. He blushed a little and leaned forward to where only I could hear him. "Community service for vandalism."

"Is anything the matter here, Minx?" Miss Gopher asked, coming over.

"No, not at all," Emma said sweetly. "Mr. Minx was just taking our orders."

"All right, then. Order away, darling." Miss Gopher winked at us and moved on to help another customer that'd just walked in.

I think she was aptly named with her short ears and small nose. Those two features made me think of a gopher, whenever I thought of her. Thankfully, she didn't have extra-long teeth, or else I would want to know why the Good Lord would let someone have not only the last name of an animal, but the facial features, as well.

"What would you like?" Minx asked me.

"I guess I'll have the mint sundae, please." I finally relented and ordered something.

"Extra nuts, too?"

"None for me. I have braces, remember?" I again flashed my tinsel teeth at him.

"Oh, sorry. I forgot. Anyhoo, two sundaes coming right up." He took our orders and disappeared into the kitchen.

"Well, this is a nice surprise."

I turned around in the seat to see Officer Snout standing behind us. "Afternoon, Officer Snout."

"Afternoon, ladies. Enjoying a little snack?"

"Yes, sir."

"Won't you join us?" Emma invited.

"No, I'm looking for a friend of mine." He glanced around the store. "But the turtle isn't here, yet. Oh, Crystal? I meant to ask you what was wrong with Mr. Russell, yesterday?"

"Oh, uh," I desperately fumbled for an answer. "I don't

know if you know, but his wife's been sick, lately. He thought something was wrong with her, because she'd been to the doctor." My voice trailed off. I couldn't think of what else to say, without saying too much.

"The way you were holding onto him, made me think you were trying to anchor him into the ground or something." Officer Snout looked levelly at me, as if trying to decide if I was telling the truth or not.

C'mon, think of something! Think of something! I managed a nervous chuckle. "He's getting on in years, and I didn't want him going too fast, or else he might keel over or something." *Could I have said anything more lame? I don't think so!*

"Well, is his wife all right?"

"Yes, she's doing fine."

"Good. We wouldn't want something to happen to her." He made it sound like he was a close personal friend or a relative. "I'm going to take a seat and order some grub. I'm so hungry, I could eat a hippo."

Emma wrinkled her nose and stuck her tongue out. "Ick! Nasty!"

"They taste mighty delicious, actually. Take the time I was in the military, and we were in Africa."

Emma and I both quietly groaned at the exact same time. It looked like Officer Snout's story was going to spoil our appetites for ice cream, however, the Good Lord in His mercy sent someone to rescue us from our distress. Minx.

"Here are your orders." The boy set them down in front of us.

"I'll leave you to your ice cream before it melts. By the way." Officer Snout put his elbows on the counter and leaned toward Emma, dropping his voice to a mysterious whisper. "Why does your sister have more ice cream than you do?"

Emma's head instantly whipped around, and as she studied our sundaes, I saw Officer Snout slyly take the cherry off her sundae and pop it into his mouth. He winked at me before sauntering over to a booth.

"Did you give her more ice cream than me?" Emma demanded to Minx. "'Cause if you did, then you're not being fair!"

"No, I gave you both the same amount. Honest and truly, I did," Minx defended himself. "I like my job and I aim to keep it."

"Well, okay." She picked up her spoon to dig in, when she noticed her cherry missing. She whirled around in her seat so fast, she nearly went spinning to the floor. "Crystal Elizabeth O'Mally, that's not funny. Eating my cherry. You pig!"

"It wasn't me, it was Officer Snout. I saw him take it." I was humiliated Emma would call me a babyish name like 'pig'. Minx, obviously amused, wore an ear-to-ear grin.

Emma grew quiet as reality set in and she realized why Officer Snout had distracted her. She blushed, and then reached over to give me a hug. "I'm sorry for calling you a pig, Crystal."

I returned the hug. "No hard feelings." I gave her my cherry. "Here, I don't really like these cherries, anyway."

"You don't?" Minx looked shocked. "But, they're the best part."

"Minx." Miss Gopher came over. "I need you to wait on those two gentlemen in the booth, right away."

"Yes, ma'am." He hurried away.

Emma put her finger into the whipped topping and stuck her finger into her mouth. "Mmm-mmm!" She wiggled her shoulders. She always did a little happy dance whenever she ate something she really liked. She looked at me. "Aren't you going to eat your ice cream?"

"Yes, I am." I picked up my spoon.

"Hey, why'd he give you more whipped cream than me?" She frowned. "I don't like him. He's a cheesecake."

"Don't you mean *cheapskate?*"

"Whatever he is, I don't like him."

I slid the two sundaes side by side, and saw what my sister had said, was true. I *did* have a little bit more whipped topping than she did, but it was such a small amount, no one would notice unless they were looking for it. *Why did Minx give me more than my sister?*

"I think he likes you," Emma declared, stuffing a big spoonful of ice cream and fudge into her mouth.

"He does not."

"Does, too."

"Why do you think he likes me?"

"'Cause, anytime a guy likes a girl, he always gives her special treatment."

"He must not have been paying attention." I crammed some chocolate chips and mint into my mouth. The chocolate melted instantly, running like butter down my throat, while the mint left a refreshing taste in my mouth.

"So." Emma looked up at me, chocolate rimming her mouth. "What are we going to be doing later? Snooping some more?"

"Probably, but I want to see how much I can find out about fedora guy, and I think the only place to look is in the police files."

"Then, let's hurry up and go." She started eating faster.

"Wait, they won't let me just waltz in there and start going through files. I'm not even a registered detective, nor am I on the police force."

"Why don't you go sign up for a day, look through the files, and then quit, tomorrow?"

"It just doesn't work that way. We've got to find another way of getting information on our suspect."

"I think I can help."

I was right in the process of bringing a spoonful of ice cream to my mouth, when Minx's low voice startled me. The ice cream slipped and before I knew it, I had a cold, green blob in my lap. "Perfect!"

"Oh, I'm really sorry. Here." He handed me a napkin dispenser.

"Thanks." Grabbing one, I cleaned myself off the best I could. Luckily, I was wearing a jacket and could just tie it around my waist like an apron on the walk home. "You can help? How?"

"I overheard you say something about a fedora guy. Was he tall and thin with shoulder length hair?"

Before I could respond, Emma piped up. "Yes, but wait. How would you know what he looks like?"

"He was in here, not too long ago. He had a to-go order and I took it. I got his name," Minx whispered.

"Lemme see it," Emma said, spewing ice cream and chocolate on the counter top in the process.

"Hang on." He went into the kitchen and after about two minutes, reappeared with a yellow slip of paper. "Here it is." He leaned over the counter, held out the ticket, and pointed to the name 'Kyle Gregory'.

Odd, a guy having two first names. But then again, it was better than a name like Minx. "What did he look like?"

"He had long, white hair pulled back in a low pony tail. Looked kind of freaky, if you ask me."

"Well, we didn't," Emma interrupted.

"What was the color of his eyes? What color is his tongue? Did he have a fever? The whole shebang," I pressed.

"Why would we want to know what color his tongue is?" Emma demanded.

"To give Minx a general idea of what features I'm looking for."

"Oh."

"He had sky blue eyes, almost the color of a cloudless sky," Minx answered. "His teeth were perfect, like a movie star's, and he had a youthful smile. He looked like a lady's man."

An alarm went off inside my brain. "Did he have a dimple anywhere on his face?"

"Yeah, as a matter of fact, he did."

Stellen! He was in here, in town. I tried to appear calm despite my shaking fingers, as I used my cell phone to type down everything Minx said. The description he just gave, perfectly matched the man in Mr. Russell's photograph. "Thanks." I pocketed the phone. I suddenly noticed Officer Snout watching us out of the corner of his eye. I squirmed uneasily, wondering why he was staring at me so intently. Craig Stellen was in the area, going under an alias name. I had to somehow warn the Russells, they were in danger.

"Hey, Crystal? Do we have Officer Snout's fingerprint?" Emma whispered.

"What for?" Minx wanted to know.

"None of your business, nosy," Emma shot back.

"Whoa, hey there, now." Minx threw his hands up in surrender. "I was just curious, is all. Don't tell me you're never curious."

"I am, at times."

"It's a long story," I told Minx, just as a pair of customers came in. "You might want to wait on them, so you don't get fired."

"Oh, okay." He strangely didn't seem too happy about it, though. "Do you girls like your ice cream?"

"Except for one thing. Why'd you give Crystal more whipped cream than me?" Emma demanded. "Do you have a crush on Crystal or something?"

"Emerald Grace O'Mally!" I poked her in the rib cage. "You didn't need to ask him about the whipped cream."

"Mama and Daddy always tell the waitresses when they're unhappy with an order," she retorted.

"That's totally different." I looked up to see Minx's face was a beet red. It was so red, his black goatee stood out. He gave us a weak grin before going to tend to the two lady customers seated one stool down from me. As I put another spoonful of ice cream in my mouth, the conversation from the newcomers reached me. I looked at them out of the corner of my eye. One of them was kind of large, while the other one was as skinny as a rail.

"I still refuse to set foot in the thief's store. I'm appalled the police haven't arrested him and are letting him continue to stay in business," the stout one said, in a huffy voice.

Uh oh. This conversation does not sound like a pleasant one, I thought.

"Oh, come now, Edith. The townspeople insist he's very trustworthy, and has been for almost twenty years," Edith's friend insisted. "Besides, I've seen some of what he sells in the newspaper. I think he sells very lovely pieces and it'll be worthwhile visiting his shop."

"You can go if you want to and get your valuables stolen," Edith huffed. "I'm going to be wise and stay as far away from there as possible."

My stomach felt like I'd just swallowed an entire carton of ice cream, freezing cold. I pushed the rest of my treat away from me. I looked at Emma and saw her eyes wide with shock and my heart dropped into my socks. She'd overheard the comment.

She also pushed her sundae away from her, and hopped down from the stool. I silently handed her a napkin to wipe her mouth as we went to the cash register.

"Was everything to your liking?" Miss Gopher smiled as she took my change.

"Yes, as always." I pasted on a polite smile, feeling like it was super-glued to my face. I wore it all the way out of the diner, and once on the street, the glue melted and the smile vanished. Emma's hand slid into mine. "Want to go to the playground for a bit before heading home, so we can work off all that sugar?" I made my voice light, hoping she'd at least grin. Instead, she simply nodded and pressed against my thigh. My heart filled with pity for her. Five minutes later, I was sitting on the squeaky playground swing next to her, staring at the mulch.

I was angry with God. *Why didn't He just show us where the criminal was? Why did Emma have to hear other people slamming Dad? It wasn't fair!* I looked up at the blue sky. Clouds chased each other across the vast blue field, reminding me of lambs frolicking in a pasture. I wished I could be as happy, light, and carefree as those clouds. At the moment, I felt anything but happy and carefree. I felt like I was at the bottom of an ocean with cement shoes strapped to my feet, and there seemed no hope of ever coming up for air. A tiny sniffle caught my attention.

Emma was also staring at the mulch, but I could see her face was red and streaked with tears. I pulled her as close to me as the chains would allow. "Why'd the fat woman say those nasty things about Daddy?" she snuffled.

I was too mad at God, at life, and at the criminal, to bother telling Emma to be nice. "She's nasty, that's why."

"I wanna' go home," Emma pleaded.

"Okay." We left the playground and slowly set our course for home.

When we arrived, Mom was cooking supper. It smelled like she was cooking Brunswick stew. The scent of pork and other vegetables teased my nose. Brunswick stew is one of my favorite dishes, and I usually hover around the kitchen until Mom gives me a small bowl of stew and shoos me away.

However, today I kicked my shoes off in the foyer and padded down the hall in my socks to my room. Emma went to her room, also. I sat in my desk chair staring listlessly at the setting sun as it left behind trails of pink, yellow, periwinkle, and lavender sprays of light, before making its way to some other part of the globe. I couldn't stop feeling bad for Emma. I was older. I could take insults, but to have my eight-year old sister hear it? *Ahem, she's only eight-stinking-years-old, peoples. She doesn't need to be hearing strangers insulting her dad.*

I clenched my hands into fists at my side. "The only way to get this stupid business over with, is to find the crook and make him pay for what he's done," I told myself through clenched teeth. I rolled over to my desk and started feverishly pouring over notes. After a few minutes, I became so engrossed in my work, I didn't hear someone knocking on the door. It wasn't until Mom was standing at my elbow, I came back into the real world.

"Crystal Elizabeth O'Mally!" Mom's hands were on her hips and her hair seemed to bristle.

Oh, boy. She was mad.

"What did you do to your sister?"

"What do you mean? Is she throwing up or something?" She hadn't finished her ice cream, so she couldn't be sick.

"No. She's curled up underneath her bed and she refuses to come out. She only hides under her bed when the two of you have had a shouting match. What did you two argue about on the way home? And how many times have I told you..."

"She heard someone slam Dad," I cut her off.

Mom's face instantly softened. "Where?"

"At the Gopher's Hole. I took Emma there for a sundae... a small one, don't worry... and some woman called Dad a thief." Tears stung my eyes at the memory. "She said she wouldn't do her shopping there." Anger bubbled up inside of me, as I thought about the other comment the lady had made. "And, she also said the police were wrong to let Dad continue running his business. Said Dad needed to be arrested, because he's a thief."

Mom laid a hand over her mouth, tears filling her own eyes faster than water in a bathtub. "Oh, sweetheart. I'm so sorry for accusing you of shouting at Emma."

"It's okay, Mom." I slumped further down in my chair, rubbing my forehead. "It's not your fault."

We were quiet for a few minutes. The only sound in the room was my wall clock ticking away the passing minutes. "Pray," Mom said suddenly, startling me so bad, I nearly yelped aloud.

"Excuse me?"

"Pray for the woman who slammed Dad. The only reason she ran her mouth, was because she's scared she'll be robbed. If the diamond had never been stolen in the first place, she would never have said what she did. I'm sure if she was in another town and the jeweler there had something valuable stolen under his watch, then she would have said the exact same thing about him or her."

Praying for the woman was the last thing on the planet I wanted to do. I wanted to flatten her pudgy nose. I swallowed hard and whispered, "Yes, ma'am."

"I know it won't be easy." Mom took a deep breath and I saw a spark of anger in her brown eyes. "I have to fight back the urge to hunt her down and teach her a thing or two."

"Why don't you teach her a thing or two?" I eagerly stood up.

"It'd be a waste of time, not to mention waste of breath. She sounds like the type who won't listen to reason, but I'm going to forgive her for saying those things about my husband, anyway."

"Why?" It didn't make sense. *How could Mom forgive someone who was nasty to her husband?*

"Hating her won't benefit me at all, and it won't make her apologize to Brian."

"Oh, I see." Not really. I still didn't understand this whole forgiveness thing.

Mom headed toward the door. "I'm going to see if I can get Emma out from underneath her bed, now."

"When you first came in wanting to know what I'd done to her, I thought she'd eaten too much ice cream and was sending it back up or something."

Mom chuckled. "Thank goodness she's keeping her ice cream right where it belongs."

After she left, I sat back down in my chair with my head halfway between up in the air and above my knees. I rubbed my hands together, trying to think of something to say to God without being disrespectful. I wanted to tell Him exactly how I felt, how angry and hurt I was. *That woman was so vicious! She had no right slamming Dad the way she did.* A verse from Matthew danced across my memory.

'You have heard it said, 'You shall love your neighbor and hate your enemy.' But, I say to you, love your enemies, bless those who curse you, do good to those who spitefully use you and persecute you.'

My temper finally burst as I looked at up at the ceiling and cried, "Why isn't the stupid thief in custody yet?" My eyes fell on the latest headlines, partially shoved underneath my desk. I reached down, picked the paper up, and against my better judgment, read the article.

'At least five more people around town hit by jewel thief.

Police are baffled, and still no word about the Alamo diamond.'

And underneath it, in smaller print,

'Police still haven't apprehended the mysterious jewel thief, as he continues to help himself to the precious and most valuable jewels in Alamo.

Why is the thief suddenly appearing now?

Why not fifty years ago, when the diamond was first discovered?

Why the Alamo diamond?

Why not the Klopman diamond?'

I chuckled, knowing Papaw was referring to the famous diamond gag used on the TV show 'Garfield and Friends'. I slowly clapped my hands together, blowing out a frustrated breath. I felt like God was letting me down, big time. I was kind of hoping for... *like say, oh, a thunderbolt to come down from the sky...* followed by a booming voice telling me where the bad guy was.

I lazily picked up the recorder and hit play. Mr. Russell's story swirled around me, but I was only listening half-heartedly. I heard the doorbell ring and ignored it, thinking one of Mom's quilting friends had come over with either a quilting question or help for a design.

My cell phone rang and I could tell by the ring tone, it was an unknown number. I answered it, anyway. "Hello?"

There was a silence on the other end, then an eerie voice crackled through some static. "Heed this warning!"

"Who is this?" I demanded.

"Heed this warning," the voice cackled again, and then I heard a distinct click on the other end of the line.

Talk about the scariest thing I'd ever heard in my life! Chills raced up and down my spine and I shivered, even though it was seventy-five degrees in my room. After a few seconds, the creepy feeling wore off and I grinned. "It just means I'm finally getting on someone's nerves. Awesome!" I picked up the recorder, once more. The bomb meant they wanted me off their tail, but the call meant I was getting on someone's nerves.

"Crystal," Mom called from behind my partially closed door. "You have a visitor."

"Coming." I tossed the recorder on my bed and went to see

who my guest was. "Minx!" I stared at him like he was an extra-terrestrial. "How'd you know where I live?"

He blushed again, his Adams apple bobbing up and down like a bob on a fisherman's pole. "Your name's only on your mailbox. I...uh... never did get to thank you for getting me off the hook. Your good word helped get us out."

"You're welcome." I felt more awkward than I'd ever felt before in my life.

"Do you know Minx?" Mom asked.

"We go to the same school together," he offered.

"We do." I hated to admit the next part, no matter how true it was. "We even share some of the same classes together."

"Good. I wanted to make sure he was telling the truth. Minx says he has something for you."

Like what? Roses? Chocolates? A moonlit ride to the middle of nowhere? I wasn't interested. I wanted to be left alone, for now. I looked at Mom, using my eyes to telegraph a message, 'Get him out of here, puh-lease!' Instead, she regarded me with an odd little smile and a raised eyebrow. I glanced over my shoulder, mentally biting my tongue to keep from snapping at our guest. I saw my reflection in the hall mirror and noticed how my face was as red as a turkey's gobbler.

"I brought some information for your case," Minx blurted out, holding out an orange manila envelope.

I sighed and slumped my shoulders, hoping Mom would get the hint. I didn't want any more help than I already had. I was an independent detective, and those types rely solely on themselves... but it was becoming harder and harder to *stay* an independent detective.

"Why don't you two come into the den and work on it there?" Mom suggested.

I rolled my eyes in exasperation. Mom was acting hopeless. I had no choice, but to sulkily follow the two of them to the den. I sat on the leather chair while he sat on the couch. After a few seconds of awkward silence, both of us started speaking at the same time.

"I've been... "

"I don't think..."

We stopped and looked at each other.

"You first," Minx said.

"No, the guest can go first."

"Ladies first."

"Age before beauty."

He opened his mouth to object, but closed it with a snap. "Can't argue with you there." He held out the envelope again. "I... I hope you don't mind. I've been doing a little bit of detective work."

"Have you now?" I wasn't exactly thrilled by his announcement.

"Go ahead and check it out." He held the envelope out again.

Before I could accept it, I heard Emma's startled cry resound through the house. "Crystal! There's a strange man in your room!"

What the heck? I jumped up and tore for my room. Emma was cowering in her doorway. She looked like she didn't know whether to dive back under the bed, or find out who my mysterious visitor was. The recorder was still playing. I'd forgotten to turn it off before I went to entertain Minx. "It's okay, Em. I just forgot to turn off the recorder. See?" I held it out as proof. It was still playing, but the sound was down too low to hear anything Mr. Russell was saying.

"I heard someone laughing crazily," she told me.

I frowned. *I don't remember Mr. Russell laughing while he told me his tale of woe.* Puzzled, I turned to go to the den again and rammed into Minx's chest. "Sheesh! Follow a little more closely next time, will you. Why were you following me, anyway?"

"I just wanted to see if I could be of any help," he stammered.

"What's wrong?" Mom poked her head around the corner.

"I just left a player on in my room, and Emma thought I had a strange man in there," I explained.

"Just so long as no one was killed. Supper time, in ten minutes." She disappeared into the kitchen.

I swallowed a groan as I trooped to the den. I had to suffer through ten whole minutes in Minx's company. *Oy!* I sat down on my throne and Minx held the envelope out to me for the third time. I placed the recorder in my lap and opened the envelope. A series of photo copied yellow tickets slid into my lap. I studied them. They were all to-go orders for different people. *Big whoop. I'm not in the restaurant business, so how did Minx think this would interest me?*

"Read ticket eighty-seven," he directed. "At least, read the name on it."

"Lee Morgan," I read it aloud. "What significance does the name hold to my case?"

"Don't you have a person on the police force known as Stan Snout?"

"Yeah." I couldn't keep my impatience in any longer. "What concern is it of yours? I mean, all of the sudden you want to start helping me on a case. I was doing just fine, solving by myself." *Well, kind of.* "Why the pretend interest?"

Minx glanced at the doorway and scooted from the couch to the floor at my feet. I instinctively shrank away from him, as if he were covered in poison ivy. "I couldn't help but overhear the comments the lady made in the Gopher's Hole, earlier this afternoon."

I scowled. "And why are you here, then?"

He sighed and looked down at the vanilla colored carpet, as if the answer was written down there in script form or something. He finally looked up. "I saw the effect it had on your little sister and it tore at me."

I was again skeptical. He could just be trying to play with my feelings and win my sympathy. How did I know he wasn't a brutal woman beater? I didn't know *anything* about him, other than the fact he'd been arrested for vandalism, he had a cute looking goatee, and he could fix a mean mint chocolate chip sundae. Oh, and he wanted to be my sidekick. "Do you have any siblings of your own?"

"No, I don't. Mom wasn't able to have any more, after me. Which really stinks, because I always wanted a little brother or sister, and we didn't have enough money to where we could adopt. I like kids, and I hated seeing your sister have to listen to..." He bit back an obvious colorful description of the woman, and quickly substituted it for another word. "That woman just sitting there, waiting for her ice cream, and slamming someone's father as if she were talking about the weather."

"So, what does this have to do with your appearance on my front stoop and you handing me these tickets?"

"I must confess, I overheard Emma saying something about being detectives. So, are you two pretending to be any famous detective in particular?"

"No!"

"Then, who are you pretending..."

"No one," I cut him off. I glanced at the clock and saw we only had five torturous minutes left. "So, what's the purpose of these tickets?"

Minx's face fell. He was obviously hurt by my abruptness with him. I squirmed uneasily under his puppy dog eyes. I couldn't help it. I had a mystery to solve, and I couldn't waste any valuable time talking to some teenage boy who went to school with me, and was just trying to ask me out on a date.

He pointed to the ticket on top of the pile. "Stan Snout's been in the diner a few times, and each time he comes in, he always orders his meals as Lee Morgan. He even had a credit card with 'Lee Morgan' on it." Minx produced the sales slip.

I was impressed, but wasn't about to show it. Well, maybe if I feigned interest, he'd take the hint, pack up his bags, and go home and play video games or whatever boys played, now-a-days. "Good work."

His face brightened up somewhat.

Uh-oh. Maybe it wasn't such a good idea, after all.

"I've been wondering why he'd order his meals using a fake name, then today, I thought, 'Hey. Why not take it to some brains, and see what she can do?'."

"Time to eat," Mom called loudly.

Those words had never sounded sweeter to my ears, than now. I literally jumped out of my chair and whispered an excited, *"YES!"*, under my breath. "Be right there, Mom," I called aloud.

Minx slowly stood to his feet. "Thanks for accepting what little bit of information I had to give you."

"Hopefully, it will help."

He awkwardly stuck out his hand. After mentally making a face, I shook it, and then wiped my right hand against the back leg of my pants. "See you later."

"See you tomorrow." He all but ran down the street, no doubt to moon over me or something, and think I liked him.

Well, I didn't! I wrinkled my nose at his departing figure and shut the hard door as tightly as I could, as if the action would keep him out of my life and house, forever. I decided to put Minx's little 'present' into a shoebox, and shove it into the farthest and darkest corner in my closet. As I picked up one of the tickets, the name 'Gregory' stood out, worse than a dirty pig in a clean kitchen.

I feverishly flipped to the ticket containing Stellen's alias name. The name 'Kyle Gregory' was written in the corner of the yellow slip of paper. I thumbed through the rest of the tickets, noting different names on some of the tickets. Lee Morgan's name appeared on two more of them.

Other names, such as 'Oliver Creed', 'Nevel Anderson', and 'Stow Peter' were written on the last three. I instantly felt a little bit of pity for Stow Peter. *What a name to have, especially when you're supposed to be a hardcore criminal.* I could almost see and hear him getting picked on and tormented by his fellow partners in crime.

"Crystal." Mom stood in the doorway. "Did you not hear me say it's dinner time?"

"Hmm? Oh, yes, ma'am. I'm just picking up my little mess here." I scooped up the papers to prove my point.

"Just don't let your food get cold," she warned, heading back to the kitchen.

I placed the papers in my desk drawer, just as a thought hit me. *Better start adding them to the list.* I hastily jotted down the new names to my suspect list. It wasn't much, yet it was a nice start. My little list of suspects was slowly, but surely, growing. My only wish was to remove Terra's name from the list, however due to her suspicious behavior, I had no choice *but* to put her name down. I hoped against hope, she would do something to redeem herself and I could take her name off, and add at least ten more new names.

Chapter VI

The Recording Spills The Beans

"Aw, how sweet of him. I think he likes you," Emma chanted in a singsong voice, running a finger up and down my arm. "Woo-hoo!"

She'd come into my room after dinner the previous evening, wanting to know all about Minx's visit. I had shooed her out of the room, telling her to let me do my Science in peace. She backed off, until the next day when we saw Minx at school. She kept badgering me even as we were walking home, hours later. I told her if she didn't hush up, then I wouldn't tell her anything. It worked, until she came into my room after dinner wanting to know everything. I told her what had happened, hoping it would get her off my back. Instead, she started teasing me.

"Would you cut it out?" I shrugged her finger off. "Besides, I don't have time for romance, dates, and everything else involved in having a boyfriend."

"Aren't there some detectives who are married and date?" she pronounced the word 'detective', very slowly and carefully.

"Some detectives might manage to find dating time, however *this* detective," I pointed to myself, "doesn't have time for such frivolities."

"What's a frav... fravolroly? Sounds like some disease or a rotten piece of fruit."

"*Frivolity*. Parties, and such."

"It wouldn't be a *party*," Emma insisted. "You two could go out to the Gopher's Hole after school, or something. And then, when you've sweet talked him over into adoring your luster beauty, you pump information from him."

"I think the word you're looking for is *luscious,* not luster. And no, I am not interested in dating Minx, at the moment. There's something I want you to hear."

"Like what?" She pulled her notebook out of her shirt.

How the heck does she manage to keep things in there, without it falling out? Probably, because she tucks her shirt in.

She snatched one of my pencils, and as an afterthought asked, "May I?"

After you've already helped yourself to it, yeah, why not? "Sure." I pulled the recorder out of its hiding place underneath my mattress. So far, Dad hadn't noticed it missing, which made me wonder why he bought in the first place if he wasn't going to use it. "Now, this is Mr. Russell talking."

"How'd you manage to talk to him without being stuffed in his closet or something?" Emma looked at me in shock.

"Would you knock it off already? Dad and Mom have both told you Mr. Russell wouldn't do anything like steal little children."

"Why hasn't he told me himself?"

"Because he's about to, if you'll let him." I was getting exasperated. It was late, and Emma was wasting time.

"Really?" She looked at the door, clearly expecting him to come walking in and start explaining why he wasn't going to kidnap her. Rolling my eyes in annoyance, I clicked the 'PLAY' button, and both of us leaned in close. Emma's pencil was cocked and ready to start writing down her notes.

Mr. Russell's bass voice came from the little instrument, repeating everything he'd told me a few days ago. I hadn't managed to visit the Russells lately, like I'd wanted to. My mind began to wander, instead of paying attention to what was being said. Something he had said was starting to attach itself to another puzzle of the mystery. I could almost literally see the pieces clicking together in my head.

Mr. Russell had told me Stellen had wanted him to come to a tiny town as an undercover detective, win the peoples' confidence, and then steal the diamond. For some odd reason, it made me think of the Snouts. Terra had become more withdrawn than ever before. I couldn't believe it. She'd talk to me every few days, if I was lucky. Dad told us she'd called in sick a few times. I'd been too busy of late to swing by her house and wring a confession from her, like excess water from a dishrag.

Now, why am I thinking of the Snouts? I haven't thought of them, lately. I couldn't understand it, until I thought of how long they'd been here in comparison to the Russells. The latter had been here for a year, and they had more rumors circling around them than flies around manure. The Snouts showed up seven years ago, and within a month, they won the hearts of the community. Officer Snout saved the town's only bank from some robbers not once, but twice, in a three month period. *They come here, everybody loves them, and they're well established citizens.*

Terror grabbed my heart. *No, Lord! No! Not the Snouts!* It was starting to make sense. Mr. Russell had said Stellen wanted him to win the town's affection, hang around for a few years, and then steal the diamond. *No... no... Officer Snout has diplomas hanging on the wall of his office saying he actually went through colleges, and...* I cut myself off, as I thought of how all of my mystery heroes had encountered more than one person with either phony papers or a phony certificate.

Tears scalded my lids as I thought about how Terra was looking more and more guilty, with every passing day. *You're not being fair here, God. Why does my best friend have to be involved in something as ugly as this?* I suddenly remembered reading somewhere in the Bible, how God gave man freewill to decide how he wanted his life to go. *But, why did Terra have to choose to be a crook? Huh?* I desperately tried to think of something that could put my mind to ease, and assure me Terra was innocent.

"Who's him?" Emma interrupted my deep musing.

"Who's what?" I shook my head.

"He's the guy I heard laughing, last night. He sounds like a *maniac!*"

I didn't hear anyone laughing, but then again, I didn't recognize the voice talking. I realized it wasn't Mr. Russell's voice. It was someone else. I frowned, knowing I hadn't interviewed anyone other than the janitor. "I wonder who this is," I muttered, more to myself than to Emma. I clicked the 'REWIND' button, and rewound it for a few seconds. What came up was a noise like a crash. I heard a voice I instantly knew as mine. *I didn't turn the recorder off, like I thought I did.* I felt my eyes widened. *What a perfect way to waste battery juice.* I heard myself muttering, and heard a sound like two objects being clunked together.

"What happened?" Emma whispered.

"I probably put the recorder on the window sill," I whispered back.

There was dead silence, then we could hear someone talking in the background, and a door slammed shut. Slowly, the talking grew louder, until the voice was audible enough to be understood. I kind of recognized the voice, but not enough where I could place it right off the top of my head.

"Yeah, everything's going according to plan, so far." His voice, even though it was low, carried clearly to us. He was quiet for a few seconds, as if waiting for something, and then spoke again. "Oh, no. I'll take care of her. She paid us a visit the other day, and nearly ruined the whole thing." Quiet...

"I think he's talking on the phone," Emma whispered.

"Sounds like it," I agreed.

"She's hot on our trail. I only agreed, so she wouldn't get suspicious." Pause... "Hey, don't worry about it. I'll make sure she's gone, and anyone else who tries to stick their nose into our business... which is none of theirs. I've been following your orders for the past seven years. Can't you at least trust me to take care of those little peons?"

"Ooh, gross!" Emma made a gagging noise, sticking her wide tongue out as far as it would go. I chuckled and paid attention to the mystery person.

"Oh, no need to worry about Crest. I'll make sure he does everything he knows he's supposed to do." The man chuckled eerily, sending shivers up and down my spine. "Just make sure everything goes according to plan on *your* end, or else we're sunk. All right. Mmm-hmm, bye." Footsteps faded away, and I reached down to turn the recorder off, just as more footsteps echoed through the hall.

"Stow!" The faint cry reached us, and we leaned forward to

try and hear what was going to be said next. "You big ox! What are you doing here?" It was the man who'd just finished his phone call, and he didn't sound the least bit pleased.

"You know I was supposed to show up with your next orders." Stow's gravelly voice was a little clearer than the first speaker. "So, here I be."

"I just got off the phone with Stellen and told him you didn't need to show up."

"He didn't call me in time to give me my new orders."

"Okay, fine. Here are your new orders. Scoot, before someone starts to wonder why you keep coming here, so often. Strangers draw unwanted talk from the townspeople."

"Hey, Lee, I'm just following the boss' orders, here," Stow growled. "If you don't like it, you kin take it up with Stellen."

Lee blew out a long, frustrated breath. "Listen, you're going to put me under suspicion by coming to see me, so much. People are going to not only start wondering why you're coming in here, especially the motor-mouth receptionist, but they'll start asking questions, too."

"I wear a different disguise, each time I come."

"How about you call me from now on? Got it? And, we can meet somewhere else. Maybe at the Gopher's Hole, like we did last week."

"Fine by me. Just so long as you get your orders, and I get paid."

"Now, you can scram! I've got work to do." Without another word Lee left, and Stow must have left, for we heard a distant door bang.

The slamming noise was soon replaced by another door slamming somewhere. A second later, we heard running footsteps and heavy breathing. I knew it was me coming back to get the recorder, and finally turn it off.

"How'd you do it, Crissy?" Emma whispered in awe.

"I just left the recorder on, without knowing it. It was a total mistake."

"Neat! You should make those kinds of mistakes all the time."

"Maybe. Hey, if it's just the two of us, why are we whispering?"

"For *dramatic emphasis*."

"Okay." I spoke in normal volumes. "So, what'd you get out of Mr. Russell's story?"

"Mrs. Tellers was right. He did go to jail. He's a bad man."

"No, he was framed."

Emma raised her eyebrows, and I could almost envision what was going on in that carrot top head of hers. She could see him walking around, with a giant picture frame around his neck.

"Meaning he was set up." I tried to think of how to break it down for an eight-year-old. "Someone lied about him, and got him sent to jail."

Thankfully, she comprehended that. "So, he didn't really steal the lady's necklace?"

Part of me wanted to say yes, while the other half wanted to say no. I needed more proof, yet I didn't know how to get any.

"He says he didn't," I finally replied, staring at the ceiling. "But the real question is, how are we going to go about finding out whether or not his story's true? And how do we find out about this Stow guy?"

"Why don't we start interviewing people?"

"We could, but who would we start with?"

"How about the motor-mouth resip... resepting... The motor-mouth lady Lee was talking about."

I couldn't stop myself from laughing softly. Emma was going to have a much broader vocabulary by the time this mystery was solved. "It's pronounced *receptionist*. It's a lead we can try, but the only thing is, we don't know which receptionist he was referring to. There are at least five different receptionists who work at the police station."

"Then, alls we have to do is talk to them, and see which one likes to talk the most."

She made it sound so easy, like all we had to do was waltz right into the station, strike up a conversation with each of the receptionists, and find out who jabbered the longest. "I guess we can give it a try," I said reluctantly.

"Great." She gave an enormous yawn, which made her face disappear.

"Next time, cover it. You'd better go to bed now."

"Okay." She gave me a kiss on the cheek before scurrying out of the room.

I decided to read a Chapter out of Proverbs before going to bed, since I hadn't had my devotional time this morning. I felt guilty, because lately I'd been skipping devotional time more and more. I opened it to Proverbs 16 and began reading. I felt my eyebrows lift in surprise when I read verse three.

'Commit your works to the Lord and your thoughts will be established.'

It felt again, like God was telling me He wanted to be part of this expedition. He wanted to help me. I wasn't so sure about it. I'd felt so let down when Emma overheard the rude lady's conversation. I felt if God really wanted to help, He would have somehow prevented my younger sister from hearing the awful slander. "I'll think about it," I told God.

I continued reading without really seeing any of the words on the paper. My mind was on the Snouts. *Terra...* I had to talk to her. I couldn't take it, anymore. This distance between us was starting to become more than I could bear.

As soon as I saw I'd reached the end of the Chapter, I put my Bible on the nightstand, turned off the light, rushed through my prayers, and pulled the covers over my head. As an afterthought, I set the alarm before pulling the covers back over my head. The sandman took his merry old time in paying me a visit. I mulled over the mystery while waiting for him. I decided to take Emma's advice, and talk to some of the receptionists at the station. They varied from day to day, so this aspect of the investigation was going to take longer than I preferred.

Another thing I needed to somehow do, was verify if Mr. Russell's story was true. The only way to verify anything, was to pay another visit to the Russell household. It was right then, the sandman dumped his load on me. I closed my eyes, and next thing I knew, my alarm was screaming in my ear. I responded by smacking the life out of it.

Twenty minutes later, I trudged into the kitchen where Emma was wolfing down her omelet. I was amused at how eager she was to get to school. Normally, she'd take her time and whine, whenever she was told to hurry up or else she'd be late.

"Morning, sweetie." Mom handed me my omelet on a paper plate.

I instantly knew there'd been another burglary, because her soft voice was visibly strained and there were dark circles underneath her eyes. "Thanks, Mom," I mumbled, shuffling to my seat.

Emma, thankfully, was too intent on finishing her breakfast to notice Mom's distress.

"Where's Dad?"

"He's in his office," Mom answered, preparing another omelet.

"Is he sick?" Emma asked, taking a gulp of her orange juice.

"No, he's busy, Emmy." Mom gave Emma an obviously forced smile.

Emma was more astute than I'd realized, because she looked at me and mouthed, "What's wrong with Mama?"

"Tell you later," I mouthed back. I somehow managed to eat my breakfast, before heading to Dad's office. The door was slightly ajar, and what I saw made me pause in my tracks. Dad was on his knees in front his leather chair, his forehead resting against his folded hands. I felt awkward catching Dad at such a sovereign time. I started to step backwards, but stepped right on a creak.

Dad looked up and saw me in the doorway. He gave me a tired smile. "Come right in, lass." He got up and sat in the seat.

"I don't want to disturb you," I said, slowly coming into the room.

"I was just chewin' God's ear, I was."

I perched on the edge of his desk. "Any new developments?"

"Mrs. Tellers lost her gold watch, last night."

"You mean the one worth fifty thousand dollars?"

"The very one." He sighed heavily. "Crystal, I may have to close the shop."

My stomach dropped into my socks, and I nearly fell off the desk. "What? Why? Were you cleaned out?"

"It's gettin' to where people are becomin' too scared to purchase anymore jewelry, on account of it bein' stolen from them almost as soon as they buy it. The tourists are continuin' to drop off at a rapid rate." He leaned forward and put his face in his hands.

I suddenly couldn't stand it, anymore. This thief was destroying my family. A feeling of intense rage filled my gut and I clenched my fists at my side, vowing this villain would pay for his deeds... *and he would pay dearly! Oh, yes he would! I'll definitely see to it!* I hated feeling so helpless.

I wanted to comfort Dad in some way, since he'd always been there for me whenever I needed to be comforted. I hopped off the desk and wrapped my arms around his neck. He reached up and patted my narrow hands with his strong hands. I sighed mournfully, and tried to think of some good news I could give him in an attempt to cheer him up.

I suddenly thought of the recording, and decided to let him hear it. "I'll be right back." I raced for my room, grabbed the recorder, and went flying back to the office. "I have something I want you to hear, Dad." I placed the recorder in front of him.

"I wondered where this went." He looked up at me.

Whoops! I silently gulped. "Uh, I was going to ask... uh... I mean, tell you... but... Well, you see..."

Dad stopped me with an upraised hand. "It's all right, lass. I trust you with it. What do you have to show me?"

"I want you to listen to something. It's rather long, but I'd like your input."

"Crystal? Where are you?" It was Mom. "You're going to make your sister late."

"Coming." I looked hesitantly at Dad.

"You go right ahead, Crystal. I'll listen to it and we can discuss it after school." He gave me a loving kiss on the cheek.

As I threw my backpack over my arm... the weight of the pack nearly sending me to the floor... I thought about the recording. Lee had said he was going to make sure 'Crest' did everything he was told to do. *Who was this mysterious Crest person, and why was he so important?*

I tripped over my own feet, as I walked down the sidewalk to school. I daydreamed through almost every period, and nearly got sent to the principal's office. The last bell was truly heaven sent, and I didn't waste any time in grabbing my things and tearing out of the building.

"Crystal, wait for me!" Emma's high-pitched voice carried easily above the chatter of my fellow classmates and other kids standing around doing nothing more than yakking. She ran toward me. Her hot pink backpack stood out like a sore thumb against her dark green sweater and her skirt poofed out with every step she took. She skidded to a halt in front of me and gave me a big, toothy grin. "Ready, Detective O'Mally!"

I wished she wouldn't say stuff like that in front of strangers. I swallowed a groan and plastered a metal grin on my face. "Let's go, partner."

"So." She skipped beside me. "Where we going?"

"To the Russells."

She stopped in her tracks. "Nu-uh, I ain't going there! No, siree, Bob."

"For one thing, my name's not Bob, and second, you said you wanted to help me with this mystery. Well, it involves visiting people who might creep us out, a little."

"Ha! You just admitted he creeps you out, too," she shot back defiantly.

"I did not. I merely stated... Oh, bother it all. You're wasting precious time, Emerald. Are you coming or not?"

"I'm staying right here." She planted her feet on the concrete and crossed her arms over her chest.

"Fine. I'll just let King get you." I turned and started racing down the street, knowing she'd be by my side in an instant.

Sure enough, I heard her howl, "NO!" and a second later, she was right by me.

King's the Doberman Pincher who lives in the doghouse across the street from the school playground. His ears are clipped and stand straight up, looking almost like horns. Emma's terrified of him, and runs screaming into the school or the nearest place of shelter whenever she sees him out.

Five minutes later, I was ringing the Russell's front doorbell. We heard muffled voices on the other side of the house.

"He's stealing someone!" Emma started to run for the street.

"No, he's not." I grabbed her pack and yanked her back next to me. "I'll go and check it out. You wait here and make sure no one comes."

"I want to go with you and be a witness when he grabs you and stuffs you in his black bag."

"Emerald! He's not going to stuff me in any bag. It just sounds like he's talking to someone. I'm just going to check out who's back there."

"I'm going with you. It's more fun than standing out here like a statue and doing nothing."

I knelt in front of her. "Emma, being the lookout is more important than spying, because you," I jabbed her chest for emphasis, "*you* have to alert me, the spyee, when someone's coming. I'm depending a lot on you."

She puffed her chest out with pride. "All right, Crystal. I'll be your little watch dog."

"Thanks." I stood to my feet and tiptoed 'round to the back. The muffled voices became a little clearer, and as I peeped around the corner, I received one of the biggest surprises of my life.

Officer Snout was there, yelling at Mr. Russell. Both men's faces were beet red, as if it were a scorching summer day instead of sixty-nine degrees. Mr. Russell's eyes seemed to shoot fire, as he pointed a finger at Officer Snout and yelled, "I ain't doing it, and I mean it! Now, get off my property, before I call the police on you!"

Officer Snout gave a chilling laugh. "You seem to forget, Sam. I *am* the police. It'll be my word against yours, and you'll wind up in jail, again. With your wife on the road to recovery, we wouldn't want you to be in jail, now would we?" His voice had turned to one of mock pity.

Mr. Russell's face turned at least five shades of scarlet, and I thought he was literally going to kill Officer Snout right then and there. The detective must have sensed he'd gone too far, as well. He took a step back and raised his hands as if in surrender. "Calm down, Sammy old boy. No use breaking those old blood vessels, all because you know I'm right and you're wrong."

"I ain't helping you and Stellen. End of discussion. I know'd there was something low down about you from the first day I laid eyes on you. I shoulda' started investigating when I had the chance."

"Well, it's too late now," Officer Snout snapped. He took a step closer to Mr. Russell, who took a step backward, as if he couldn't stand to be so close to a man he obviously detested. "Now, all you have to do is help us out, and if you do, we'll back off. Why, we'll even leave your Carol alone, too."

"Carol? If you've done anything to her, I'll… " Mr. Russell extended his hands like claws and started for Snout.

"Just help us, and we'll leave you alone forever," Officer

Snout shouted, growing more impatient by the minute.

"I ain't helping you skunks with anything. Get out!" The last word was bellowed so loudly, that even I jumped and started high tailing it for the road.

"Crystal!" Emma started after me. "Hold up!"

I slowed down to catch my breath and to let Emma reach me. I wiped my sweaty forehead with my sleeve, panting hard as if I'd just run ten or twelve miles.

"What happened?" she wanted to know.

"Officer Snout was there." I rasped out.

"Snotty Snout?" She wrinkled her nose. "What was he doing back there?"

"He and Mr. Russell were…" 'Talking', was anything but an adequate word to describe the discourse I'd just witnessed. "Hashing something out." *Why had Officer Snout called Mr. Russell 'Sam', when his name's Todd? It didn't make sense.*

"You mean like finishing up an argument."

"Kind of, yeah. C'mon. We've got some more visiting to do."

"Where to next?"

"To the automated newsstand," I replied, without any enthusiasm.

* * * *

"And, you should have seen him when he walked in here. Ah! He was the most ghastly sight I've ever seen. He had coffee stains on his shirt, his hair needed to be combed… Oh, it was awful." Mrs. Tellers carried on in her dramatic way, fluttering her fingers as if she were shooing away a dog. "And, to think he's one of the most respected men on our detective force. And, he's been so moody lately, too."

My stomach grumbled loudly and I clapped my arm around my waist, hoping Mrs. Tellers hadn't heard me. It didn't take her very long to get going on how Officer Snout had been receiving poorly dressed 'relatives' lately, and how the man had been dressing rather poorly, himself. It sounded so unlike the impeccable Snout I've known since I was nine-years-old.

Mrs. Tellers had been rambling on for at least two hours now, and it was dinnertime. My stomach wasn't about to let me forget Mom was fixing lamb chops for supper tonight. "Were you able to catch the relative's name?" I quickly interjected. Emma was practically dancing with impatience at my side. I didn't blame her.

"Oh, merciful angels. What was his name?" She frowned and pushed her spectacles further up her bulbous nose, as if the action would somehow bring the name to her remembrance. "Bob? Taylor?"

"Stow?" I asked. "Stow Peter?"

"Peter. Yes. He gave me his name as Peter Smithen, but I wasn't told anything about a Stow." She looked at us over her gold rims. "Is there something I need to know about?"

"Naw." I tried to make my voice sound nonchalant. "I was just throwing names out there, hoping you'd catch one and it'd help ring a bell." I began scooting toward the door. "Gosh, Emma. Mom's going to be mad if we don't hurry home."

"You're right." She caught onto what I was doing, and played along. "And, I don't want to get grounded again."

"Thanks for talking to us, Mrs. Tellers." I opened the door leading to the wonderful outdoors.

"Anytime, darlings. And, if there's ever a time you're lonely and need someone to talk to, don't hesitate to call." She blew us kisses.

"You could give me all the dolls in the world and I wouldn't call her if I was lonely," Emma burst out, as we ran down the sidewalk.

I didn't comment. I was too busy processing what Mrs. Tellers had spent the last two hours telling us. Officer Snout had become rather moody lately, snapping at everyone on the force. They were patient with him, because they attributed his mood swings to the baffling case.

I'd overheard Dad tell Mom last night, Mr. Wington was getting extremely antsy and wanted his diamond recovered as soon as possible. If it wasn't recovered in the next two weeks, then he'd press charges against Dad.

"Why on earth would he press charges?" Mom cried indignantly.

"The diamond was in me care at the time of the robbery," Dad replied, sadly. "The police force has cleared me name, but Mr. Wington is getting so anxious, he's pointin' the finger at anyone and anythin' to get his jewel back, he is."

"Jesus knew what He was talking about, when He told us not to be anxious nor worry about anything." Mom sighed. "Therefore, do not worry about tomorrow, for tomorrow will worry about its own things. Sufficient for the day *is* its own trouble."

My anger simmered in me as I recalled the frightening

conversation. I again swore when the criminal was caught, I'd see to it he would pay dearly for all of the trouble he'd caused my family.

"Earth to Crystal!" Emma called.

I felt my foot catch on the hose and I was suddenly free falling, arms flailing in perfect windmill imitation. I landed on my back, all of the air whooshing out of my body. I was chasing birdies round and round my throbbing skull. I shook my head and they flew away. In the gathering twilight, I hadn't realized we'd reached the edge of the yard. My back was going to be quite tender for a few days, as was my head.

"Ouch! Are you okay?"

Okay, birdies. You can come back now, I thought, closing my eyes and wishing I could be surrounded by an entire flock of birds. I recognized Minx's tenor voice, and this time, I didn't bother to cover up my exasperated sigh.

"Crissy." Emma's voice was low and teasing. "Minxy's here. Woo-hoo!"

I opened my eyes and made out Minx's tall form towering over me, his hand extended to help me up. I grudgingly accepted it, and slowly and painfully stood to my feet. "What brings you here this late?"

"Just wanted to drop by. I... uh... have some new developments on the case for you." He let go of me.

I turned to Emma. "Em, would you mind taking my backpack inside for me, and then start taking notes on what we heard today?"

"No prob." She took my backpack, grunting as she did so.

"What do you have in here? A dead body?" Still grunting, she disappeared into the house.

"Do you need help inside?" He started to put his arm around my waist to support me into the house. "Just…"

I abruptly stepped aside. I was frustrated, tired, and sore. My temper was dangling by a rapidly fraying thread. "Why do you keep coming here? Why don't you go hang out with your two buddies, Celine and Cory?"

Even in the gathering darkness I could tell my shot hit home, because a pained expression covered his face. "They've been sent to their grandparents as punishment for vandalism. They'll be back in a few days. I don't have anything to do, and… and, I've learned there's more to life than going around and destroying other peoples' property."

Like annoying detectives? "Then, why pick me to hang out with? You've ignored me for the past two semesters, and then suddenly you want to be best buds? How does it work?"

"There's something different about you. I've wanted to hang out with you for a while. I could just never work up the courage to do so, 'cause you were always hanging out with your small group of friends or at the police station."

I couldn't believe it. This boy was two fries short of stalking me. "So, I see you know my life very well, Mr. Minx."

He opened his mouth, made a squeaking noise, and closed it again… looking like a total idiot, and no doubt was feeling like one, too.

"Kids, suppertime," Mom called from the porch.

"Coming, Mom." I turned to Minx. "Maybe if you would

have *asked* in the first place, I might have accepted your help." *You know that's highly unlikely,* a little voice inside my head scolded me. I knew the voice spoke the truth, but I wasn't about to admit it aloud. "See you in chemistry, Minx."

"Um, yeah. Bye." He turned to go.

"Minx, you can stay for supper," Mom invited.

"What?" I stared at her, not believing what I was hearing.

"Oh, it's all right, Mrs. O'Mally. I wouldn't want to impose."

Smart boy!

"It wouldn't be imposing, at all. Call your parents and see if it's okay with them, and then afterwards, you and Crystal can finish your detective work." Giving me a sly wink, Mom vanished inside the house.

Behind me, I could hear Minx on his cell phone, obtaining permission to dine with us. I just stood and stared at nothing, my jaw hanging open while my mind refused to believe this was reality. Some strange boy was going to be eating with us, and all because my parents thought we were detective partners.

"Better close your mouth," Minx advised, standing next to me. "The squirrels are just looking for places to hide their nuts."

If looks were daggers, I would have killed him at least a million times with 'The Looks' I shot him, before stiffening my back and marching inside.

Chapter VII

The Falling Out

I rubbed a tired hand across my eyes and gave an exaggerated yawn. It was only seven o' clock, but I was itching for Minx to go home. He'd brought more photocopies of tickets from the Gopher's Hole, and drawings of the guests whose names were on the tickets.

When I got a look at Stow, he immediately reminded me of one of those old time prospectors you see in the movies. He had a scruffy gray beard, wild salt and pepper hair, and he was slightly stooped around the shoulders. He fit the description of the robber Mr. Russell had in his closet. Oliver Creed had eyes as dark as the sky, right when a tornado's approaching. His soft brown hair was a total contrast to his eyes which had meanness about them, and one of his lips was pulled up at the corner. Nevel was a broad shouldered man, with straw blond hair and brown eyes. He was stocky and had a barrel chest. I silently gagged when I saw yellow chest hair sticking up out of his shirt. "Nice," was my only comment, as I handed Minx's drawings back to him.

"I'm glad you like them. I wasn't sure whether or not you would." He looked pleased with himself.

"They look like the drawings you see on the news." I faltered, as a puzzled frown creased his handsome brow. "You know, like during a trial... and the press isn't allowed in there, but there's some artist in the courtroom drawing pictures."

"Oh, yeah. Now I see what you're getting at." He nodded, his Adams apple bobbing up and down.

Emma was dozing on the leather couch across from me. Her

hair was pulled back into two pigtails and she was in her pajamas. She was snoring softly, which I hoped Minx didn't hear.

I found myself studying him from my viewpoint on the footrest. I could tell he was deep in thought by the way his eyes were as dark as the nighttime sky, without any stars out. His square jaw was missing its goatee. *When had he shaved it off?* His ears kind of stuck out from his head, and his lips... *Ah, hold it right there, Crystal Elizabeth.* I mentally shook myself. *You are not in any way, shape, or form, going to be attracted to this boy.* "So, why did you pick these guys to spy on?" I broke the silence.

"They looked rather shifty to me," he answered. "I thought I'd better draw them, just in case they were criminals or something."

"What if they're average, every day, normal Americans?"

"Then, I'll burn the drawings and forget I drew them in the first place."

My head was hurting and I was more impatient than ever for Minx to go home. Dad was working late at the shop, and I wanted him to hurry it up and come home so we could discuss the recording. As if in answer to my wish, I heard his footsteps on the front porch. "Three, two, one," I counted down with my fingers, and pointed at my sleeping sister. Right on cue, Emma suddenly rolled off the couch and went zooming for the doorway.

Minx's eyebrows went up so fast, they almost left his forehead. "I thought she was asleep."

"She was. She just has this built in sensor for whenever Mom or Dad comes home. She's always there to greet them, almost like a little puppy."

"Must be nice to have someone to come home to." There was the wistful tone in his voice, again. I debated whether or not to start prying about his personal life, when he started talking. "My parents are working, both of them at the same time, so I come home to a house with nobody in it."

"If you're their only son, then why do both of your parents have to work?" I frowned. It didn't make sense. Mom and Dad just had Emma and me, and only Dad was working. Mom was home to take care of us.

"They said they'd rather be safe than sorry. Meaning, they want to make sure they have enough money saved up for my college tuition and retirement… instead of if only Dad works, and we find out at the last minute, we don't have enough." He sighed heavily. "Their only free day is Sunday, and they're usually too worn out to do anything else except go to church and to lunch, afterwards."

I couldn't help but feel sorry for Minx. Truly sorry. I couldn't imagine not coming home to Mom's smiling face every afternoon. I tossed my ponytail over my shoulder and abruptly changed the subject. "Anything else you wanted to show me?"

"Yeah, this is the guy who signs his checks as Lee." Minx held another picture up. "But, I've heard other people call him Stan."

I instantly felt dinner sticking in my throat. Stan Snout's lean face was staring right at me. His pickle green eyes looked irked. His lips, which were usually turned up in a smile, were turned down in a scowl, and there was hardness on his face I'd never seen before. I peered closer and saw a tiny scar right next to his left eye, a small detail I'd never noticed, until now. Another piece of the puzzle clicked into place, and fear gripped my heart. *Dear God, this can only mean Terra is...* I didn't even want to think about it.

"So, yeah. This is the guy," Minx said, obviously unaware of my shock. He placed the picture in my lap. It was only then, he seemed to notice my face. "Hey, you okay, girl?" He put a hand on my arm, and for once, I didn't try to shrug it off.

How could You, God? I closed my eyes and swallowed hard. *How could You let someone like Terra, be mixed up in a criminal act, like this? It isn't fair! She's my friend! Don't You care she could be sent to jail, and I might never see her again?*

"Crystal." Dad's voice ended my little pity party.

I popped my eyes open and saw him standing on the threshold. He was holding a tray in his hands as he came and sat down on the couch. I scooted off the footrest, so he could use it as a table. Nodding his thanks, he quickly prayed, and then pulled the recorder out of his pocket. "I wanted to talk to you about this."

"Now?" The word just kind of popped out on its own accord. I couldn't keep the disbelief out of my voice.

"Catherine told me Minx has been stoppin' by almost every afternoon lately, sayin' he has items for your case... so I assumed it'd be all right for him to hear it as well, since he *is* your partner." Dad started attacking his green beans.

I pursed my lips and shot Minx 'The Look'. He, in turn, wiggled his eyebrows, but looked extremely uncomfortable. *Good! Let the punk squirm. It would serve him right. He made his bed, now he has to sleep in it.*

"Todd's story is very interestin'," Dad began, after he'd swallowed his food. "What amazes me even more, is how open he was about everythin'."

"Kind of makes me wonder if the story wasn't fabricated," I commented.

"Ahem."

I looked over my shoulder to see Emma standing behind me, holding my notebook in her hands. "Thanks." I took the notebook and she snuggled up next to Dad.

She looked up at him and gave him a loving smile, before nuzzling his arm. He, in turn, popped a forkful of green beans into her mouth. I looked down at my notes, embarrassed. Minx didn't hide his snicker, and I quickly kicked him in the leg for it.

"Mind if I join the party?" Mom came in, carrying a mug of coffee. "Anyplace interesting in your mystery, Crystal?" She sat down next to Emma.

"We were discussing the recording Crystal got," Emma announced importantly.

"The one you showed me this morning, Brian?"

"Yes. Minx, have you had a chance to listen to it?"

"No, sir. I haven't."

"Well here, by all means, help yourself." Dad handed him the recorder.

When did this get so out of hand? I wondered, groaning softly. *I didn't want any help in the first place, and now look where I am. Why, I wouldn't be surprised if in the next few days, all of Alamo was helping me look for the crook... even the criminal himself!* Without a word, I stood to my feet and quietly left the room, my anger again simmering.

I slipped outside in my socks, not bothering to put any shoes on. The sun was shedding its last few rays on the Northern Hemisphere, before it made its journey to the other side of the planet. I stood on the deck, relishing those last few drops of light, before they faded and dusk began to place her cloak on everything. I leaned against the railing and looked at the rolling plains. This was a lush part of Texas, thankfully. I'd have hated to have been stuck somewhere in the desert, especially since my skin burned so easily.

Ash trees dotted our yard, along with a few Bradford Pear trees, and at least an oak or two. I walked along the length of the deck, my finger running along the rough grain of the railing. As I stopped at the opposite end, the one closest to Mom and Dad's bedroom, I thought about the mystery. Terra was truly guilty. There was no other way about this. *Why hadn't I seen it before?*

It was all starting to make sense, now. Officer Snout's interest, when Emma told him Dad was going to clean the diamond. I recalled the way Snout's eyes lit up, as Dad walked out of the museum with the slip of paper in his hands. It made me wonder the significance of the paper. And then, there was Officer Snout's hesitancy at letting me join the 'force'. Him trying to throw suspicion on Mr. Russell, who still wasn't totally cleared.

And then, there was Terra, withdrawing. Only a guilty person would withdraw from her best friend, because if she was truly innocent, then she would have absolutely nothing at all to hide from me. "God, I didn't ask for this when I signed up to be a detective," I called up to the sky. "I knew it wasn't going to be easy, but I didn't think it was going to be insane."

I felt like sinking to my knees and bawling like a one-year-old. A sound prevented me from doing just that, and bursting into tears. It was the sound of someone slipping and hitting the ground with a loud thud. I was instantly on the alert. Having heard nothing but crickets chirping and cicadas singing to one another for the past ten minutes, my ears were very sensitive to 'non-nighttime' sounds. This particular sound seemed to be coming from the direction of Mom and Dad's master bedroom window, the one overlooking the garden. I ran lightly down the deck steps and hurried to the garden.

At first I couldn't see very well, but then the dim light from the quarter moon enabled me to make out a silhouette of someone starting to climb in through the window. For starters, coming into the house through the side window is not a very good way to make a perfect impression on my parents, and second, it's called breaking and entering. *Unless it was Uncle Felix paying us a surprise visit again, like he did last year*, but I preferred to be safe than sorry.

Sprinting forward like I cheetah, I reached our 'visitor' just as he was getting ready to haul his long, spider-like legs in through the window. I grabbed them and tugged as hard as I could. What I'd overlooked was if I tugged downward, he'd... *yep, land right on me...* which he did. He landed on my chest, squishing all the air out of me. I made a noise that sounded like a cross between a dog getting hit and a dying cow.

"Brat!" the deep voice spat at me. He struggled to get up, but I wasn't about to let go. He managed to free himself of one of my hands and started to stand up, but my flailing fingers grabbed a hold of his pocket.

I heard a few things hit the ground, including pocket change. *Uh-oh, please don't tell me I just heard a rip, and saw a flash of white against those black pants.* I never saw the blow coming. One second, I was tousling with Jack the Ripper, the next, it was lights out.

* * * *

"I found her, she's right here."

The shout resounded through my foggy brain. *I must have fallen again,* I thought, trying to move my head. Every little motion sent a spasm of pain shooting across my head. It felt like someone had taken the world's biggest sledgehammer and whapped me upside the noggin with it.

"Can you hear me? Are you alive?"

Someone shook my shoulder, and an agony-filled cry burst through my dry lips.

"She's alive!"

I couldn't place the speaker's voice. It sounded too young to be Dad's.

"Crystal? Are you dead?" Emma's cry sounded far away. "Please say something, so I know you're not dead!"

"Something," I groaned, not sure if she heard me or not. I felt light being shined in my face and heard voices babbling all around me. I made out Dad's baritone voice, wondering aloud what on earth I was doing in the middle of the rose garden. *Tiptoeing through the tulips,* I thought wryly. *You know, since they're not really giving me a chance to speak, I think I'll just keep my mouth shut.* So, I just lay there, limp as a ragdoll in the cedar mulch.

I felt myself being lifted, and couldn't repress a groan. My head ached mercilessly. My little journey didn't last very long. I heard doors being opened and shut, before being laid on something soft and fluffy. I recognized it as my bed and finally dared to open my eyes. My poor pupils were stabbed viciously by the light as soon as my lids parted. I shut them again very tightly, before slowly opening them again. My vision swam underwater for a little bit, and then slowly adjusted.

Emma's nose was literally pressed against mine. "She's alive!" Her joyful shriek made me wish I was unconscious. She grabbed me around my shoulders and hugged tightly. "Why didn't you say something when I told you to?"

"I did," I croaked out. "I said, 'something'."

"She's awake, Mama and Daddy!" Emma hollered, without leaving my bedside. "She isn't dead. Minx, you can come, too."

Minx! Now I recognized the voice. He was the one who'd found me first. I fumbled around for my plush pillow, wanting to suffocate myself in it. Anything to spare me further humiliation. *Why do I always make a dunce of myself whenever he's around, and then he has to play the knight in shining armor and come to my rescue? It's stupid!* I squeezed my eyes shut as tight as I could.

"Crissy, open your eyes." Emma poked me in the arm.

"Crystal, honey, can you hear me?" I felt Mom gently lift the upper half of my body and hold it close to her heart. She stroked my tangled hair, and when she spoke, her voice shook with emotion. "Please open your eyes, baby. Can you hear me?"

"Yes, ma'am."

"Do you hurt a lot, pumpkin? And if so, where?"

I gingerly reached up and touched the lump growing on the left side of my head, directly on the hairline. "My head hurts." I finally opened my eyes and saw tears filling Mom's eyes.

"Thank God, you're alive." She held me close. I could feel her arms quivering, but I could also hear the soothing rhythm of her heartbeat.

"Crystal!" Dad appeared out of nowhere and wrapped Mom and I in his arms, holding the two of us tight. I heard him draw a shaky breath, obviously trying to keep his tears at bay. "Doc Crawton's on his way," he finally said, in a voice filled with relief. He relaxed his grip and looked at me. "What in God's green creation were you doin' outside at this time of night?" he demanded. "You know better than that."

"I was simply getting a breath of fresh air," I replied as innocently as I could. It was then, I suddenly remembered our mysterious visitor. "Did he steal anything?"

"Did who steal what?" Mom asked.

"Did the thief steal anything from your room? I saw someone climbing into the house through your bedroom window, and tried to stop him," I explained, feeling frustrated for two reasons. One, it looked like my parents didn't believe me, and two, the fact the thief had gotten away. My first chance to be a real hero, and I had to bungle it.

Without a word Dad disappeared, and was back within two seconds, his face tight. "She's right. Someone did try to break in."

Mom gasped. "Did he take anything?"

"No. The window had been forced open." He turned to me and planted his hands on his hips. "Crystal Elizabeth."

Emma came in and handed me an ice pack, which I promptly put over my bump. I gasped as the freezing cold came in contact with my injury. "What'd I do wrong now?"

Mom gently laid me back down on the bed.

"A very risky thin', me lass. You could have come inside and alerted us, but instead, you chose to get the fiend yourself. He could have injured you worse than he did." Dad surprised me by grabbing me in the world's biggest bear hug.

I dropped the ice pack and it bounced off the bed and landed on the floor.

"I could have lost you, and then where would I have been without me precious Crystal?" He leaned back and I saw tears in his eyes, making them glitter like emeralds underneath an artificial light. "You're me most precious treasure, and I couldn't bear to lose you."

Tears stung my eyelids and I clung to Dad. *Okay, why am I acting like a little baby?* I wondered.

A ten-second silence stretched between us, before Emma broke it by coughing roughly. Both of us looked at her and she held out the ice pack.

"Oh, thanks." I plopped it back over my bump.

The doorbell rang and Mom went to see who it was. Dad stood in the doorway, moving aside to let Minx stand beside him. The latter looked like he felt exceedingly awkward standing in my doorway. I slowly lay back down, so as not to cause myself any more pain.

"You feeling okay?" he asked.

"Yeah." I closed my eyes, not wanting to look at him. I

heard him shuffle across the room and knew when he was standing by my bedside, because even though my eyes were closed, I sensed some of the light being cut off. I cracked my eyes open a wee bit and made out his tall form standing over me. My heart took to the stage and started tap dancing as fast as it could.

"You have one giant knocker on your head," he stated the obvious.

"I know, ain't it purty?" I said sarcastically. I really wished he'd take the hint and leave.

Dad was still standing in the doorway while Emma decided to perch on a stool at the foot of my bed, so I knew as long as Minx's visit was 'chaperoned', it was okay for him to be in my room. "You gave us all quite a scare when we found you out colder than Alaska, in the rose bed."

"I guessed as much." *God, why isn't he taking the hint? Do You have any thunder bolts to spare? And if so, can You hit him with one? Maybe, that'll help him get the hint that I want him to leave.*

"I overheard you telling your parents you were trying to catch a thief. Don't you know how risky it was, Crystal? I wish you would have alerted us."

I felt like a pirate as I peered at him through one eye. This was the first time he'd ever called me by my first name, and to be honest, I liked hearing it and wanted to hear him say it, again. I heard a snicker and knew it came from Emma. I glanced at her. She clasped her hands over her heart in a dramatic way and fluttered her eyelashes at me. I looked back up at the boy standing by my bedside, and suddenly saw him as a man... not as a troublemaker who liked to go around painting peoples' property for his own amusement.

Doctor Crawton came in just then, and Minx stood off to the foot of my bed. He had his hands in his jean pockets and he looked oh so very casual, and oh so very... well... *handsome!* His crystal earring glittered as it caught some of the light, and sparkled like a star in the night. *Will you cut it out already, Crystal?* I scolded myself. *Focus on the mystery at hand, not on someone like Minx.*

He has helped you in this mystery, the annoying little voice in my head reminded me.

Yeah, but I've made so much progress by myself in this mystery, I think I can handle it on my own.

Have you really made a lot of progress by yourself? the little voice asked.

I didn't realize until now, just how little progress I'd made on my own. Sure, I'd gotten the confession from Mr. Russell, and a few other clues here and there. But, it was Emma who had helped me uncover some of my most important clues, such as the note in the box. And then, there was Minx, with the copies of the tickets he kept bringing to me. In a way, I had made more progress with others helping me, than I did by myself. *How, where, and when, did I get all this help?*

"Crystal? Are you still with us?" Doc Crawton was calling me, and I was so caught up in my little fantasy, I hadn't heard him at first.

"Yes, I'm still here. I'm sorry. I just zoned out for a few seconds."

He chuckled. "You're fine, just so long as you're conscious."

Now, you always read about how doctors are either as skinny as a rail or as roly-poly as a little piglet. Well, Doctor Crawton was physically fit. He was young, too. His chestnut waves were slicked back and his light brown eyes were bright and alert. His long fingers gently probed my bump, and I kept biting back urges to grunt, yell, or holler every time he touched me. "She's got quite a prize there," he stated at last. He went through an exam with me, asking me how many fingers he was holding up, how well I could see things off in the distance, and where else I hurt… the usual doctor stuff.

Ten minutes later, I was drinking a mug of coffee, much to my disgust. I hate coffee. Doc Crawton said I shouldn't go to sleep for at least another four hours. It was eight o' clock, and by twelve o' clock, I could bunk down for the night.

Everyone else, including Minx, had left, after being assured I wasn't going to die. Before he left, Minx turned to me, his dark eyes more serious than I'd ever seen them before. "I think you should check up on our Officer Snout or Morgan, whichever name he goes by."

"And, how would I check up on him?" I wanted to be left alone. Sleuthing was the farthest thing from my mind, at the moment. My head was aching, despite the aspirin I'd been given. I wanted to lie down and sleep for a million years.

"Find out where he went to school, and go from there."

I sat at my desk for a long time after Minx had left, staring at the oak grain pattern. *Why hadn't I thought of that before? I mean, I'm supposed to be the detective here, yet people I haven't even asked to help me are doing it.* I didn't know what Emma's motives were for helping me, but Minx's are as clear as the zit on the end of my nose. He just wanted to be with me, and I didn't *want* him to be with me. I shoved my chair away from the desk and hurried down the hall to the main computer in the den. Luckily, no one was using it, and I turned it on.

Officer Snout's diploma said he'd gone to Harvard University. I went to their web site and tried looking up names of past students, but met a dead end, there. I finally wrote down the school's phone and fax number, as well as their email address. After I'd closed the Internet, I nibbled on the end of the pen, pondering the best way to contact them. Email might take too long. I didn't know how to send a fax, and they might be closed already. I decided to try and give them a call first, telling myself I'd pay my parents back for the long distance call, later.

"C'mon, c'mon, c'mon!" I said into the phone, as it started ringing on the other end. "Please, someone pick it up."

"You've reached Harvard University. I'm sorry, but we're closed, right now. If you could please leave your name..."

"Never mind." I clicked the 'END' button and decided to email them, hoping I could get to the email before my parents saw it. I didn't want them to see how in-depth my investigation was becoming, lest they pull me from it entirely. I pulled up our email account and with shaky fingers, quickly typed out a message requesting information concerning a student from previous years.

My index finger hovered above the 'S' key. *Should I use the name Stan Snout or Lee Morgan?* I worded it this way.

'His name was either Stan Snout or Lee Morgan. If you could please send me any information concerning his records with your school, I would very much appreciate it.

Sincerely, C. Mally'

I purposefully left out the 'O' before 'Mally'. It's a detective measure, just in case someone receiving your email is in league with the crooks.

"How come I have to go to bed and Princess Crystal gets to stay up later?" Emma's indignant cry reached me from further down the hallway.

"Because she got bumped on the head, and Doc Crawton says she shouldn't go to sleep, just yet," I heard my patient mother explain to my younger sister.

"So, if I go and bump myself on the head, then I get to stay up later, too?"

"Maybe." I could hear Mom hustling Emma into her room. "However, for the time being, you're going to bed when I say you are."

"But, Mama..." Her bedroom door was shut, cutting off anything else she had to say.

I chuckled and turned and stared at the field of wild flowers on the computer screen. I had an overwhelming urge to check the email, but I knew it would take a while to receive a response. I decided to go and read some mystery novels to pass the time, however, I couldn't concentrate on the words in front of me, and found my mind constantly wandering.

If only the thief would've left behind some kind of clue, like a broken watch or a candy wrapper, or... I shot up in bed so fast, my head spun. *Maybe, our mysterious guest left some footprints behind!* Snatching my flashlight I went over to my window, and after removing the screen, quietly hopped out. My window faces west, which is at the back of the house where Mom and Dad can't catch me in my sleuthing project. I turned the flashlight on and hurried to the rose bed. Where mulch had been, the bare ground was now exposed.

My light picked up pocket change, some breath freshener, and more change. I dropped to one knee and shone the light on some partly visible footprints. They looked like they were working boots, or maybe they were tennis shoes. I wasn't as well versed in shoe knowledge as I would've liked to have been. Discouraged, I turned to go, just as my light picked up something white at the base of the window. I bent down and found it to be a note, or the lower half of one.

'We can get the ten thousand cheese, and beat it. Morgan is the man to go to.'

That's where the note ended. Puzzled, I hunted around in vain for extra clues, but didn't find any. I went back to my room and got in the same way I got out, only I remembered to put the screen back in the window. As I opened my folder to place the note in there, I caught sight of the paper Emma had found. My hand froze and my breath caught in my throat. I mechanically placed my note at the bottom of the first one, and found them to be a perfect match. I read the note in its entirety.

'If you can grab Russell's jewel as well as O'Mally's, then we can get the ten thousand cheese, and beat it. Morgan is the man to go to.'

'Morgan', the name Minx had given me this evening, along with a picture of Officer Snout. *Terra, why couldn't you just be honest and tell me the truth in the first place?* I silently cried out, closing the folder.

By the time bedtime came a few hours later, I was more than happy to flop onto the covers and bury my face in my wonderful pillow. I'd just closed my eyes when a buzzing noise arrested my attention. It sounded almost like a fly wanting to get out, but as I looked at my desk, I saw my phone was all lit up in an eerie blue color, and the buzzing noise was coming from there.

I rolled my eyes, wanting to just get to sleep. I flipped the phone open and squinted as the blue light revealed I had a text. I hate those things. Why I even have the texting option on my phone, I don't know. I saw this particular message was from Minx. *How in the Sam hill did he get my phone number?* I know I didn't give it to him. I probed my poor, tired mind for some answer and couldn't find one. I'd confront him about it tomorrow, before chemistry.

'Did you have any luck with our guy? Hope you feel better by tomorrow. Minx.'

Our guy? Our guy? What cheek! Did I even invite him to be my crime-solving partner? No, I did not! He invited himself, and boy, did it infuriate me. I turned my phone off and tossed it in my hamper, before rolling back onto my side and eventually falling into a dreamless sleep.

* * * *

'C. Mally, we regret to inform you we are unable to share any information concerning any of our past students.

Sincerely, John B. Graham'

The sound of the grandfather clock was the only sound in the room, as I stared mutely at the screen. I couldn't believe it. *How rude and totally unfair!* I closed the program, turned the modem off, and went storming to my room. It was six forty-five in the morning, and I could hear my parents starting to stir in

157

their room. I tried not to bang things around as I brushed my teeth, but I was so ticked! I was still wearing a scowl when I appeared at the breakfast table, thirty minutes later.

Mom placed a big plate of pancakes in front of me, and I smiled in spite of myself as I smelled the aroma of apples, honey, cinnamon and ground allspice. She'd made her special batch of pancakes she normally reserved for birthdays, special occasions, and sick days. "Thanks, Mom."

"No problem, hon." She lovingly ruffled my hair, then turned back to her cooking.

"Did you sleep well last night?" Dad asked.

"I did. Thank you for asking." I didn't tell anyone about the bummer email. I silently ate my pancakes and thirty-five minutes later, was jogging up the cement steps to the school building.

A flash of orange caught my attention, and I turned to see Celine giving me the evil eye. Cory was standing right next to her, also giving me a dead stare. It appeared they didn't stay too long at their grandparents. I didn't blame the grandparents for sending the kids back early. I rolled my eyes like a Ping-Pong ball and hurried inside.

"There's the ugly girl," Emma whispered, as I took her to her classroom.

"Emerald Grace, would you be nice?" I chided her.

"It's true," Emma defended herself. "Her hair looks gross and she wears Halloween makeup."

"It's called mascara, and yes, she does wear too much of it. You be good for Mrs. Fellops today, okay?"

"Yes, Mother." She gave me a quick hug and scampered into her classroom.

I made my way through the growing throng of kids, toward my locker. Someone bumped me along the way and I stumbled, nearly hitting the ugly grayish, white tile floor.

"Careful, there." Minx grabbed my arm.

I straightened up and politely removed my arm from his grasp, trying to control the butterflies fluttering around in my chest. "Thanks."

"No, problem." He fell in step with me as I went to my locker. He leaned casually against a green metal locker and watched as I entered in my code to unlock my door. His aftershave drifted to me on the slightly stale air, and I found myself taking in deep breaths of his suede scent. *You ninny! Would you knock it off already?* "I got your text. How'd you get my number?"

"I asked Emma," he replied, casually.

It figures! I thought, still staring at him like an empty-headed dope. His next words brought me crashing out of orbit.

"Any luck on our culprit?"

"Our culprit? *Our* culprit," I nearly shouted. A few students looked our way, but for the most part, the chattering of everyone else drowned me out. "Since when has my culprit, become yours, as well?"

Minx stepped back, clearly startled by my outburst. "Hey, I thought we were in this together."

"No offense, I never invited you to come and help me. You just invited yourself." I flung open my locker door, and jumped back with a frightened yell as something lunged at me. I crashed into at least two other students, who also went tumbling to the floor. Books and papers went flying, as if a cyclone just ripped through the room.

Something was scratching my face, feeling like zillions of needles puncturing my skin. Whatever was attacking me was yowling in a high-pitched tone, almost like a baby who's just a few minutes old. I grappled for it and tried to grab whatever was on me, and when I finally pulled it off, I saw I was holding a tiny kitten. It hissed at me and extended its claws in a threatening gesture, which said, 'Touch me, sucker. I dare you!' The kitten was a solid black with yellow eyes narrowed into slits. It had to be a couple weeks, if not a month or two old.

"What's going on here?" Principal Laurence shoved some of the students aside, as he came to see what the ruckus was about. "Crystal O'Mally! You know it's against school rules to bring your pets to school."

"But, I didn't bring him… her… it," I defended myself. I could feel the cuts on my face starting to swell, and it felt like some of them were starting to bleed a little, too.

"She didn't bring the cat in, sir," Minx piped up. "It was in her locker when she opened it."

"Did anyone see who put the cat in Crystal's locker?" Principal Laurence asked, looking at the students and a handful of teachers.

No one had, until one tenth grader spoke up. "I saw a guy in a janitor's outfit standing next to the locker, a few minutes before Crystal walked over. I didn't think much of it, because it looked like he was just wiping the lockers down. His shoulders were kind of stooped."

Stow! I thought frantically. *He's somehow managed to find out where I go to school.*

"Crystal, are you okay?" Principal Laurence helped me to my feet. I could hear some of the kids around me snickering and snorting, trying to hold back their laughter.

My face felt so hot, I was almost sure my hair was about to catch fire. "Guess so," I mumbled. The kitten must have guessed I wasn't going to harm it and settled down, somewhat. Its eyes were still narrow slits, however. I began petting it and its body slowly relaxed.

"You'll need to get your face taken care of," said Principal Laurence. "Come with me, please." I wordlessly followed him as he cut a way through the kids and to the nurse's office. I kept my head down, eyes riveted on the floor, as I followed him passed the mahogany door and into the pristine clean office.

"What in the world happened to you?" Were the words I was greeted with, as soon as I entered the office. Ms. Denise, the head nurse, was staring at me, her eyes bugging out of her head.

"Apparently, someone played a prank on her and left the kitten in her locker," Principal Laurence explained. "I'm going to call the humane society and see if they're missing a kitten from any of their litters."

"Here, I'll take the kitten for you." Nurse Gretchen held out her hands for the kitten.

Much to my surprise, the little bugger didn't want to go to her. It pressed itself against my chest and hissed at her. I grinned, in spite of myself, and winced as the sore skin around my lips stretched. The kitten was eventually transferred over to

Nurse Gretchen, but not until after she'd gotten her hands punctured a few times. She muttered under her breath about de-clawing the kitten and took it away.

"Now, Crystal, if you'll just sit right there, I'll examine your injuries," said Ms. Denise.

Injuries. She made it sound so final.

* * * *

"What happened to you, Crystal?" Emma stared at my face, which had at least half a dozen Band-Aids on it.

"I got into a tousle," was my only response.

"With who?"

"A kitten. She obviously didn't like me." I peered inside my locker to make sure there were no other hidden surprises. There were none. *Thank You, Lord!* I grabbed a stack of English papers.

"A kitten!" Emma squealed in delight. "Where is it? Can we keep it?"

"I don't know where she is, and we can't keep her." I didn't tell Emma, I'd overheard the principal telling Nurse Gretchen the kitten had been stolen from the pet shop, about thirty minutes before it appeared in my locker.

As I opened my backpack to stuff the papers in there, I noticed the stack was a little lumpy. *Great!* I was in a hurry and didn't have time to sort through the papers, however, I got on my knees and began thumbing through them to find out what was creating the lump. What I saw caused my eyes to widen in shock. A small, brown paper package with the handwriting '***To: Crystal From: Minx***' on the top, lay in my hand.

"Auhm, Crystal?" Emma saw the package, and trailed her finger up and down my arm. "He's got it bad for you."

I found myself grinning. *Why am I smiling?* I crammed my papers into the pack, and then neatly laid the parcel on top. "C'mon. Let's get going."

"We've got more of the mystery to solve." Emma grabbed my hand and skipped beside me.

Minx was waiting for us right outside the glass double doors. He was whistling the 'Andy Griffith' theme song, and he stopped as soon as he saw us. "Howdy. How's your face, Crystal?"

I touched the Band-Aids dotting my face. "Stiff, but I'll be fine."

"Good to hear it." He looked genuinely relieved. "Mind if I accompany you gals home?"

"You gonna' help us more with the mystery, Minx?" Emma asked. "Yow!"

I'd elbowed her rather hard in her shoulder and shot her the evil eye. It was bad enough he'd already invited himself to join our little troupe, but him joining us on our investigations was where I drew the line. I turned to Minx. "Don't you have to be at work, sometime soon? We wouldn't want you to be late. See you tomorrow." I nearly pulled Emma's arm out of its socket as I pulled her along beside me.

"I don't have to be at work until five." Minx was by our side in a flash, his hands stuffed casually in his jean pockets. "I wouldn't mind accompanying you lovely ladies to the scene of the crime. Maybe we could take a look at the email."

"What email? Crystal, are you keepin' secrets from me again?" Emma scowled up at me.

"I didn't want to get your hopes up in case it was a false lead," I said lamely. Luckily, she believed me and fell silent. I glared at Minx who looked back at me in surprise. *Lord, why'd You make men so slow?* I silently demanded. *There's only so much I can take from this guy, before I make like an atomic bomb and seriously blow up. For his sake, please let him take the hint before I detonate!*

Unfortunately, either God was ignoring me, or Minx was ignoring God, because the boy didn't leave. I swung by the Russells' house, wanting to talk some more with Mrs. Russell.

Emma balked and refused to enter the driveway. "I'm staying right here, so I know to run if he grabs you, Crystal." She crossed her arms across her chest.

"Oh? Is he a child snatcher, then?" Minx looked at me curiously.

"No, nothing of the sort," I said in exasperation.

"He went to jail for stealing," Emma told him.

"Cut it out, Emma," I said impatiently. "Minx, you wait here with her." I jogged down the gravel driveway and up the cobblestone steps. I rang the doorbell and stepped back to wait. A few seconds passed, and nothing happened. Now, normally I don't like wringing a doorbell twice, but this was an emergency. I rang it two more times, and still no response. I even knocked, and then started walking around the house. The windows all had shades pulled down, signaling no one was home. *Odd.* I'd of at least expected Mrs. Russell to be home.

"Anybody home?" Minx asked, as I joined them.

"No. I'll try back later." I headed for home.

"He's probably out either stealing, or snatching people," Emma muttered, in disgust.

I jammed my hands in my pockets to keep from backhanding her. She was acting impossible. I tried to get rid of Minx, but the scamp went with us all the way to the house and even dared to come inside.

My mom was in the kitchen entertaining some women from her quilting club. She smiled and waved at us as we entered the kitchen. "Help yourselves to the cookies." She nodded toward the fresh-from-the-oven sugar cookies sitting on a rack.

"Thank you, Mrs. O'Mally." Minx flashed her a charming smile. He asked for directions to the bathroom and went to wash his hands.

I groaned as I overheard a few of the ladies comment on how, "Crystal picked herself a right polite boyfriend."

Lord, I'm coming this close to taking an iron skillet to his thick skull, if You don't do something soon. I took three sugar cookies, knowing I'd be 'entertaining' a guest with cookie dough stuck in my braces. At this point I was getting desperate, and hoped he'd be so grossed out by my poor manners, he'd leave and never come back. We took our snacks and went into the den.

Emma excused herself and hurried to her bedroom. I pulled up the email and showed it to Minx. He leaned over my chair as he studied it. His face wasn't four inches from mine, and I scooted as far away from him as the chair would allow me. I picked up a cookie and promptly started munching on it. The sugar melted like snowflakes on my tongue, and the sweet vanilla flavor lingered in my mouth even after I'd swallowed.

Bits of soggy cookie mush stayed in my braces.

"Hmm," he said at long last. "Here's something you could try. Tell them it's a police investigation. That might make them talk."

Okay, I've had it! He was acting like he was the head detective here, and it was the final straw. I shot up out of the chair and glared at him. "Who invited you into this investigation, Minx?"

"Emma did." He looked puzzled.

"No, she invited you over to the house." I jabbed a finger at the front door. "I didn't invite you to join us in our investigation, you merely invited yourself, which was really rather rude."

Much to my surprise, Minx planted his hands on his hips. "Is it not right for a guy to want to be with a girl?"

"When they're not invited? Yes!"

"But, you never told me you didn't like having me around."

"I tried being polite and discreet about it, hoping and praying that you'd get the hints I was dropping. Instead, you stayed like…" I nearly added, 'Like a bad dream', but decided it was too mean.

He was quiet for a few seconds. "How long have I been getting in your hair?"

"Since the day you showed up on my front porch."

"Oh-ho, so this is your house, is it? You make the monthly payments and everything? You pay the utilities and the electric bill?"

"You know what I mean, smart-aleck." I was almost to the point of infuriation. "Look, if you don't have anything nice to say, then leave me alone."

"I wasn't being mean here, Miss O'Mally."

The boy had more cheek than he was worth. I wanted to grab him by the collar and hustle him out the front door… however, he was at least five inches taller than me and he had muscles, so he could easily shove *me* out the door, instead of the other way around. "Minx, if you can't be a gentleman, then stay away from me." I shoved the chair away from me so fast, it nearly skidded into the couch ten feet behind me. I stormed past a shocked Emma who had her arms full of dolls, and marched to my room.

"You drove Minx away." Emma's high-pitched voice was filled to the brim with accusation. "What'd you say to him, meanie?"

"Leave me alone, Emerald," I snapped at her. I wanted to be left alone. There were a lot of things I wanted in this world, but knew I was never going to get them… and it looked like peace and quiet was going to be two of them.

"I'm not leaving until you tell me what happened." She plopped herself down on my partially made bed and crossed her legs, Indian style.

"Well then, you're in for a long wait," I growled. "Because, I'm not going to tell you anything." I grabbed a mystery novel and tore out of the house.

In no time at all, I was curled up in a corner of the tree house, munching on a banana, as the master sleuth and I trailed the criminal from the restaurant to his hotel room. I peered over the detective's shoulder, itching to go and grab our villain. Just as I started forward, someone knocked. I had to blink several times, before coming back into the real world. *Oh, I was in the tree house, not standing in the lobby of some fancy hotel.* I rubbed my eyes as the knocking intensified. "Come in."

Dad came in, and without a word, sat down next to me. He stretched his long legs in front of him, bending one into an upside down 'V' and resting his arm across it. He looked down at me. "I see I don't need to use me shotgun, after all."

"Huh?" I closed the book and set it down in my lap.

"I was worried with Minx showin' so much affection toward you, I was goin' to have to brin' out me shotgun, just in case I needed to drive him off. But, it seems like you've done a fine job of doing it yourself."

"Emma told you, huh?"

"She did. She was pretty upset and she said she's taken a likin' to Minx."

"Dad, he's a former vandal. Why should she be attached to him? I mean, he ignores me for a few years, and then suddenly he wants to be my boyfriend... or whatever he thinks he wants to be."

Dad was quiet for a minute. He stared out the window, as if the bird cleaning itself on the branch outside, held the utmost fascination for him. "You know, he's been tryin' to call on you for a while, now. At least a week, or so. He came into the shop a few times, and waited around for at least thirty minutes. I finally asked him if he was waitin' for someone. He asked me if I was your father, and I said I was. Well, he said he was waitin' for you, in hopes he could show you some 'clues' he'd picked up. He produced a brown manila envelope from his backpack, and showed me some pictures he'd drawn of people he claimed were suspects you were tracking. Anyway, he told me the two of you were friends."

I snorted, sounding like an agitated horse. "Friends? Yeah right! He's ignored me for a long time. Well, he did speak to me, sometimes. And we're merely *classmates* at school, not *friends*." I couldn't believe the gall of this guy… not my dad, but Minx.

Dad again fell silent, and stared at the plywood wall across the room. "I personally think this would be a good time to have a man in the mystery, at least as your sidekick." He gave me a mischievous grin. "You seem quite attracted to the lad."

I was ready to say I wasn't attracted to Minx at all, yet, it would have been the blackest of all the black lies. I *was* becoming attracted to him, which was *so* not cool. I mean, I wanted to solve this mystery on my own, and somehow I was accumulating help along the way.

"I'm not tryin' to be the voice of gloom and doom here, sweetie, but there may come a time where you can't do somethin' by yourself and you'll need help. It would probably be a good idea if you had someone there to help you. Just somethin' to think about." He planted a kiss on my forehead. "Now, show your dear old father exactly what you've uncovered so far in this mystery."

I laughed softly and proceeded to tell Dad about the suspect's list and how it had begun accumulating. At one point, I leaned forward to grab the leather folder, and Dad suddenly took my small chin and turned my face to him. "What on earth happened to you, me lass?" he demanded.

"What do you mean?"

"You've got at least half a dozen Band-Aids speckled across your face. I didn't notice them until now."

"Oh, well… " I knew Dad would start worrying if I told him about the threatening message I'd received, and then the cat in my locker. "I just got into a small tousle with a kitten. Don't worry, it wasn't born on the streets or something. It was from the pet store." I made light of the matter and proceeded to grab the folder.

"I wondered where me book went."

"Um, Emma wanted to go as pro-detective as she could… and, well… it meant taking anything 'professional looking' she could lay her hands on."

Dad merely chuckled, a light warm sound like the spring breeze outside. "Again, just so long as I get it back at the end."

I opened the book and showed him the list of suspects, as well as the note we found in the diamond box and the fingerprints. The fingerprint list was starting to grow rapidly. We'd collected Minx's fingerprint, Mom's, Mrs. Tellers', Miss Gopher's, Papaw's, and so on. Emma had been a busy little beaver the past few days, collecting fingerprints while I'd been busy talking to different townspeople.

Dad was obviously quite impressed and gave me a hug. "Well done, Crystal, dear."

I beamed with pride. "Thanks, Dad."

"Have you decided what you want for your birthday?"

"Yikes! My birthday's in two weeks. Uh, unfortunately, no sir. With all of the mayhem going on, I haven't had much time to think about it. I will, don't get me wrong." I thought hard for a few seconds. "Well, I'm not really sure. Maybe, another mystery book or two. I can't think of anything else, for right now."

"Well, keep on thinkin'." He gave me a soft smile.

In the afternoon light, I saw there were worry lines around Dad's mouth and eyes where laugh lines normally were. I wished I could give him the world's biggest squeeze and erase all of his worries, but I couldn't. In order to erase the worries, I had to solve this mystery and bring the criminal to justice!

After he'd left, I picked up my book and resumed reading. Fifteen minutes later, I was done with the novel and I started regretting saying what I'd said to Minx. "I wish I could take it all back, but I can't. What's been said has been said." I sighed sadly, letting my head rest against the wooden wall. *Wait, what about the present he'd given me?* It was still in my backpack, waiting to be opened. I hurried inside the house to go and get it. My fingers trembled a little as I took a pair of scissors and cut it open.

What fell out instantly took flight across the room, and I crab crawled backwards until I smashed into my wall. I lay there, panting like a dog, before I finally worked up enough courage to crawl over and take a closer look at my 'present'. The dead mouse lay next to my heater vent, where he'd crash-landed.

Thankfully, he hadn't blown to bits when he landed, because I threw him pretty hard. His eyes were open in a fixed stare at nothing in particular, and I could easily count all four of his teeth. This time my fingers weren't trembling from excitement, as I took the package and shook it. A piece of paper fell to the ground, face up. I read the bold print.

Leah Pugh

'Next time, it won't be the mouse!'

Chapter VIII

Running Against Time

"…And another thing, O'Mally, if you don't recover my diamond soon, I'll have you behind bars so fast, your head will be whirling for the rest of your life!"

"But, Alex, please listen. I'm doin' the best I can."

"Your best just isn't good enough anymore, O'Mally. I'm giving you five days, and if you haven't produced my diamond by then, you're done."

The receiver was slammed down, and I winced as I glanced at Emma, whose eyes were as wide as our fifty-seven inch TV screen. I quietly set the receiver down, hoping Dad hadn't heard the click. It'd been a week since my blow up with Minx, and pride kept me from going over and apologizing to him. I guess pride was keeping him from apologizing to me as well, because I saw him hanging out with Celine and Cory. His rejection stung for some odd reason, especially when I saw Celine flirting with him, and he seemed to take delight in it.

I pushed Minx from my mind, and concentrated on the task at hand. I was going to call Terra, but Dad had been on the other end, talking to Mr. Wington. Emma and I couldn't resist eavesdropping on their conversation. Now, I wish I hadn't been so curious.

"I hate him!" Emma declared viciously.

"Emma…"

"Oh, Crystal. I'm fed up with you saying what's nice and what isn't. Were those men nice? Huh? The ones who stole the diamond? Why don't you tell them to be nice, instead of always telling me, huh? And, Mr. Wington, he was mean as a snake to Daddy. Why isn't he told to be nice? Why is it always me?" She ran from the den and I knew she was running for the safety of her bed, or at least under her bed.

I sat in front of the computer and pulled up the email once more. I'd taken Minx's advice… *yes, shocking, I know…* and re-emailed the University, telling them this was an investigation and I would appreciate their cooperation. And boy, did they *ever* cooperate. Mr. Graham apologized for his abruptness in his last email, and told me they had no records pertaining to either a Stan Snout or a Lee Morgan.

Pain filled my heart, and I began banging my forehead against the maple desk. "Why, Terra?" I demanded. "All these years, and you lied to me? Why? You know your jerk of a husband was nothing better than a worthless thief, and you didn't say anything? How could you?"

The Russells were gone. They'd left town about a week ago, and no one knew where they went. Mr. Russell hadn't even left a word of warning at the police station. He was there one day, and then gone the next. I realized the only way to get an answer for anything, was to pay Terra a little visit.

* * * *

"Crystal! Um, I… uh… can't talk, now."

The door started to close and I stuck my foot in the doorway, wincing as the hard wood slammed on it. "You have no other choice, Terra," I said in a voice I didn't recognize as my own. It sounded so mechanical and lifeless. The door opened just a crack, and I slipped my skinny frame inside.

Terra was in her orange, fluffy bathrobe and matching fluffy slippers. She reminded me of a walking pumpkin. One of the stems on her glasses was taped, her normally well-kept hair was in total disarray, she had a bruise on her left cheek, and her eyes were wide with fright. *Hold on... she had a bruise on her cheek?* "Terra, what happened?" I stared at the bruise, as if I'd never seen one before.

"Nothing." She instinctively covered her cheek with her hand. "Now go, before I call the police."

"And have me tell them your husband stole the diamond?" I challenged her.

You'd have thought I slapped her by the way her eyes widened even more, and she drew back a step. "You're lying!"

"I am not! I just investigated it, and found out those diplomas your husband has on his office wall at the police station are as phony as instant coffee." *No offense to all you coffee lovers, out there.*

"Oh, really?" She tried to appear unfazed by my announcement, but I saw her hands were trembling. "And, what else did you learn in your little investigation, *Miss O'Mally?*"

Now, *that* felt like the world's biggest insult, and my temper flared. I drew myself up to my full height and shot back, "For your information, *Mrs. Snout*, your husband never even applied to Harvard. The dean had never even heard of him. Oh, and by the way, your last name isn't Snout. It's Morgan."

"What makes you so sure?"

"I personally contacted the dean of Harvard myself, and there are no records of a Stan Snout *ever* attending Harvard. And another thing." I reached into my pocket and pulled out the photocopied meal tickets from the Gopher's Hole. "Your husband never pays for his meals at the Hole in the name of Stan Snout. Instead, he uses the name Lee Morgan." I continued to go down the long list of reasons of how I knew her husband was a crook.

Terra's face drained even further of what little color was left, and I saw my harsh words were striking her hard. "I can't believe it," she whispered hoarsely. "All these years, and he's lied to me."

"Terra?"

She didn't seem to hear me, but kept talking to herself. "He spent all of my hard earned money… on what? Definitely, not schooling. And the last name? I always thought Snout was the dumbest name on the planet. When we were dating, I couldn't even find it in the phonebook, and yet, there were plenty of Morgans. Oh, my word!" She sank onto the bottom step and stared at the white wall behind me, her face totally covered with shock.

I instantly felt guilty and awful for coming over in a complete rage, and taking it out on Terra. This wasn't just *any* Terra. This was my best buddy, my best friend… and I was treating her like she was just some jerk from down the street. I sat down next to her not knowing what to say, yet feeling too awkward to say anything at all.

After about four minutes of sitting like statutes, she snapped out of her revere and looked at me with enormous eyes. They looked like eyes off an anime character, they were so big. "Are you sure, Crystal? Where did you get your information?" Her voice cracked with emotion.

"I… I emailed the school," I stammered. "I told them it was

an investigation, and they were most cordial in assisting me." I winced, wishing I could take those words back, as Terra's eyes filled with tears. They started spilling down her face and landed with plop-plops on her robe. I reached over and squeezed her hand.

Before I knew it, she was squeezing me so tightly, her arms felt like a noose around my neck. It startled me and I just froze for a few seconds, before slowly reaching up and wrapping my arms around her. I could almost literally feel the ice melting between us, like God was sending a Chinook across the vast plains and to us, in order to melt the tension that had been with us all these weeks. She rubbed my back very gently. It still tickled a little, but all I did was grin into Terra's plush robe. We drew back, hands still on each other's shoulders, and started giggling like a couple of empty-headed ninnies.

"I've been suspecting something's been up, for quite some time," Terra said. "About a year ago, Stan stopped letting me use his laptop. Made some excuse about the Internet being crummy, and bought me a laptop for my birthday. A few months ago, he got a different landline for the phone in his office. And then, back in December, he started getting strange mail from western Texas. He refused to say anything to me about why he got a different landline, and why he was getting envelopes with cattle skulls on the front.

"Whenever I'd ask him about any of it, he'd just laugh and politely tell me to mind my own business. I accused him of having a girlfriend somewhere, and threatened to leave unless he told me what was going on. He finally 'broke down'." She made quotation marks with her fingers. "And told me he was just corresponding with some old buddies of his. He even showed me some of the emails and letters he'd received." Her eyes clouded over as memories marched across her mind.

"I thought he spoke the truth, and naively believed he was still the wonderful man I married, even though…" She took a deep breath, and I could hear a sob trying to climb its way out of her throat. "Even though a little nagging voice in the back of my head, tried to tell me otherwise. I should have listened to it."

I couldn't think of anything to say. What *could* I say? Nothing really came screaming to mind. All I could do was sit there and hold Terra's hand. I think me being there for her, was more comforting than offering an encouraging word, or three.

"Morgan." She let the name roll off her tongue. "I like it. Sounds a whole lot better than Snout. What's the first name?"

"Lee."

"Lee Morgan," she whispered, looking up at the ceiling. "The name actually sounds kind of dreamy."

I couldn't stop myself from wearing a grin a mile wide. *YES! The old Terra was back! My good ol' friend had returned to me, at long last.* I stuck my hand out. "Welcome home, partner."

She stared at me all funny like for a couple of seconds, before smiling and shaking my hand, cowgirl fashion.

I didn't want to ask the next question, even though it had to be asked. It was part of my detective work. "What happened to you? No offense, but it looks like you ran into a semi-truck!"

"It kind of feels like I got ran over. Stan… er… Lee… whatever he calls himself, today… and I, got into an argument earlier this morning. It was about how he's started blocking me off certain sites online. I informed him I was twenty-six, and too old for wall blocks online. Before I knew it, he smacked me. *Hard.* He's been in sour moods lately, and was in one this morning before he left for work.

"Actually, it was more of a rotten mood. We had a shouting match. I used to take singing lessons and am a soprano. Needless to say, I easily outmatched him. Naturally he was ticked to be out-yelled by a girl, and when he hit me, he not only smacked my cheek, he also broke my glasses."

"Terra, one last thing." I squirmed uneasily on the worn step. "Who was the guy with the fedora? The one you wouldn't tell me about?"

"He's some guy named Craig Stellen." She squeezed her robe between her fingers, and a guilty look washed across her face. "I must confess, I acted like a schoolgirl around him. He's so handsome, and handsome men have always been a weakness of mine. I know the Bible says it's wrong, especially if you're a married woman, but sometimes I forget and drool over handsome men.

"Stellen invited himself over here, said he was a good friend of my husband's. I didn't object to it, yet when I told my husband, I'd never seen Stan so livid. I could literally see one of the veins on his neck bulge out. He stood right in front of me, and said in a threatening voice, 'Don't you dare tell anyone you met Craig Stellen. Do you understand me?' I instantly demanded to know why he was talking to me in such an angry tone.

"Well, he hemmed and hawed for a little while, before saying something about Stellen being an undercover FBI agent he brought in especially for the diamond case. I never knew the FBI had cute looking guys on their force."

I started to laugh, but slapped my hand over my mouth. "So, you don't know anything about this Stellen guy?"

"You mean other than the fact he's good-looking, wears a ponytail and an awesome hat? And, he's probably not an FBI agent? No." She stood to her feet. "Want some hot chocolate?"

"Sure." I followed her into the kitchen and sat down at her oak table as she bustled around, preparing two mugs of hot chocolate.

"So, how's your man doing?" she asked, pouring some hot water over the cocoa powder.

"My what?"

"Your man. Minx. At least, I think your dad said the boy's name was Minx. Told me the boy was quite taken with you." She looked at me and wiggled her eyebrows mischievously.

"He's not my man." I fingered the green place mat. "We're not speaking to each other." I found myself telling Terra all about how I'd wanted to solve this mystery by myself, and I'd somehow wound up with helpers.

"But what about Emma? Do you not want her help, either? Or is it just the boy's help you don't want?" she interrupted at one point in the story.

"Emma's all right, because she has the childish innocence to where she can snoop someone out and no one would be the wiser."

"Right."

"Minx, on the other hand, just invited himself to join the party, which seriously ticked me off. When I told him I didn't appreciate his barging into my investigation, he got mad and left. And now, it's back to Emma and me."

Terra set a mug of hot chocolate in front of me and spooned a generous portion of whipped cream onto it. She sat across from me and removed her glasses. Her face was lined with worry, something which set me on edge. "I think you should include Minx in your list of aides."

"Why?" I took a sip of the creamy sweetness and burned my tongue.

"If I know my husband, which I'm sad to say I do, he won't let anything, or anyone, stand in his way. He's also prone to violence, as you can see." She pointed to her bruise. "I don't think he'll take it easy on you, just because you're a girl and a teenager. His temper must know no bounds. Even though he did a good job of keeping it hidden for the past six years, I could always tell it was there... bubbling under the surface, and ready to break out at a moment's notice." She shuddered.

"But, I only have five days to solve this stinking mystery!" I argued. "I don't have time to go around asking people for help."

"Who set the time limit?"

"Mr. Wington. He said if Dad didn't produce the diamond in five days, then Dad would wind up behind bars. The waddling mass of a person said so, himself." All of the bitterness I'd locked up for the past few weeks began to spill over, like the hot chocolate was doing onto my hands. I merely dabbed the liquid up with a napkin, but it wasn't as easy to erase my anger.

"Crystal," Terra started to say, but the slam of a car door brought her to her feet as if she'd been shot in the backside. "You've got to hide, girl!"

"What? Where?"

"Here." She dragged me to a pantry and stuffed me behind the vacuum cleaner and dust mop. As I crouched behind the cleaning equipment, she tossed some rags onto my head. When I started to object, she said, "Don't worry, this closet is usually pretty messy, anyway. No one will take notice, since it's always like this." She quickly shut the door, enshrouding me in darkness.

I could smell the tangy scent of lemon Lysol and the dirty water scent from the mop. It felt like little dust bunnies were hopping down my back every time I moved. As I tried to shift my shoulders and get the bunnies out of my shirt, I nearly knocked the mop over.

"How was your morning, dear?" I heard Terra ask.

"What business is it of yours?" Officer Snout growled.

"It's what I always ask whenever you come home for lunch, and you know it. Now stop being a grouchy old bear."

"Who'd you have over?"

"What? Why?"

"There are two mugs of hot chocolate on the table, and they're still warm. Now tell me, woman, before I get rough."

"What business is it of yours?" Terra mimicked Officer Snout's tone.

Get some, Terra, I silently cheered her on.

"You had the O'Mally brat over here, didn't you?"

"She's not a brat, Stan. At least she has better manners than someone else I could name."

Wham!

I winced as if I'd been the one just slapped. Terra's startled cry got to me, and it was all I could do not to go lunging through the door and right at Snout's throat.

"Quit sassing me, Terra. Now tell me who you had over, or I'll tear the place apart looking for them." His tone said he was going to follow through on his warning, if Terra didn't say something soon.

I couldn't believe the menace I heard in his voice. It was so unlike him. My heart began to pound so loud, I was more than certain Snout could hear it loud and clear. Sweat broke out on my forehead.

"Go ahead. I don't care. As of today, I'm leaving. I've had enough of your bullying."

"Terra, sweetheart, you shouldn't be this way to someone who's loved you for six years." His tone had turned cool and suave, more like the Snout I'd grown up knowing.

"You can sweet talk me all you want to, *dear*." She said the word as if it were poisonous on her tongue.

"You must understand me, here. The case has me…"

"No more excuses. You've used the same playing card one too many times in this game."

"Oh, really? Well sometimes a man's forced to use the same card more than once."

"And another thing, you keep changing your voice. One second you're a tenor, then the next you're an alto. It's getting on my nerves."

"A man has special reasons for why he does what he does," Officer Snout retorted.

I had to clap a dust-covered hand over my mouth to keep from exclaiming aloud. *Snout's voice matched the one on the recording! The person who'd taken the phone call... Lee. Had Snout been disguising his voice, all along?* I strained as hard as I could to hear the rest of the conversation, or argument, as it were.

"Forget it, Stan. I've had it with your mood swings. You're an angel one second, and then mad as a hornet the next. I'm leaving." Her footsteps stomped up the stairs.

"You betcha' you're leaving, but not where you think you're going." His footsteps marched after her.

"Stan! What are you doing? Put me down! Help!" Terra's screams vibrated through the house.

Glass was smashed and footsteps thundered up and down the stairs. Something struck the door and light sliced into the darkness. I cowered back, half expecting a monster to come in and get me. Shouts filled every crevice in the house, until the slamming of a door silenced it all.

For five whole minutes, I stayed in my hiding spot, too scared to come out. When I finally dared to leave, I had to really shove the door as hard as I could with my shoulder. I peered around the corner and saw a kitchen chair leg buried in the door. The leg had left a good-sized hole in the wooden door. My own legs were cramped, and it took a few moments of limping around before circulation returned to them.

The kitchen was a total wreck. One of the mugs was broken. Chocolate left a huge, ugly stain on the white linoleum floor. Something black in the middle of the brown spot made me stoop down to see what it was. It was Terra's glasses, or rather, what was left of them. One of the lenses was broken, and the stem was no longer taped to the frame.

I left the house and saw her slippers in the driveway, where they'd fallen off during the struggle. Again, rage ran through me, and I stared at the road as if staring at some unseen foe. "You better watch your back from now on, Snout!" I shouted. "Because I'm not going to play nice!"

* * * *

"Terra didn't show up for work." Dad rubbed his forehead and sighed. "I tried callin' the house, but no one answered. I couldn't even reach her on her cell phone."

I chased my green beans around my plate, and tried to get Terra's cries out of my head. They'd been playing over and over again, all throughout the afternoon. It infuriated me to know I'd been a chicken and hid, while my best friend was in danger. *What could you have done against a big guy like Snout?* my head asked me.

Poke his eyes out. Scratch his face off. Bite his hands... Anything I could think of.

But, he's bigger than you are, my head argued. *You know you couldn't have stood a chance against him.*

"Daddy, when are they gonna' catch the bad guy?" Emma asked in a small voice.

"I don't know, sweetie. Hopefully soon." He flashed her a tired smile. He had day old stubble around his face, making him look a little fierce. He'd lost some weight, and I could tell he'd also lost some sleep by the dark circles under his eyes.

Mom didn't look much better. Her face was worn and haggard. I'd often caught her on her knees in her room, praying to God.

Me? I didn't quite want to have anything to do with God, at the moment. He'd wanted to help me, but He'd been letting me down time and time again. I just couldn't take it anymore. It reminded me of the time when Jesus was on the cross, and He cried out, 'My God, My God, why have You forsaken Me?' I felt just as forsaken now, as Jesus had, two thousand years ago.

I stood up. "If you'll please excuse me, I'm not really hungry." I went to my room and plopped down in the middle of my room. I pulled my legs up to my face and buried my face in my knees. It took all of my willpower to keep the tears back. "Why, God? It's not fair! My family hasn't done anyone any wrong, and we're being attacked like this. Where are You? Why aren't You doing something? Why?"

I jumped as something slid between my arms. A fashion doll stared up at me, with a smile glued permanently onto his plastic face. His soft brown hair was spiked, and his green eyes had been colored with markers so they were now blue. Emma stood over me, holding dolls in her arms. "I thought maybe Josh could cheer you up," she whispered.

Josh, yeah. I'd forgotten this one had a particular name. I gave her a weak grin. "Thanks, Emmy."

She got on her knees and threw her arms around me, squeezing me as hard as she could. "Don't worry, Crissy. We'll catch the rotten old thief, yet. And he'll be sorry for what he's done."

A half-smile tugged at the corners of my lips. It wasn't quite a cynical smile, but then again, it wasn't a happy smile, either. "He will indeed be sorry for what he's done, Emma. He will indeed."

* * * *

"Letter for you, Crystal." Mom handed me a white envelope with Terra's handwriting on it.

I let my backpack thump to the floor and ripped the envelope from Mom's hand. As a second thought, I ran for my room without even bothering to take my shoes off. I'd most likely get scolded for it later, *but hey, I'm in a hurry to see what this letter says!* My swivel chair creaked a little as I sat down, and with feverish hands, slit the envelope open.

A single piece of yellow notepad paper fell out. Disappointment welled up inside of me, and threatened to spill over in the form of tears. I unfolded the sheet, and gave a small cry of fear as I read the following message.

'Either leave us alone, or it'll be too bad for Terra and your precious jewel.'

Why do these guys always write in bold print? Do they think I'm blind or need glasses, or something? I knew Terra was in danger, but what did they mean about my precious jewel? I didn't have any jewelry I valued with a passion. Greatly puzzled, I folded up the paper and stuffed it into my drawer.

"Whatcha' get, Crissy?" Emma came into my room and stood at the corner of my desk.

"Oh, just a letter," I responded absently. *What did they mean by my precious jewel? Are they going to be stealing more of Dad's jewelry?*

187

"Is it a threatening letter? Lemme see!" She tried to reach into my drawer and take the paper out.

I must confess to smashing her fingers, as I slammed the drawer shut. She gave a screech of pain and stuck her fingers in her mouth.

"What happened?" Mom demanded, appearing in the doorway.

"Cwystal twied to wip my fingews off!" Emma hollered around her fingers in her mouth.

"Emma wanted to see the letter I'd just gotten, and I tried to shut the drawer before she could get her hands on it. Unfortunately, the drawer got her hand before her hand could get the letter." I giggled. The sentence didn't make any sense, but it sounded funny.

To my surprise, Mom smiled and chuckled. "Well then, I guess I should scold the drawer for smashing my poor baby's fingers." She came and stood in front of my desk. "Now drawer, you did a very bad thing, smashing my Emma's fingers. Don't you ever do it again. Do you understand me?"

I pulled the drawer in and out to make it look like it was talking, and spoke in a ridiculously deep voice. "Yes, ma'am."

"Good. Now don't you forget it." Mom winked at me.

I winked back, and suddenly felt odd. I wondered what was wrong with me, and then I realized I felt lighthearted. Which was an odd feeling, after feeling nothing but heavy stress, for the past few weeks. We hadn't goofed around like this in what seemed like ever… and it felt awesome!

Mom examined Emma's fingers and went to get some ice for

them. My sister's fingers were only slightly swollen, however, she's such a princess, she has to get a tourniquet every time she gets chapped hands or something. She's so picky about bleeding and stuff.

"What'd you get?" Emma stayed in my room, her hand wrapped in an ice pack, which in turn, was wrapped in a peach colored towel.

I looked down at the towel and suddenly snorted. The ice pack wrapped in the towel made her hand look like it had swollen at least twenty-five times its original size. It reminded of a Three Stooges episode, 'Punch Drunks', when Curly smashed his glove against a metal pole... and the next shot showed him with this ginormous glove, which meant his hand was swollen.

"What's so funny?"

"Never mind." I looked out the window at the blossoming cherry tree outside my window and tried not to laugh. After a few seconds, I managed to get my giggling under control, and become serious once more.

The letter I'd just received told me the crooks were not only agitated, but they were no longer playing games with me. They meant business. It was too dangerous to let Emma stay on the case. I knew what I had to do, even though I didn't want to do it. As much as she liked to act like a pain, she was still my sister, and I still loved her. "Em, you know how at the end of Clue, when we've gathered all of the clues together, then we say who we think the criminal is?"

"Uh-huh." She nodded eagerly.

"Well, I have reason to believe it was Officer Snout, but

where and with what, I'm not sure."

"Snotty Snout?" Emma wrinkled her nose like a little piglet. "Why would he want an old honking diamond? He gets paid well enough where he is, or so Mrs. Tellers told me."

"Yeah, but don't you remember in Mr. Russell's story, how he said his boss wanted him to pose as a detective in a small town? Well, I figured out the small town Mr. Russell was talking about, was Alamo. And, another thing I remembered, is we don't know much about Snout's detective background... other than the tall tales he likes to tell."

Her eyes lit up with understanding. "So you think Snout was a phony?"

"He *is* a phony," I corrected her. "I got in touch with Harvard University, and they said he never attended their college. This means those fancy diplomas he's so proud of, are as phony as a three-dollar bill. Also, do you remember the morning the diamond was stolen, how Snout was eyeing the slip of paper in Dad's hand? I guess Snout decided to steal the diamond from Dad's shop, instead of the museum."

"How come?"

"Because stealing it from the shop, would be easier than stealing it from a museum. In the museum, there's a whole lot more security cameras and lasers and stuff guarding the diamond. Whereas in Brian's Treasures, it's only a few security cameras and no lasers, which is why he broke into Dad's shop."

"Why the little..."

"Calling him names behind his back, isn't going to help anything."

"You're right! I'll save it so I can say it to him in person." Her face suddenly fell. "But... but does it mean Terra lied to us all along? She knew what her husband was up to and she helped him, didn't she? So now she'll have to go to jail, and wear striped pajamas for the rest of her life."

"No." I took Emma's hand in mine. "I talked to Terra, and she said she didn't know anything about her husband's dirty dealings. She was just as angry about them, as you are."

"She won't have to wear those striped pajamas?" Emma asked cautiously.

"No, she won't have to wear the striped pajamas." I couldn't hide my snicker at Emma's description of the clothes a convict wears, even though her color description was a little outdated.

"But her mean ol' husband will, though!" she gloated.

"Eh, most likely." Here came the hard part, and I was more nervous than I thought I'd be. "Emma, I'm afraid I'm going to have to take you off the case."

"What do you mean?" A look of uncertainty crossed her young features.

"It means you're no longer a detective."

"What?" Disappointment and shock were written all over her face. She looked ready to cry.

"It's becoming too dangerous. We're near the end, and if you've read any mystery novels, you know something bad usually happens right around the end."

"Like what?" She tried crossing her arms across her chest in a defiant manner, but only managed to cross one arm due to her swollen hand.

"Like someone gets kidnapped, drugged, or something much worse could happen." *Lord, she isn't getting the picture, here. Please, help her to see how dangerous it's becoming.*

"But, the good guy always merges victer… victar… The good guys always wins in the end, no matter what happens."

"I think the word you're looking for, is *victorious*. And yes, the good guys always do emerge the winner… but Emma, something bad always happened, before something good."

"But you'll be there to protect me, Crissy," she objected, turning on the puppy eyes. "If you let me stay on the case, I'll never ask you to play dolls with me for as long as I live." She crossed her heart.

Ooh, it sounded way too tempting. I opened my mouth to say, 'Deal', but then I really looked at her. As the older sister, I had an overwhelming responsibility to take care of Emma, and protect her in every possible way. *If something were to happen to her, like she was killed, how could I explain to Mom and Dad their Emerald was gone, forever?* I couldn't. It was an unbearable thought. I couldn't handle it, if anything happened to her.

"Please, Crystal."

"I'm sorry, Emma." I stood up and hugged her. "I'm doing this in your best interest. I don't want anything to happen to you."

She punched me in the stomach with her good hand and I staggered back a little, completely shocked. "You're not doing this for my best interest," she spat angrily. "You're doing this so you can get all of the glory for capturing the criminal, and see your name in the newspaper. You're not being fair!" She ran from the room before I could recover my breath and contradict her.

"I just want to protect you," I whispered to no one in particular. I slumped dejectedly into my seat, and stared at the calendar in front of me. My birthday was coming up soon, and I didn't feel any excitement. Normally, I'd be bouncing off the walls, inviting people over and driving my parents nuts with party plans. Not this year... *and I was turning sweet sixteen, for crying out loud. This should be the mother of all celebrations, here. Instead, I'm spending the days leading up to my special day, arguing with annoying guys... as well as my sister... and chasing some insane wacko who wants to keep this girly, pink diamond.*

Okay, I'm at the end of my mystery, here. I'm getting ready to scope out the bad guy. What to do next? I thought of Carolyn Keene's novels, and pondered how her books ended. "Well, apparently my next step is to find the location of the robbers' hideout." Unfortunately, this was something I hadn't even taken into consideration. I decided to start at the Snout home.

It was still light outside at five o' clock, and supper wasn't for another hour. I put my flashlight in my front pocket, slipped my cell phone into my back pocket, and tucked Dad's recorder into the other back pocket. "Mom, I'm heading out," I called as I shrugged into my jacket.

She came to the foyer, wiping her hands on her apron. "Where to, angel?"

"The Snouts."

"Good. Maybe you can see if poor Terra's not feeling well."

Poor Terra, is right, I thought, zipping up my black jacket. I gave Mom a kiss on her cheek. "Be back later."

"Try to be back in time for supper."

Aloud, I said, "Yes, ma'am." To myself, I added, *Sorry, Mom. Can't make any promises.*

I jogged down the sidewalk toward the Snouts' home. Along the way, I saw Minx, Celine, and Cory go into the Gopher's Hole. Celine's hand was possessively on Minx's shoulder, and she was batting her eyes up at him in a stupid way. Bile filled my throat and I had an urge to go decorate Celine with it. *She was so disgusting!*

Ten minutes later, I arrived out of breath at Terra's front porch. Fortunately for me, the front door was unlocked, and I quietly slipped in. Sour milk permeated the room, smelling like dirty socks that hadn't been washed in a week. I gagged and quickly moved on to the room on my left, which was Officer Snout's home office. Someone had been here recently, and left mud prints on the carpet. I dropped to one knee and felt them. They were fresh and hadn't even crusted over. They went right up to the tiny computer table at the far end of the room.

I went over, and using my knuckle so as not to get any fingerprints, hit one of the buttons. The computer was on and instantly woke up. Someone had been map-questing an address. I scrolled down and saw the name 'Brian O'Mally', as well as his home address. *Why would they look up our address? All they would have had to do was go to Dad's jewelry store, and see him there.* It was quite puzzling. I went to 'history' and saw it had been deleted. *Darn!* Someone obviously knew they needed to cover their tracks. Too bad I'm not a computer hacker.

I left the office and headed for the upstairs. The master bedroom was a total disaster. It looked like a hurricane had ripped through there at 120 miles an hour. Clothes were everywhere, the mirror was smashed, and Terra's makeup was spilled all over the place. A cheesy picture of Terra and I, taken at the fun park last summer, lay on the floor, the glass cracked. We'd been sticking our tongues out at the camera and pushing our noses up with our fingers, making us look like a couple of pugs. *What had the thief been looking for, or had Snout done this?*

I found some of Terra's winter gloves on the floor, put them on, and began an investigation. I was right in the middle of opening a drawer, when my cell phone rang. "Hello?" I answered it, not stopping my work.

"Crystal, it's Dad. Is Emerald with you?" Dad sounded frantic.

"No, sir. Last I saw she went to her room. Isn't she there?" Tingles of fear electrified through my spine. Something wasn't right, here.

"Han' on." I could hear him talking to Mom in the background.

She was crying and I couldn't understand what she was saying. The only words I could make out were "My precious Emerald."

Dad came back on the line. "She's not anywhere on the property. Crystal? Crystal? Are you still there?"

I'd opened the drawer, and what I saw made me freeze in my tracks. A note glared wickedly up at me.

'Time's up, sister!'

My name and address was next to it, and I knew that note had been intended for me.

"Crystal!" Dad's frantic voice helped me pull myself together.

"I'm still here, Dad. I'm still here."

"Get home as fast as you can," he ordered. "If Emma doesn't show up in another two hours, I'm goin' to call the police."

"Yes, sir." We hung up and I stared at my ten different faces in the mirror, as it spider-webbed in all different directions.

The last piece of the previous note finally made sense. *Emerald!* Not only it was the name of a valuable jewel, but it was also the name of my sister... who was one of the most valuable things in my life. *How did she manage to get herself kidnapped?* A feeling of helplessness engulfed me, and I fell to my knees in the middle of the messy room. I didn't know where to begin... where to look... nothing!

What would my storybook heroes do in circumstances like this? Nothing came to mind, other than they'd try to remain calm... but staying calm, was out of the question. *This is my little sister, we're talking about here! I just can't stand around and make myself think rationally.* I was panicking, because for once... I couldn't think of a single thing, any of my heroes would do.

"God help me!" I cried out. "I don't know what to do! Help me, here." As I began to cry hysterically, Minx's image flashed through my mind. *Yes, I had to get Minx.*

"God, if he doesn't help me, then I guess it's just You and me!"

Chapter IX

Crystal's Decision

"Minx!" I ran up to him and grabbed his arm.

He nearly choked on his cola as he pulled it away from his lips. He wiped his mouth with a napkin. "Crystal? What are you doing here?" He frowned. "I thought you hated my guts."

"Come to chew on him, some more?" Celine taunted me, leaning forward. Her orange hair had been dyed a fiery red.

"Or, have you come to beg for his help, *Detective O'Mally?*" Cory added mockingly.

Minx must have told them about the blow up. I'd get him for it, later... for now, Emma was in trouble. "Emma's been kidnapped," I told Minx, ignoring the others. "Please, help me! I'm afraid they're going to murder her, or something." If I would have been calmer, I'd have seen how ludicrous I was being... but I was hysterical, and didn't care how stupid my sentences sounded.

Without a word, Minx jumped up, grabbed my arm, and we ran out of the Gopher's Hole together. "Where and when was the last time you saw her?" He got right down to business.

"At my house, in my room at about five o' clock. We... uh... we had a slight argument. I told her I was taking her off the case, because it was becoming too dangerous. She got mad and left my room."

"Hence, why it's called an argument."

"It was the last time I saw her." Tears filled my eyes. "Minx, I'm sorry for how I treated you. I was jealous over the fact you were coming up with all the solutions. It was wrong of me to act the way I did. You can forgive me, later." I added this next part, under my breath. "If I live long enough."

"It's okay, Crystal. I understand your frustration." He put his hand on my arm in a comforting gesture. "By the way, do your parents know where you are?"

"Kind of... no, not really. They can hang me for it, later. Minx, they're going to wait another *two hours*, before reporting my sister missing. I can't wait two hours, and I'm not going to!" My Irish stubbornness was really coming through, then.

Minx grinned. "Trait number one, I admire about you. Your stubbornness and determination to see things through. Do you have any idea where to look?"

"No." I threw my hands up helplessly. "Nothing."

"Good. Then you won't object to going to the police station first, will you?"

"Why there?" Then, it registered. Snout worked there, and maybe he'd been careless enough to leave behind some clues.

We were two dark blurs racing down Main Street, as twilight started to arrive. Adrenaline coursed through me every time my feet pounded the concrete. Those suckers were going to pay dearly for messing with my family. It was bad enough they nearly ruined my Dad, but they touched my sister... *and boy, were they were going to be so sorry! It was going to take them until Judgment Day, before they didn't feel guilty anymore!*

Luckily, the police station was still open.

"I'll catch you in a second." Minx veered to the left of the building, next to the garbage cans.

I saw a flicker of light and rolled my eyes in disgust. Of all the times to smoke a cigarette, he had to do it now. I ran inside and up to the window. "I'd like to see Officer Snout," I said breathlessly.

"Officer Snout's not in," Mrs. Tellers told me. She'd obviously had a long day, and wanted to get home as soon as it was her quitting time.

"But, may at least see his desk?" I begged.

"No. It's time for me to go home, and I think you'd best do the same, dear." She pushed her chair away to emphasize her statement.

"But... but," I stammered. "Please, this is an emergency."

"Well, if you want to, you can talk to Officer Olav, over there." She jabbed a long, pointy finger at the barrel-chested officer, as he walked through the doorway leading to the offices.

"What about me?" he looked puzzled.

"Officer Olav, you've got to come with me." I ran over and tugged on his hand. "I think my sister's in trouble, and Snout's the one to blame."

"What grounds do you have to make such an accusation?" He didn't budge.

"I've been receiving threatening notes, and the last one said if I didn't get off the case, then something bad would happen to my little sister." I tugged harder. "And besides, I think Snout's the one who stole the diamond."

"Listen, Crystal." Officer Olav sounded tired. "Snout took the day off, today. Said he was really tired, and needed a rest from this baffling case. To be perfectly honest, I could stand to use a little vacation, myself. Have your parents called the station to report your sister missing?"

"No, sir, but…"

"Well, as far as I know, your parents haven't reported your sister missing."

"But, if you'll just come with me to the Snout home…"

"Another thing, what proof do you have to uphold your claim about Snout being a thief?"

"Hang on." I fumbled in my pockets, hoping to come up with something, but all of my evidence was at home. "Please, just come with me, and I'll show you all the proof you need."

"Stan Snout is a respectable citizen of this community. He wouldn't do something as low down as steal a diamond." Officer Olav shook his head. "Go on home, Crystal. You needn't worry about the case, anymore. Go home and work on homework, or something else constructive." He turned and went back into the offices.

"You've got to believe me," I whispered, tears sliding down my cheeks. I felt a gentle hand on my shoulder, and I turned around to see Minx standing directly behind me. He jerked his head toward the door and I followed him silently outside. *Why, God? Why didn't the officer believe me? It's not like I have a history of lying. Is it because I'm just a kid, he didn't believe me?*

"Hey, Crystal. I found something I know will interest you." Minx held a piece of smelly, wrinkled paper out to me.

"Where'd you find this?" I asked skeptically.

"I went rooting through the trash," he said bluntly.

I silently gagged and was about to refuse, when I realized I was still wearing Terra's gloves. Taking a deep breath, I gingerly took the paper from his hand. I felt my eyes widen and I inhaled sharply. I was staring at a blueprint for Dad's jewelry shop. There was also small piece of paper taped to the side. I tilted the blueprint to my left, and saw the paper contained information on how Dad's security system worked. "So, this is how the crook was able to shut the security cameras down and do his dirty work without being detected."

"Told you it'd interest you." Minx sounded proud of himself. "While you were in there, I went rooting through the garbage in the back. I found this in a plastic bag, along with a few other pieces of paper."

"What else did you find?"

"This." He took the blueprint and put another stinky, crumpled piece of paper in my hands.

I looked down and Mr. Russell's wrinkled face looked up at me. It was a mug shot, like the one you see in police movies, and such. His pudgy face was full of sorrow and dejection. Stubble covered his face, making him look like a biker. I squinted and studied his eyes more closely. They had a look of betrayal in them, and for once, I felt honestly sorry for him. I knew what it was like to be betrayed by someone you trusted and looked up to. It hurt worse than a bee sting.

"Who's the guy in the picture?"

"Todd Russell," I explained. "He is… was… the janitor here. He was framed for a robbery and earned ten years for it."

"Ow! That's got to be hard."

"You're telling me."

"Would you look at this!" Minx gave a low whistle, and held a sheet of paper up for me to see.

It contained a rather long list of people around town. *Where had I seen those names before?* A light bulb went off above my head, as I recognized those names as people who'd been robbed.

"So, this is their hit list, huh?"

"Looks like it is." I saw something yellow in the dirt at my feet and scooped it up. It was a smudged sticky note with a message written in pencil.

'Crest's skipped town. Hunt him down at all costs. In the meantime, don't forget six o' clock. Bring girls and diamond. Tonight we leave.'

"Crystal?"

I handed the note to him and watched his eyes widen in disbelief.

"But, the only bad thing is, we don't know *where* the meeting's going to take place."

"We have over a five mile radius, from which to choose from." Minx thoughtfully tapped his chin with his forefinger.

Lord, help. Where are the criminals having their farewell party? A mental image of the torn note flashed in front of me, like a picture on a movie screen. "Morgan is the man to go to!" I blurted out.

"Huh?" Minx stared at me, clearly thinking I was having a nervous breakdown due to the stress.

"Emma and I found a note, ending with the sentence, 'Morgan is the man to go to'. And since we know Stan Snout is also Lee Morgan, we're going to Sesame Street."

"Great work, Crystal." He beamed proudly at me.

"Thanks." I blushed and looked away. "The Lord helped me, with that one. Now, let's go!" I stopped and looked down at Minx's filthy hands. "Please, do me a favor and wash your hands. They smell like garbage."

Minx rolled his eyes before running into the building. He was gone for about a minute, and when he came back, I could still see water glistening on his hands from the nearby street light.

"Thank you." I straightened my jacket collar. "Now, let's get going!" But before I could go flying down the sidewalk, Minx grabbed my arm with his damp hand.

"Crystal, perhaps we should ask the Lord's protection on us."

I stared at him, dumbfounded. "You never told me you were a Christian, before."

He kicked at an imaginary pebble on the ground. "It's just, well... I mean... I've never felt comfortable sharing my faith with others. I'll be the first to admit I've been straying from the 'Straight and Narrow' lately, such as doing vandalism, but spending time with you, seemed to help bring me back around to what Revelation calls my 'First Love'. I've asked Christ to forgive me, and have come back to Him. I hung out with Celine and Cory, because they were the only friends I had for the longest time."

I remembered how Celine had been fondling Minx's arm. "Celine looked like she was getting pretty cozy with you."

"Yeah, she's the biggest flirt I've ever seen, and I've been trying to break her of the habit. So far, it hasn't worked. Anyhoo, moving right along, for now let's get back to the moment at hand. Do you want to ask the Lord's protection, before we head out?"

I started to say, 'We don't need to', but then I had second thoughts. We didn't know what we were getting ourselves into, and I didn't like the idea of coming home in a pine box. I nodded quickly. "Yes, I think we should."

The two of us held hands and stood underneath the streetlight. I squeezed Minx's hand, telling him he could lead the prayer. He cleared his throat nervously and began. "Heavenly Father, we come before You this night to ask for Your guidance and protection. Please, protect us and every innocent person involved. Please, help us rescue Emma…"

"And, Terra," I interjected.

"Terra?" Minx looked at me, his eyebrows raised in shock.

"Proceed." I bowed my head.

"And help us rescue Terra, as well. Let us all make it home safely in one piece and in good health. Um, I guess that's all. In Jesus' Name. Amen."

I added my own hearty, "Amen", at the end.

"Let's get this show on the road!"

We ran down the street, both of us wearing dark jackets, which enabled us to blend in with the nighttime shadows. Ten minutes later, we approached the Snouts' house. To our surprise and delight it was lit up like Christmas, even though the blinds were drawn. I forced my pounding heart under control, as we slowly crept up the driveway and to the nearest window, which luckily had only a half-drawn blind. Someone's back was blocking our view, so we moved on to the next available window.

I saw Snout, Nevel, Oliver, Stellen, and Stow. The diamond and the girls were nowhere in sight. The men were standing around drinking beer out of glass bottles, laughing, and having a jolly old time. The window was open a crack, and I could smell the foul odor of cigarette smoke and beer. I gagged as I studied the characters on the inside.

Stow's salt and pepper hair looked wild and he was standing straight up, no shoulders hunched. Stellen's shoulder length hair wasn't pulled back into a ponytail as usual, but rather hung loose down to his shoulders. Nevel was busy picking his teeth with a toothpick, while Snout was busy guzzling his drink. Oliver took a long puff of his cigarette, before flinging the butt into a trash bin.

"And, then what?" Stow asked in a slurred voice. He must have been drinking for quite some time, already.

"We get the ransom money for the kid," Stellen shot back, waving a ring-covered hand toward the ceiling as if Emma was super-glued up there. "You think I'm leaving this beautiful town without something to remember some of the citizens by? Speaking of which, show me some of the 'merchandise' you boys have picked up for me."

One by one, the stolen items were displayed, with boldness and the utmost cockiness.

"Well done, Morgan." Stellen slapped Snout on the back with a loud thump, causing the latter to lurch forward a bit. "I knew I could trust you better than Crest, who was nothing more than a yella' coward."

"Yeah, I was sure surprised he moved to Alamo, considering the job you were trying to give him," Snout commented, picking up Miss Gopher's sterling silver necklace and admiring it in the light. He put it back in the box. "We'll, I've got my prize." He elevated a sapphire and kissed it. "Crest thought he'd won, after he got this for his wife. Well, he thought wrong, because when I want something really bad, I ain't stopping until I get my hands on it!"

A dull thumping noise overhead arrested my attention. It must have been louder in the house, because the men looked up at the ceiling, their faces full of annoyance.

"Tell them dames to knock it off, or I'll knock them off myself!" Stellen ordered Nevel.

The latter nodded and without a word, left the room.

The rest of the men were cajoling with each other, when Emma came spiraling into the room like a top, and landed with a crash at Stow's feet. Terra soon came flying in and made a crash landing, as well.

At first, it looked like Emma had a purple lollipop stuck to her left cheek, but as I squinted and looked harder, I saw it was a giant bruise. "Why those...!" I started for the front door.

"Duck!" Minx yanked me down.

"Let me at them," I growled. "They've gone one step too far, hitting my sister. I'm going to let them have it!" I tried to get up again.

"No, Crystal. I think this is where we bring the police in."

"The what? Why?"

"Uh, *hello*! It's two teenagers against five grown men."

"Weren't you the one who just prayed for God's protection?"

"Yeah, but there's also something called using common sense. You know we'd be pummeled, trying to take these punks on."

I blew out a long, frustrated breath, knowing full well what Minx said was right. "Fine, we'll get help."

We stole into the nearby bushes and I pulled out my cell phone. To my horror, it had only one bar left. I had to make this call count. I quickly took the gloves off and flipped through my list of contacts, but couldn't find any personal police numbers. Why didn't I take that into consideration before? *You didn't think you'd get into a situation like this!* I told myself.

"Why don't you just dial 911?" Minx made me feel like a complete idiot.

"I was hoping to get a hold of just one police officer, in particular," I tried not to snap at him as I dialed '911'. It rang twice, before someone picked it up.

"This is 911. How may I help you?" A woman's voice I didn't recognize, answered my call.

"The diamond thieves are at the Snout place," I said in a hurry.

There was a hesitant pause on the other end. "Say again?"

Lord, I don't have time to play games! "The diamond thieves are at the Snout place, and they have two hostages," I repeated, as patiently as I could. "Here, listen in for yourself." I hurried back to the window, and pressed the phone up against the screen.

"You big bully!" Emma cried, her back pressed against the wall.

"Jest tell us where your sister's gonna' be next, and we'll let you go home to your nice beddy-bye," Stellen said. "And, you can see your mummy and daddy."

"You gonna' steal Crystal, too? Like you stole the diamond and me and Terra?"

"Steal you?" Stellen sounded hurt. "Would you boys listen to her? This little chipmunk, accused us of stealing." He fell against Stow's shoulder and pretended to sob loudly. "Don't it plumb hurt your feelings, fellas?"

"Talk about disrespect for your elders." Snout spat something into a metal trashcan, and it made a loud ringing noise as it hit the bottom.

"You stole the diamond from my daddy, and now he's gonna' get in trouble. It's all your fault!" Emma was clearly growing more and more terrified, with each passing minute. Minx literally had to hold me down, to prevent me from tearing in there and ripping those guys to shreds.

"It jest so happens, I like pretty jewelry, and the diamond will go nicely in my collection," Stellen gloated. "Your pappy thought he was perty smart with his high tech security gizmos, but we outfoxed him." A chuckle of approval ran around the room. "As soon as your old man pays us to get you back, we is gonna' put that beautiful hunk of money in my library, where it belongs."

"It belongs in a museum," Emma retorted.

"My library *is* a museum."

"Thief."

"You're running your jaw, one too many times," Stellen growled, starting for her.

"Could you hear everything?" I crouched down and whispered into the phone. "Hello? Hello?" I looked at the screen and groaned in dismay. My phone was dead, and Minx didn't have his phone with him. "We can only hope and pray they received the message and sent help." I pocketed the now useless instrument.

"Amen." Minx nodded

"You leave her alone." Terra's shout caused my head to come springing up faster than a jack-in-the-box. She was standing between Stellen and Emma. "Touch her again, and you'll be sorry."

"Whatcha' gonna' do, Tiny?" Stellen laughed rudely.

"Now, baby, don't be snapping at my boss." Snout laughed loudly.

"Well he ain't *my* boss," Terra shot back. "I think he's a sorry excuse, for anyone's boss."

"Watch your mouth, woman," Snout snapped, coming to stand in front of his wife. "It's been a might too flappy, lately."

"Has it? Oh, I'm sorry. Well then, I guess something else besides my mouth should 'flap'."

"You just keep your mouth shut, Pipsqueak." Snout towered over Terra's five-five figure. He was physically fit, and I could see his well-toned muscles tensing up underneath his thin, cotton shirt. Terra looked like she was no match for this giant jerk.

"I'm warning you, back off." Terra's bird-like voice was filled with steel. "Or you'll be sorry."

"You're no match... *Pulg!*" Snout doubled over, as Terra's bare foot launched itself into his stomach. He crumbled to the floor, writhing in pain. His buddies held their stomachs and roared with laughter at his agony.

"Look at Emma!" Minx pointed.

I saw her creeping toward the front door. I finally realized Terra was trying to create a distraction, so my little sister could escape. *Go, Emma, go!* I silently cheered.

Unfortunately, Oliver saw her as well, and pounced on her like a cat pounces on a mouse. "It looks like we have ourselves an attempted jail break," he leered at her. His voice was high pitched, but at the same time, it sounded heavily drunk. "What do we do with escapees, Boss?"

"Throw 'em in the dungeon," Stellen answered. "Or in this case, the basement. Take 'em both away."

"I'm not waiting any longer!" I told Minx, and stole for the back door.

I heard him snort something about me acting stupid.

I reached the back door and opened the dog flap. No one was inside the dark kitchen. About a year ago, Terra had locked herself out and had me crawl inside through the dog flap. I'd grown, since then. Taking a deep breath, I squeezed through the rubber flap. I could make it, but just barely. The linoleum was icy cold, as was the rest of the room... as if something foreboding was lurking in the shadows, waiting to jump on me. A heavy stench hung in the air, almost like someone hadn't taken the garbage out for two weeks and it had been left to sit there.

"A little help."

"Minx!" I clamped my lips together to keep from laughing aloud. Minx's body was halfway in and halfway out of the dog flap. His broad torso was a tad too wide to fit through the doggy door. I crawled over to him, grabbed his black hoodie, and began tugging.

"Watch it, sister! You're ripping my favorite hoodie." He was starting to disappear, as the hoodie slid over his face.

"Can't help it. I... *Oomph!*" I sat down hard on my backside, Minx's hoodie in my hands... and Minx, in his white undershirt, was still in the doorway. "Oops."

"I'll get myself out of here. You go and try to help the girls," he ordered.

"But, I can't leave you here."

"I got myself into this pretty mess, and I can get myself out of it, thank you very much. Now go!"

"Yes, master." I crawled on my hands and knees to the den.

The cigarette and beer stench was even stronger in here, than it had been when I was outside. Nevel was busy puffing on a cigarette. His gorilla-like figure spilled out of the antique chair in which he sat. His boots were caked with mud. *Those must have been his footprints I saw earlier,* I thought excitedly. I slowly reached into my back pocket and pulled the recorder out. After hitting 'RECORD', I put it on the wooden floor, and quietly slid it like a hockey puck under the coffee table next to Stow.

"Any word from the O'Mally family, yet?" Stellen asked Stow.

"Nary a word, Boss. I can't seem to raise anybody at the house. Every time I call, I get the busy signal."

"Maybe they're trying to call you." This came from Nevel.

I was surprised he had such a musical sounding voice. Bass baritone, I think they called it… nice and deep… but in this instance, his tone was cold and creepy. *Lord, where are the police? Please, let them be on their way!* I took a second glance at Nevel, and noticed his nostrils were rather large. *He must have been the UPS man who attacked Terra!*

"Think the little twirp's onto us?" Stellen asked Snout, who was sitting at the computer table.

"She ain't no idiot. Of course, she's onto us," Snout spat angrily. He was, no doubt, still humiliated about the fact his friends had witnessed his wife getting the best of him.

"Why'd you even let her on the case, in the first place?" Nevel demanded.

"I didn't want her getting suspicious and trailing me everywhere I went. All I could do was warn her about the dangers of being a detective, and try to scare her off the trail. I sent her a scary message over the phone, after I got her number from Terra."

"It was my idea to put the kitty in her locker." Stow sounded like he wanted some of the glory. "And I did it, too!"

"The dead mouse was my idea," Snout said. "As well as the

works bomb."

"Enough of my horse is bigger 'in your horse," Stellen growled, showing impatience for the first time. "The kid's parents had better call soon, or else the police will be on our tail."

"Why can't we scram without the money?" Nevel sent a gray plume of smoke at the ceiling. "Have them email the check to us, or something."

The men laughed uproariously.

I decided to let the recorder do the rest of the eavesdropping, and went to rescue Terra and Emma. As I crawled to the basement, I heard someone stomping up the carpeted steps. I flattened myself out on my stomach, as the door burst open and Oliver staggered up. His face was scratched and I saw teeth marks on his arms. He passed me without a second glance. *Must have mistaken me for a throw rug, or something.*

Luckily, the door hadn't been shut all the way, and I was able to open it. The hinges squealed their protest as loud as they could, as the door opened. It grated on my already tense nerves and I hit the floor once more, covering my head with my hands. My heart thumped against the floor, making me wonder if the crooks thought we were having an earthquake.

After a few minutes, which felt like hours to me, I cautiously lifted my head and looked around. No one had heard me. Breathing a quiet sigh of relief, I slithered like a snake on my stomach down the steps. It was dark, and my flashlight made an uncomfortable lump in my pocket. The lump hit my leg every time I went over a step. I wished I'd had enough sense to take it out earlier, but I hadn't been thinking rationally. My hand groped for the next step, and felt nothing but air. My body was still moving downward, and I crashed onto the floor. "Ow!" I couldn't keep the small groan in.

"Serves you right, you fat old frog," Emma said.

"Ribbit!" I croaked, rolling over onto all fours.

Pause... "Crystal? Is it really you?"

"Yep. Hang on." I turned the flashlight on and waved it around, until I caught sight of the two girls huddled in a far corner of the basement. Their hands were tied behind their backs and their ankles were bound tightly. Terra was busy wiggling her ankles. I 'Army crawled' over to them. "Are you girls all right?"

"I'm better now that you're here to rescue us, Crissy," Emma whispered.

Her bruise looked even worse close up. It had a splotch of yellow in it, as well as red, black, and blue. Her emerald green eyes were enormous with fear, and there were tear tracks racing down her face. Rage ran through me, as well as an urge to go take out everyone upstairs. "Hang on, sweetie." I began working on the knots. Even though Oliver was drunk, he'd managed to tie some pretty tight knots. I tugged at them until my fingers were hurting. "Try wiggling your ankles," I directed my little sister, who promptly began wiggling her little feet, like a worm wiggles on a hook.

"How'd you know where to find us?" Terra finished kicking herself loose.

"What the...?" I demanded, totally shocked.

"Oh, I kept my ankles apart a little as the lug tied me up. He never even noticed. His main intent was to get the job over with, and get back to the booze upstairs. The rest was easy, on my part." She began moving her arms.

"Is there a knife anywhere, around here?" I was becoming antsy, not knowing how much time we had to get out of here, before we were discovered.

"In the drawer, behind you," she directed.

"Thanks." I looked around and finally located a small table behind me. I opened the drawer and pulled out a Swiss Army knife. "Sweet!" I positioned the flashlight on top of the table, so I could see what I was doing. My cell phone fell out of my jacket pocket. Annoyed, I slapped it on a nearby crate and got to work.

"The knife's really Stan's, but you can use it." I didn't miss the sadness and bitterness in her voice.

"How'd you get yourself into this mess, Emmy?" I grunted as I sliced at the thick ropes.

"After you took me off the case, I decided I was gonna' prove to you I could be a good detective, like you. I slipped outside and decided to go to the police station. I didn't get passed the hedge, 'cause this stinky man jumped out and grabbed me. He smelled like a horse stable. I tried to scream, but he put his smelly hand over my mouth and took me here."

I didn't say anything as freed Emma's feet, and then her hands. Before I could move onto Terra, Emma was on me, her small arms wrapped tightly around my neck.

"I love you, Crystal Elizabeth."

"And I love you, too, Emerald Grace." I patted her head and

rubbed her back. A few minutes ago, I was almost certain I'd never hold my sister again on this side of eternity. I see now, I was dead wrong.

"Not to interrupt your little party…" Terra said.

"Sorry." I released my sister as Terra turned around, and I cut at the ropes binding her wrists.

"Thanks, girl." She flexed her chaffed wrists.

"No problem."

"How'd you know where to find us?" she re-asked her question.

"It was Minx's idea." *Minx!* I'd forgotten I'd left him in the doggy door. I wondered if he was still there.

"Minx?" The two of them chorused in astonishment.

"Yeah, he's been helping me."

"You made a good choice," said Terra.

"Not to mention a cute choice," Emma added.

"Let's get out of here." I grabbed the flashlight, wishing they'd cut out the teasing.

All three of us crouched low and hurried for the steps. I turned the flashlight off and let my eyes adjust to the sudden darkness, before crawling like a baby up the steps. We made it safely to the top, and I poked my head around the doorway. No one was in sight. A heated argument reached me on the stuffy air, and I knew it wouldn't be long before we were discovered.

"Where to?" Emma whispered, holding tightly onto my sleeve.

"To the kitchen. Let's see if we all can't get out through the dog door."

"I should be able to fit," Terra whispered.

Moving like three little mice, only we weren't blind, we scurried for the door. Minx was gone. His hoodie was still where I'd tossed it, however. Emma made it through the hole, no problem. The door must have been made for a German shepherd or something, because Terra was able to just barely squeeze through.

I was halfway out, when something grabbed my legs and yanked me back inside. Something that smelled like it'd been doused in beer and cigarettes, was clapped over my mouth. Kicking like a mule didn't benefit me any, only helped to puncture the air. I was carried for a few seconds, before being tossed on something with springs. I bounced off of whatever it was, and then landed with a thud on the floor. I blinked a few times and found Snout's face two inches from my own. I recoiled at the heavy smell of beer on his breath.

"Hi there. What did I just say?"

"How'd she get in?" Stellen yelled.

"I caught her sneaking in through the dog door in the kitchen," Snout announced, scowling at me. "Must think she's a mutt, or something."

"How long were you there?" Stellen stood in front of me.

I stood to my feet. My legs were quaking so badly, I was surprised they could support me, at all. "In the dog door? Oh, about five seconds, before I was given a roller coaster ride by the jolly green giant over there." I waved a hand at Snout. "It wasn't breaking and entering. Terra lets me go in and out through the little door."

"Well, Terra isn't here," Snout informed me. "So, I classify your action as breaking and entering."

"Do you really?" I feigned surprise. "I didn't break anything. If anyone did the breaking, it was you. You nearly broke my skull open when you jerked me in here." My mind was busy running a million miles a minute. *Okay, what would my heroes… no, forget about what my heroes would do in a time like this! What would you, Crystal, do at a time like this?*

Hmm, let's see, I'd panic big time. Yeah, panicking is always an option, but not exactly a helpful one. Stalling for time until the police arrive here is my only other option, but I'm not good at stalling, unless I'm trying to stall punishment time.

Then, just pretend you're stalling with one of your parents.

Okay. Why am I carrying on a conversation with myself?

"Who is she, anyway?" Stellen snapped at Snout.

"You mean, you've been trying to throw Crystal O'Mally off your stinkin' scent all this time, and you don't even know what she looks like? You're dumber than I thought you were." Snout snorted in disgust, as he shot a nasty look at his boss.

I bit my lower lip to keep back a squeak of amazement. Being this close to Snout, I was able to see the scar next to his left eye. There was something familiar about the shape of his face. It took only a second, before I remembered where I'd seen his face. He was the cowboy in the picture Mr. Russell had shown me… the one with the weird green eyes and beard. A quick glance at Nevel, who was staring at a bottle of beer, told me he was the cowboy… the second, mysterious cowboy in the photo… only his hair had been bleached, then.

"Nobody calls me dumb," Stellen warned, in an icy tone.

"All I'm saying is, I'm surprised you don't recognize Crystal O'Mally. The girl you've been trying to get rid of," Snout yelled.

These men had obviously been helping themselves to the liquor, and were on the brink of a drunken quarrel... something I had absolutely no desire to be a part of.

"Shut your mouth, Morgan," Stellen warned. He studied me, and a split second later, his face lit up with recognition. "Now, I remember you. You're the brat who nearly ripped my pants off me, when I tried to pay you a visit."

"Yep, it was me. I found out where you lived, and came to buy you a new pair of pants," I said, with all of the sarcasm I could muster. "I needed to know your size, before I could get the pair. Didn't want to buy too big a pair, though with your 'physique'," I made quotation marks with my fingers as I said the word, "I was afraid I'd buy a pair, and it'll be too small."

Everyone else around him hooted with laughter, while Stellen's face turned a tomato red. "She's just as bratty as her sister," he snarled. "What'll we do with her?"

"I say we throw her into the basement, with the other two," Oliver volunteered. "It'll teach the young whippersnapper a thing or two about crashing parties."

"Good idea." A cruel smile spread across Stellen's face. "Then we can get twice as much for her, since we have *both* of O'Mally's kids."

"This is the police. We've got you surrounded. Come out with your hands up." Chief Stuart's bullhorn sized voice, boomed out of nowhere.

"The cops are here!" Stow shrieked. "How'd they find us?"

"I don't know." Stellen turned to Nevel. "Bring the other two prisoners up here. We'll use them to get a bargain, if not the money."

My heart sank like a stone as Nevel ran from the room. I could only hope the girls were safe by now, if there weren't any guards around the grounds. *Oh, Minx, where are you?* My fear was mounting like someone stacking blocks on top of one another. Red and blue lights danced around the room, like little fairies chasing one another in a game of tag.

"They're gone," Nevel roared, charging into the room like an angry bull.

"What?" Stellen whirled around to me. "You little scamp! You let them go, didn't you?"

"No harm done," I shot back.

"Craig Stellen, this is Chief Stuart. We've got the house surrounded. Come out slowly, with your hands up. You, and your entire gang."

"It ain't over yet, boys." Stellen reached over onto a table littered with bottles, and pulled out a small pistol. It was a lethal black color and it looked deadly. He went over to the window and flung it open. "It's me, Stuart. We've got Crystal O'Mally in here, and we ain't coming out 'til you promise me none of us is going to jail!"

"I can't promise you that, and you know it, Stellen."

"Then, I can't promise you Crystal's gonna' be able to get out of here."

I started quaking all over, but forced myself to hold my

head high. I couldn't let these creeps know I was frightened out of my wits. A verse from the book of Job, came to my remembrance. I think it was Job 5:19.

'He shall deliver you in six troubles, yet in seven no evil shall touch you.'

"Lord, I'm wallowing in trouble. Please, deliver me from it all," I whispered.

It literally felt like someone grabbed my chin, and turned my head in the direction of the entryway leading to the foyer. *The steps!* Maybe I could sneak out a window upstairs, or something. I tried scooting to the steps leading to the first floor. No one seemed to notice me, since they were all focused on the negotiations with the police chief.

I'd just put my foot on the first step, when Stow caught sight of me trying to escape. "Come back here, girly, or you'll be sorry!" He started toward me, but was too drunk to take more than a few steps, before he hit the floor with a giant crash.

I tore up those stairs like a frightened child. I was passing a room, when someone grabbed my arm. I lashed out and punched as hard as I could. I'm no Jackie Chan, but I can pack a mean whopper.

"Yow, Crystal!"

"Minx! How? Where? Who?" I was totally dumbfounded.

"I got in through the emergency exit," he explained in a rush, grabbing my arm and tugging me through the doorway. "Hurry. We don't have any time to waste."

I could hear the men falling over themselves as they tried to run after me. Their yells filled the whole house, making it sound like it was haunted or something. We reached an open window with the screen missing. Minx scampered through the hole. I hesitated for a fraction of a second, totally unsure, but then proceeded to follow him. There was an oak tree growing directly outside the window. The pause cost me, because I'd wrapped one arm and both my legs around a branch, just as someone grabbed my right arm and began pulling me the other way.

"Up there!" I heard Emma shout.

"Crystal, hang on! Don't let go!"

A spotlight was shone on us, blinding me and making me feel like I was in a circus, or something.

"Hang on, Crystal," Minx cried.

He says it like I he thinks I'm about to let go, or something, I thought, rolling my eyes. I looked backwards and saw Snout's hate-filled eyes staring back at me. He tugged as hard as he could, and my grip started slipping on the tree limb. "Minx, help me!" There was a giant splinter of wood somewhere in the house, followed by a tremendous roar and some gunfire. My right arm felt like it was on fire, as there was a tug-of-war for it. My right leg had just slipped off the branch, when there was an inhuman yell directly in my ear.

Minx jumped onto Snout like a tiger jumps on its lunch, and the two men started wrestling. Now I'd been let go, I was dangling like an ape from the thick branch, about ten feet off the ground. I was holding on with just an arm and a leg.

"Don't worry," Chief Stuart boomed.

"Try to stay calm, Crystal. We'll have you down in a second."

"I have no intentions of letting go." No sooner had I made the proclamation, than I could feel my leg starting to lose its grip. A fine sheen of sweat broke out like zits on my forehead, and my mouth went bone dry. A ladder was placed underneath the tree, however, I knew they wouldn't get to me in time. By the time one of them would come even close enough to reach me, I'd have fallen off the tree like a ripe piece of fruit.

"Lord Jesus, help me!" I cried.

Chapter X

Happy Ending?

My arm had gone from fiery hot, to icy cold numb. The fingernails on my left hand were filled with bark, as I held on with a death-like grip. Just when I knew I was about to join Grandma in heaven, I was grabbed from behind… and for the second time tonight, yanked backwards. My head hit something hard, and the birdies immediately resumed their dancing around my rolling eyes. I lay there, too dazed to really do anything except watch the birdie show. They flew away, one by one, and I became aware of being gently slapped… and the musky smell of aftershave.

"Crystal, can you hear me?" Minx called anxiously, continuing to hit me.

"What do you think you're doing?" I tried scooting away, but an arrow of pain shot up my arm whenever I tried to move.

"You're alive." His eyes were filled with tears. "I thought I'd killed you, when I pulled you in." He fingered the lump on the back of my head.

"Another trophy." I rolled my eyes.

"Crystal!" Emma came tearing into the room. She threw herself on the dusty floor, and gave me her anaconda squeeze. "I thought you were gonna' die."

"So did I, sweetie, but I guess God had other ideas." I patted her head.

Before I knew it, Dad burst into the room, and I was being smothered by his bear hug. It seemed if I wasn't going to be killed by falling, I was going to be loved to death. He didn't say anything, he just hugged me tight. "Dad, I can't breathe," I wheezed out, feeling my lungs about to come shooting out of my body.

He gave me one last squeeze, before setting me on my feet and kneeling in front of me. He was crying harder, than I'd ever seen him cry in my whole fifteen years of living.

Mom was suddenly by my side, kissing me all over the face and hugging me tightly... but thankfully, not as tightly as Dad. "Why didn't you tell us?" she was begging, over and over again. "Why didn't you tell us, what you were up to?"

"You nearly got killed," Dad spoke at the same time. "I didn't raise you to be stupid."

If this is what it's like when the reporters start flocking to my doorstep and trying to interview me in the next few days, then Lord Jesus, help me! I thought. I was overwhelmed by all the talking, and waited until their questions had died down a little before saying anything. I... I, uh..." I fumbled like a duck in a pig's mud sty. Not only was it awkward with Minx standing right by me, but also with a few of the officers standing close by listening in on the conversation. "I didn't think to call you or Mom. I was in a hurry to rescue Emma, and I wasn't thinking rationally."

"I'd say so." Chief Stuart's titanic frame filled the doorway. He wasn't a fat man. He was over six-foot-five, and had the build of a pro-wrestler... which is what he used to be, before he became an officer. "Didn't you know Craig Stellen's a mastermind thief the police have been trying to capture, for almost a decade?"

"How was I supposed to know?" I demanded. "I don't read

the newspaper, unless it's the funnies." Everyone laughed, but I was serious. Minx put his arm around my shoulder and I leaned against him.

"Did they hurt you anywhere?" Dad asked tenderly.

"My arm hurts, a little."

"The big oaf who calls himself a detective, Stan Snout, nearly tore her arm out of her socket, sir," Minx interrupted, ignoring the elbow I jabbed into his rock hard stomach.

"Where is he?" Dad was on his feet in an instant, his eyes blazing.

"Brian." Mom put a steadying hand on his arm. "What's done, is done. No use crying over spilled milk. Stan will receive justice. Let's just be thankful, our precious jewels are safe."

"Speakin' of justice," Dad looked at me. "You disobeyed us, Crystal. We told you to come straight home, and you didn't."

"But, Dad," I objected, "my sister was in trouble, and I wasn't about to stand by and let something horrible happen to her!"

"Your mother and I understand, me lass, but you didn't even tell us where you were goin'."

"I tried to get Officer Olav to help me, but no matter how hard I begged him, he didn't believe me." I looked at the man standing to my left, and he looked away... obviously ashamed he'd brushed me off, when I was right, all along.

My parents looked at each other for a few seconds, and I held my breath anxiously. *Was I about to get busted, big time?*

"For the next week, you'll have extra chores waitin' for you at home, after school... and you'll have to do the chores without gripin'. If you gripe, then you'll have an extra week added on to that week. Do you understand me?" Dad asked.

"Yes, sir." I released a silent sigh of relief. The punishment wasn't as bad as I'd expected it to be. I mean, doing extra chores every day stunk, but at least I could live with it.

Emma fingered the bruise on her cheek. "Mama? I got a bump just like Crystal had, the time she got to stay up real late. Does this mean I get to stay up late tonight, too?" Everyone in the room laughed heartily, and I could almost tangibly feel the weight of stress and fear roll off my shoulders and fall away.

Some paramedics came into the room and examined my sister and me. My arm was only badly bruised and I would probably have to wear it in a sling for a little bit, or so I was told by one of the paramedics.

Terra came into the room, her arms open wide, and a broad smile across her bruised face. "We whooped 'em," she gloated as she gave me a hug.

"We *shore* did." I said in a thick, hillbilly accent.

"Mrs. Snout?"

Both of us turned, and saw a police officer standing in the doorway with Stan Snout, alias Lee Morgan, by his side. The latter's face wore a beaten and worn out look. He almost looked like a puppy, who'd been whipped one too many times with the newspaper. I glanced at Terra and saw her jaw tighten, and a look of hatred spread across her girlish features, almost distorting them completely. "Yes, Officer?"

"We will need you to come downtown sometime soon, to give a statement," he told her.

"I'll gladly give it."

"Terra…"

"Save it, Buster!" Terra cut him off with a tired wave of her hand. "I don't want to hear it." Pain shot across Officer Snout's face and he opened his mouth to say something, but the officer hustled him out the door.

No one said anything, as a slightly strained silence fell over the group. I drifted over to the window and looked out. I saw the officers putting the criminals in the car, and felt a sudden tug of pity for them. These were men who could have led everyday lives. They were somebody's uncle, brother, cousin, father, and maybe even grandfather. *Yet, these men chose to lead a life of crime, and where did it get them? Ten, possibly twenty years, behind bars.*

Something Mr. Russell had said, came to mind. *Ten years, that I can't get back.* Now, these men were about to lose time they could never get back, ever again. Mom was right. It didn't do me a lick of good holding a grudge against these men, because the only person my anger would affect, would be myself.

"You okay?" Minx joined me at my elbow.

"Hmm? Oh yeah. I was just thinking."

"'Bout what?" He pulled me close to him.

"Once upon a time, I wanted to see these guys punished for what they did to my family. I wanted them to experience the exact same hurt and humiliation, they put my family through," I confessed.

"I think every human feels revenge, at one point or another in their life," said Minx. "It's just a natural feeling we have, whenever someone does us wrong. We want to hurt them back, and make them feel the exact same way we felt."

"I wish it *wasn't* the first instinct we felt," I said, softly. "Be nice if we felt forgiveness right off the bat, instead of hatred."

He put a gentle hand on my shoulder. "You're a good girl, Crystal."

I turned ninety degrees and looked at him in complete astonishment. "What on earth did just you say?"

For once, he didn't blush and turn his head away like a little kid, but faced me head on with the adorable grin he sometimes wears. The one where he grins out the side of his mouth, and I can count five and a half teeth. I know he has a mouthful, but when he grins all crooked, five and a half teeth is all I can see.

The little laugh lines at the corner of his eyes were visible, as he gazed fondly at me. "I say you're a good girl, because you chose to forgive, instead of holding it against them. You could have very easily chosen to hate them. Instead, you're doing the opposite. It means you're strong, just like you've been strong for the past hour."

"I didn't feel strong, when Emma went missing," I confessed. "I didn't really even know what I was doing."

"You looked like you knew what you were doing. From what Emma told me, you kept a cool head when you were rescuing her and Terra. I also noticed you didn't panic, when your own life was in danger."

"Didn't panic!" I scoffed. "I was freaking out on the inside. I just didn't want to waste energy showing it, on the outside."

"Like I said, you're a special girl, Crystal."

"Wait, you said 'good girl' the first time around. Not 'special'." Without a word, Minx put his arms around me and pulled me close. I smiled up at him. I could almost hear romantic music begin to play, *and was it me, or did the moonlight suddenly seem brighter?*

"Ooh, gross!"

I snapped out of my daydreaming and looked over at my little sister, who was sticking her tongue out and wore a disgusted look on her face. "What's so nasty, Em? I thought you liked Minx, and were trying to get the two of us together?"

"Yeah, but I didn't think you'd be smooching so soon!" She rolled her eyes.

Minx and I chuckled. "We weren't kissing," I told her.

"You looked like you were ready to," she insisted, coming to stand between us, like she was some kind of barrier.

Minx reached over and gently yanked one of my wayward curls. He cocked his head to the side, and it was then I saw the lump on the side of his face. Without saying anything, I quickly reached up and fingered the injury. "How'd you get this? Did the paramedics check you out? Does it hurt a lot?"

"Calm down, Crystal." He gently took my hand off his cheek. "No, the paramedics didn't check me out, and it doesn't hurt too badly. All I need to do is put an ice pack on it, and I'll be fine."

"But, how'd you get it?"

"You gave it to me."

"I did? When?"

"When I grabbed your arm and you swung at me. I didn't have time to duck, before you walloped me."

Embarrassment crept across my face, and I took a step back. "I'm so sorry, Minx! I didn't mean to hurt you."

"You were swinging in self-defense." He smiled, reassuring. "It's okay, Crystal. Really. You don't need to make such a big fuss over it."

I studied him for a few seconds, before sighing loudly. "Oh, okay. If you insist."

"I'm tough. I can take it."

"All right, me lassies, let's go home." Dad came over to Emma and I, arms open wide and a huge smile on his face.

"Wait." I suddenly recalled my cell phone. "Hang on a second, I forgot my phone. It's in the basement. I'll go and get it." I scampered down the steps. Minx was right on my tail. "What are you following me for?"

"Exercise, for one thing. Another thing is to make sure you're going to stay safe."

For once, I didn't object to him helping me. I was finally learning to accept help from others, and it wasn't such a bad idea. I flipped on a light switch and trotted down the steps. There was my phone, where I'd left it. As I bent down to retrieve it, I saw it was resting on a wooden crate... and a rather large one. Curious, I bent down to examine it.

"Crystal? You lose your phone, or something?" Minx came to stand next to me.

My jaw dropped and I felt my eyes bug out. I tried using my nails to lift the lid off. This felt like Christmas time, except the crate wasn't wrapped, and it wasn't underneath a giant, green fir tree… but I had a hunch I knew what was inside the crate, and couldn't wait to verify. I'd forgotten about my game arm, and gave a small grunt of pain when I tried lifting the lid with it.

"You crazy girl." Minx crouched beside me, and started lifting the lid, himself. "I guess it'll take a cast to make you remember you've injured your arm. What's so special about this crate, anyway? Why's it making you so fired-up excited?"

"Just open it already, Minx!" I squealed, excitedly.

Rolling his eyes he complied, and with a reluctant groan, the lid popped off. The scent of fresh straw greeted our noses, as soon as the lid flew off. With my good arm, I started digging around like a puppy looking for a rabbit or a squirrel. My hand struck something rock hard, and I bit back a howl of pain. "Minx, help me move the straw aside."

"Okay, you're the boss." He picked up and armful of straw and flung it aside.

Bits of straw fell like snowflakes around us. We brushed the remaining straw off of the object in the crate. His jaw fell so far open, I thought it was going to fall off his face. He gave a low whistle and looked at me, admiration written all over his face. "Well, Detective O'Mally, looks like you've struck pay-dirt!"

"Mom! Dad!" I yelled as loud as I could. Maybe a little too loud, because Minx winced. "C'mere, quick!"

"Crystal? What's wron'?" Dad hollered. He seemed to jump down all eight steps in one giant leap. It took only about two strides, before he was next to me. "What's the matter? Did you hurt yourself again?"

I pointed to the contents in the crate. I was shaking with excitement, and could barely talk. "Look… look at what Minx and I found, Dad!" I brushed back some of the straw, and the pink glow of a giant diamond was visible. Dad dropped to his knees, tears glistening in his eyes.

Mom, Emma, and Terra came thundering down the steps. Emma nearly fell down the last five. She made a beeline for me. "Crystal, are you okay?"

"Brian, is everything all right?" Mom hurried over.

"Catherine, look what she found," Dad said, in a choked voice. Her hand flew to her mouth, and Terra gasped.

"What?" Emma pushed Minx out of the way, so she could see inside the crate. "What'd Crystal find?" She ran her chubby hand along the smooth top of the diamond. "You found the diamond?" she squeaked in astonishment. "I thought it was stolen!"

"It was stolen, honey," Mom explained. "But Crystal managed to find it, again."

"You're a real detective." Emma threw her arms around me, knocking me to the floor. "You solved the mystery."

"You rule, girl!" Terra cheered.

"Minx helped me find it," I spoke up, not wanting to take all of the credit for myself.

Dad enveloped me in his arms, as soon as Emma let me up. "I'm so proud of you, Crystal."

Tears filled my eyes, as if someone had turned the 'tear hose' on inside of me. "Thanks, Dad."

* * * *

"Our breaking story today, is about Crystal O'Mally, daughter of Alamo's only jeweler. This fifteen-year-old somehow managed to not only outwit the Stellen Gang, but also aided the police in the gang's capture. Crystal may be young, but she proved..." The anchorman's nasal voice was instantly silenced, as I turned off the TV.

My injured arm was in a blue, canvas sling. It'd been exceedingly awkward, at first. The most annoying part about having my arm in a sling, was the fact I couldn't climb up the tree to the clubhouse until my arm healed. *Bummer!*

Another annoying thing was the leeches... er, I mean all of the reporters... who were flocking into Alamo. Of course they wanted to interview me, but I'm pretty well known around town, and the townspeople know I don't like publicity. Thankfully, the locals have kept their mouths shut as to where I live. My teachers let me stay at home, until things cool down.

With the sudden publicity Dad was receiving, he was now getting boatloads of tourists who were coming in almost daily to buy jewelry from him. He had to hire three new people to help accommodate the workload he now had. The museum was also receiving tons of tourists, who wanted to see the famous diamond, which had been stolen and was now recovered. Mr. Wington paid a personal visit to our house about a week ago, and gave Dad a most sincere apology. The manager also promised to help vamp up publicity for Dad's business. So far, it looks like he's kept his promise.

The criminals had broken like wet paper bags, and confessed. Craig Stellen, also known by several aliases... too many to name... was wanted on several burglary charges, and had been on the lam for almost ten years. He'd had robbery on the mind, when I caught him trying to break into our house. Thanks to me, he'd failed miserably.

Stan Snout, alias Lee Morgan, was a professional thief. He'd made his debut back in 1998, when he helped to steal fifteen thousand dollars out of a National City bank in Walla Walla, Washington. About a week or so later, he struck two more banks, making successful getaway both times. It had been Morgan's idea for the works bomb in my backpack, and it was him who tipped the newspaper about the stolen diamond. Morgan had wanted revenge on Dad, for selling the sapphire to Mr. Russell. *Talk about greed!* But the plan backfired, and it was Morgan who was ruined, in the end.

Nevel was, in fact, the 'UPS' man who'd attacked Terra. He used to be one of Stellen's best ranch hands, if not the strongest. He'd tripped and crashed into the door with his body when he was leaving with the diamond, which is how the door had gotten busted. Oliver and Stow were just two cowhands with no criminal background, but they possessed a lust for money, and no conscience. All five of them looked like they were going to face a maximum of twenty years behind bars.

My cell phone started ringing. I dug around in my back pocket for it, and managed to answer it just before it stopped ringing. "Hello?"

"Hey, Crys, what's up?"

I grinned. "Nothing much, Minx. What's up with you?"

"Wondering how you're doing. So, how are you doing?"

"I'm bored out of my gourd!" I hadn't realized until now, just how much stuff I had to do during the investigation. Now, everything was solved, back in place, and I had too much time on my hands. I sat in the overstuffed chair, and impatiently drummed my fingers against the armrest.

"A little bird told me someone's birthday's, coming up soon."

"Who's birthday?" Then I remembered, my birthday was tomorrow. "I'd completely forgotten about my birthday, in all the hubbub."

"Do you know what you want?"

I hadn't given my special day any thought, and told him so. He kept pressing me, so I confessed I'd been interested in some detective items... such as, a new magnifying glass, and maybe some fingerprint powder. He asked if there was anything else I wanted.

"Well, I wish my arm wasn't so sore," I said.

He laughed softly. "Then, you'll have to take it up with Jesus. Tell Him that's what you'd like Him to give you for your birthday."

"I just might." We chatted about little things, before hanging up. No sooner was the phone in my pocket, than the O'Mally tornado came tearing through the room and straight toward me. I didn't have time to get out of the chair, before I was struck.

"Happy birthday, Crissy!" Emma crowed loudly.

"Thanks, Emmy, but my birthday's tomorrow." I rubbed my poor ears. "Don't try and rush my age."

"I thought for sure it was your birthday today." Her brows knit together in a thoughtful frown.

"Nope."

"Are you gonna' to have a party? What kind of cake are you going to have? Can you please do chocolate with fudge icing? And, can we play pin the tail on the donkey…"

It looked like I didn't need to plan my day, at all. Little sis was doing a bang up job of doing that, herself. I let her prattle on, until she stopped to catch her breath. She suddenly turned serious, her eyes turning a deep, emerald green. "Crystal, are you sorry the mystery's over?"

"A little," I confessed. "It was fun and quite an adventure for me."

"What was your favorite part?" She sat down at my feet, like I was Granda getting ready to tell her a story.

"Ooh, I'm not sure." As I mentally went over different areas of the mystery, Emma butted in.

"Mine was when you and Minx swooped in and saved the day!"

"Okay, definitely *not* my favorite part," I told her.

"But, you saved me when I was in danger."

"Saving you from danger, was the most terrifying thing I've ever done in my life."

"Why?"

"Because I kept worrying I'd be too late, and the bad guys had done something awful to you. Do me a favor, if we ever do another mystery together, *please* do everything in your power *not* to get captured."

"I'll try."

"Promise?"

"Pinky promise." She crooked her little finger, and I crooked mine around hers.

"So, what *was* your favorite part?"

I thoughtfully nibbled on my lower lip. "Mmm, I think one of my favorite parts, was where I caught Stellen trying to break into the house. As I was pulling on him, I saw a flash of white. Oh, and by the way, he was wearing black pants." I grinned and wiggled my eyebrows at my sister.

Emma gasped dramatically, and clapped a hand over her mouth. "Crystal Elizabeth! You saw London, you saw France, you saw Stellen's *underpants*?"

"I don't know." I felt myself blushing, and yet, I was giggling. It had been an embarrassingly amusing situation, but I could laugh about it now, since it was over and done with.

Emma drifted into the kitchen to ask Mom what kind of cake we were going to have, and once again, I was bored. I stared listlessly at the silent TV in front of me, wishing I had a friend sitting next to me so I could talk with them. Suddenly, an idea sprang into my head, causing me to jump out of the chair. "Mom," I called, as I neared the kitchen and poked my head around the corner.

"Yes, sweetie?" She looked up from the pile of quilt patches she was sorting through.

"May I go and visit Terra, please?"

"Eh... I don't know." Mom looked hesitantly out the window. "I don't want to run the risk of you running into a reporter on your way there."

"I can call Terra and see if she's even home," I offered. "If she's not, then I don't have to go over there."

"Good idea."

I dialed Terra's new number and chewed the inside of my cheek, waiting for her to answer.

"Hey, girl. What's up?"

I smiled when I heard Terra's gentle voice, but noticed she was missing her usual, chippy tone. "I'm bored and was wondering if I could stop by for a visit."

"Aren't you worried the reporters are going to get you?" she teased. "How do you know I'm not hiding one here in my closet, waiting for you to stop by so they can get the drop on you?"

"Because your closet can barely hold your clothes, much less a reporter" I teased right back.

She laughed. "You got me. Sure, c'mon down."

"Be right there." I pocketed the phone and stuck my head back into the kitchen. "She's home, and she said I could stop by."

"Did you remember to do your extra chores?" Mom asked, counting the quilting blocks in her hands.

"Yes, ma'am." I went over the mental checklist… pick up clothes in room, dust bonus room, and help Emma with her homework… all had a giant check next to them.

"All right. Just call me when you get there." She stood up and came over to give me a hug.

"Yes, ma'am." I hurried to my room, jammed a baseball cap

on my head, and whipped a pair of sunglasses onto my face. This was the best disguise I could come up with, on the spur of the moment. Taking a deep breath, I rushed to the front door and opened it. Before I ventured out, I poked my head around the doorframe and peered up and down the street. With the exception of a few people walking their dogs, there was no one else in sight. Doing my best to act nonchalant, despite my hammering heart, I sauntered down the street to Terra's apartment.

After her husband's arrest, she'd moved out of her old house on Sesame Street, and into an apartment on Fifth and Main. "Please, tell me I'm seeing things," I muttered, stopping to stare at some pedestrians across the street. A man and a woman were talking together, but that's not what caused an alarm to go off inside my brain. It was the fact the man wore a suit and tie and looked exactly like the reporter I'd just seen on TV, not twenty minutes ago. The woman pointed toward the bank, and walked away.

My heartbeat accelerated and sweat broke out on my forehead, as the well-dressed man looked around and caught sight of me. He immediately started walking my way. I fully expected him to thrust a camera in my face, and start interviewing me. *Where can I hide?* I frantically looked behind me, hoping to be near an ally. Instead, I was standing directly in front of the grocer's. I quickly turned and pretended to be fascinated with the oranges, cucumbers, and apples the grocer had put on display outside his shop. There was a tap on my shoulder and I just about fainted. *Mom, maybe I should've asked you to drive me to Terra's!*

"Excuse me. I'm Steve White with the Houston Blaze. Can

you tell me where I can find Sesame Street?" the man said urgently. "I want to interview Mrs. Terra Snout."

"Uh, yes, I can." I turned and pointed to Second Street, hoping and praying the man didn't notice my shaking hand. "Just go to Second Street, and take a left onto Third and Lakeland. It's the next street to your left. You can't miss it."

"Thank you." He patted me on the shoulder. "Thank you, so much." He quickly took off toward Second Street, and I lost no time in running madly to Fifth and Main.

Five minutes later, I was climbing up the wrought iron steps to apartment two-o-nine. Before I could even knock on the door, it flew open and Terra was standing in the doorway. "Hey you!" She tweaked a red curl peeking out from underneath my baseball cap. "C'mon in." I followed her in to the tiny, one room apartment. "You look completely worn out. Can I get you anything to drink? Lemonade? Milk?"

"Lemonade's fine." I stepped inside the dim apartment and was greeted with a blast of cool, refreshing air, which took my breath away for a few seconds.

"You look like a frightened jackrabbit. What gives?" She studied my red face.

"I ran into a reporter, on the way here."

Her eyebrows shot up and her eyes widened. "Did he manage to squeeze an interview out of you?"

"No. In fact, he was looking for you, not me."

"He wanted to interview me? Did you tell him where I lived?"

"No way! He merely asked where Sesame Street was, and I

told him. He didn't ask where you lived, he only asked how to get to your old street."

She chuckled and shook her head. "You pulled a fast one, girl. Here, take a seat and make yourself at home, while I get you something to drink."

I removed the sunglasses as I nervously sat down in a second hand, scuffed up desk chair. All of the furniture in the apartment was from Goodwill. Terra had refused to bring a single stick of furniture from her old house, to her new home. After making a quick phone call to Mom, and letting her know I'd arrived at the apartment safely, I fell silent. A clock ticked noisily on the mantel, and with the exception of the noise coming from Terra bustling around in the kitchen, the apartment was uncomfortably quiet.

"Here you go, birthday princess." She handed me a glass of pink lemonade.

"Thanks." I took a quick swallow of the tart liquid, and couldn't help but make a face. "Wow! Sour!"

"Yeah, just a little." She perched on the edge of the coral colored couch, and picked at some of the stuffing sticking out of the cushions.

"Are you doing okay?" I blurted out, setting the glass on the table next to the chair.

She nodded, as tears filled her eyes and slid down her face. Her lower lip trembled and her face turned red. A sob burst from her lips and she buried her face in her hands. A lump filled my throat, and tears pricked the back of my eyes. Doing my best to swallow the lump, I got up and pulled her into an awkward one-armed hug. She rested her head against my shoulder and sobbed quietly. Tears slid down my own face and plopped on top of her head. *Why, God? I silently yelled. Why does Terra have to suffer like this? What'd she do to deserve all this bad stuff?*

After about ten minutes of sobbing, Terra took her head off my shoulder and wiped her eyes with the back of her hand. "Sorry to get your shirt all wet." She sniffled.

"Naw, it's okay. I've got lots of clean shirts at home," I said casually, not telling her the wet spot was making my shoulder itch. "Is there anything I can do to help? Anything, at all?"

"No, it'll be okay."

"Are you sure?"

"I guess. I went down to the police station this morning, and gave a statement against my former husband. It was the most difficult thing I've ever had to do." She sniffed, wiping away more tears. "I thought Stan loved me, but he was really using me for his 'looking good to the public' gag."

"Were the two of you actually married?"

"Oh, yeah. We were married. Yet, you know what he told me this morning? If he hadn't been caught, he said he was going to divorce me, as soon as the diamond was safely transported to Stellen's place. Said he wouldn't need me anymore, after his job in Alamo was complete." She bit her bottom lip, obviously struggling to keep more tears back.

"Why is this stuff happening to you?" I demanded. "What did you do to deserve all of this bad stuff in your life?"

Terra shoved some stray hair behind her ear. "When I was dating Stan, my mama warned me against him. Said there was something about him she didn't like. She couldn't put her finger on it, but she kept saying there was something shady and untruthful about him. I figured I was smarter than Mom, and she didn't know what she was talking about. I went ahead and married him anyway, against her wishes." More tears filled Terra's eyes. "Now I wish I would've listened to her. I could've saved myself all of the pain and heartache I'm going through, now." She again looked me straight in the eyes. "Listen to what your mama tells you. It'll save you from 'the three h's'."

"The three h's?"

"Hurt, hassle, and heartache."

"Oh." Another uncomfortable silence descended on the two of us. It lasted for about five minutes, before I decided to break it. "I, uh… I'm having my birthday party, tomorrow. You're more than welcome to come."

"I might." Terra gave me a sad smile. "I haven't felt very sociable lately, however, I will try to come. Your dad's been great, giving me time off so I can heal." A hard look came over her eyes, and her lips tightened. "I just don't know if I'm ever *going* to heal."

"Are… are you saying you're never going to forgive your husband?" It didn't seem like something Terra would do, never forgive someone. *Had what she'd been through been so traumatizing, she'd changed completely and forever? Please, God. Don't let Terra allow bitterness eat her alive!*

Terra squeezed her hands together, until her knuckles were totally white. "I don't know, Crystal. I honestly don't know, if I can forgive him."

I tried to lighten the situation. "Do you at least know what kind of party snacks you like?"

"Let's see." She tapped her chin with her forefinger. "I like chips and salsa… the really, really, *really* hot, kind of salsa."

"I'll have Mom pick some up from the store, just for you."

She gave me a loving squeeze and a sad smile. "It'll be all right, Crystal. I'll make it through this."

I nodded half-heartedly, feeling totally depressed by the change in my best friend. "I'd better be getting home, now. Remember, the party starts at eleven tomorrow morning."

"All right-y." She followed me to the door and opened it. "Wait!" She stuck her head out and looked both ways, and then motioned for me to step out. "I shall see you tomorrow."

"Okay," I mumbled, putting the glasses back on. The walk home seemed to last a million years, and I honestly didn't care if a reporter caught me, or not. I was too down-hearted to really care, anymore. I finally got home a few minutes later, sat on the front porch, and stared at the grass. I don't know how long I was out there, before I felt something wrap around my shoulders. "Yipe!" I yelped.

"It's just me." It was Mom. "Sorry to scare you, sweetie. I didn't realize you were so deep in thought." She took the sunglasses off my eyes, and seemed to be reading the pain in my soul. "What's wrong?"

This time the tears didn't just prick my eyes, they gushed down my cheeks, as I told Mom about my visit with Terra, and how she wasn't going to forgive her husband.

"Did she come right out and say she wasn't going to forgive him?" Mom asked, tenderly wiping away the tears from my face.

"No, ma'am, but I'm scared she will harbor hatred in her heart to the point of where she becomes nasty, and impossible to be around." More tears filled my eyes. "I… I don't want my best friend to become bitter."

Mom pulled me into her arms, and I rested my cheek against her shoulder. "All we can do right now for Terra, is pray. I know I've been telling you to pray a lot, for the past few weeks, but a little more won't hurt. She's been wounded deeply, by someone she loved and trusted."

"What would I pray?"

"Pray God heals her heart, and puts people in her life who will help her to remember the goodness in the human race, instead of the ugliness."

I straightened up. "Terra knows we're great people, and we like her a lot."

Mom smiled fondly at me and chuckled. "Yes, we do like her. Did you invite her to your birthday party, tomorrow?"

"Yes, ma'am. I asked her what kind of party snacks she likes, and apparently, she likes chips and salsa… but not just any salsa. It has to be the fiery hot salsa."

"Ooh!" Mom stuck her tongue out a little. "I guess I'd better pick up a fire extinguisher while I'm out shopping, later this afternoon." She smiled and patted my good arm. "Don't worry, honey. With a little prayer and time, Terra can get through this."

"Thanks, Mom." I smiled back.

"Crrryyysssttttaaalll!" Emma's loud call echoed throughout the house. A split second later, she hopped out on the front porch, clutching three dolls in her left arm, and holding a piece of paper in her right hand. "I made a list of some of the things we can do, tomorrow." She thrust the list in my face. "Here, take a look."

The first thing that jumped out at me was, 'Hopefully play with dolls. If Crystal's arm doesn't hurt too much.' I chuckled. "We shall see about the dolls, Em."

"Okay." She plopped down next to me. "What kind of drinks are you gonna' to have?" My sister and I passed the day making party plans together, and when I went to bed nine hours later, I kept feeling tingles of excitement about the upcoming day.

My sixteenth birthday dawned bright and early. I was the last one up and in the kitchen. Mom was at the stove making my favorite… Belgian waffles with chocolate chips in them.

"Happy birthday, Crystal." Dad came over. "You're sweet sixteen, and…" He planted the world's biggest kiss on the side of my cheek. "Kissed you are, me lass!"

"Brian! Chasing and kissing younger women!" Mom mockingly shook the spatula at him. "How dare you!" To me she added, "Happy birthday, Crystal."

"I dare very easily, I do." He winked at her, and then gave me a hug. "Happy birthday, dear."

"Thanks, Mom and Dad."

"Happy birthday, Prissy Crissy!" Emma yelled, charging into the room and knocking me into a chair as she threw herself on me.

"Thanks, Emmy." I hoped my spine was still intact. I'd finished pigging down my first waffle, just as the doorbell rang.

Faster than a shooting star zipping across the night sky, I tore for my bedroom and locked the door behind me. Part of me wanted to dive under the bed, like Emma would have done, however, I'm sixteen, and sixteen-year-olds don't hide under the bed like an ostrich hiding their head in the sand. I could hear Mom talking to whoever was at the door. It was too early for any guests to start arriving, and I did really wonder who it was. My phone rang. "Hello?"

"Crystal?" It was Mom. "Visitors for you."

"Why are you calling me? Can't you come and knock on my door?" I wanted to know.

"I figured you wouldn't come out if you knew you had guests, and calling you saves the time it would have taken me to walk down the hall and get you. So, come on out… and it's not a request."

I hate it when she says, 'it's not a request'. I stomped over to the door, and jerked it open. I purposefully dragged my feet to the kitchen, where I heard voices. *Who had Mom had let in? Some undercover newsperson, posing as an innocent pedestrian? No doubt, he had a camera carefully concealed somewhere on his person and would either take multiple pictures of me, or video tape a conversation with me… and before nightfall, have it playing on every news station across America.* I trudged into the kitchen, eyes on the floor.

"Happy birthday, Crystal."

Why did the soft voice sound so familiar? I dared to lift my head, and saw the Russells sitting at the kitchen table along with my parents. I stared dumbfounded at them, before blurting out, "What are you two doing here?" Everyone laughed heartily. It was the first time I'd ever heard Mr. Russell laugh, and it sounded like a donkey braying loudly. I chuckled softly.

"We heard about what happened, on the news," Mrs.Russell explained, as the laughter died down. "We wanted to come, and personally thank you for everything you've done."

I blushed and shuffled my feet nervously. "Gee, it wasn't all my doing, Mrs.Russell. Minx and Emma helped me."

"So your mother told me, and we've already thanked Emma. Now, alls we have to do is find Minx, and thank him." She came over and gave me a tender hug. It wasn't like the tight squeezes I'd been getting lately, but rather a gentle embrace, that said, 'Thank you!'.

Tears welled up in my eyes, and I regret to say some managed to run down my cheeks. I sniffled and blinked back the remaining tears. When she let go of me, I saw her own eyes were brimming over with tears. She gave a gentle laugh.

"Crystal." Mr. Russell nervously cleared his throat. "I think we owe you an explanation, as to why we suddenly skedaddled without a word a' warning. I feared Stellen was getting too close for comfort, and when he found out where we'd been hiding, I knew Carol wasn't going to be safe as long as the loon was out there. So, one nights, we's packed up everything, and left. I did think of leaving you a note, so you'd know we weren't skipping town 'cause I was guilty, but I never wrote it."

He looked down at his brown, work worn hands. "One thing I left outta' the story I told you, was my name ain't really Todd Russell. It's Samuel Crest. I changed it after I left prison, 'cause I knew Stellen wouldn't leave me be, and would hunt me down to make me do his dirty work." He clenched his hands into fists at his side and frowned ferociously.

"It's over now." Mrs. Russell laid a steadying hand on her husband's arm. "Stellen is behind bars."

So, Mr. Russell was the mysterious 'Crest' Emma and I kept seeing in the correspondence between the gang members. Samuel Crest, I silently tasted it on my tongue and found it rolled off much easier than Todd Russell. "I'm glad everything's over."

"We are, too. We brought you a little something." Mrs. Russell reached behind her and produced a present wrapped in bright pink wrapping paper.

"You didn't have to," I objected.

"We wanted to," Mr. Russell told us. He held it out to me. "You deserve it, gurl."

Emma came into the kitchen just then, and to everyone's surprise, walked right over to Mr. Russell. She stared up at him without saying anything for a few seconds, and then produced a bouquet of wild flowers from behind her back. A few more seconds passed, before she held them up to him. "These are for you," she said shyly.

Mr. Russell accepted the offering, a look of total shock on his face. He reached out very slowly and hesitantly, as if he was afraid Emma was going to bite him. When she didn't bat an eye, he placed his hand on her shoulder and drew her close to him for a one armed hug. She again surprised everyone by throwing her arms around his middle, and hugging him tightly.

"I guess nothing is impossible with You, God," I whispered, amazed my sister finally warned up to someone she considered to be the devil, himself.

"Your present," Mrs. Russell gently reminded me.

"Oh, right. Thanks." I awkwardly accepted the gift with one hand.

"Here." Dad stood up and offered me his chair. "Sit here, honey."

I suddenly felt incredibly shy, and wanted nothing more than to run back to the sanctuary of my room. I tried to ignore everyone staring at me, as I ripped the paper off my present. I stared at a copy of Carolyn Keene's very first book. It smelled musty and it looked almost ancient, with its forest green binding and grainy feeling. I already had a copy of this, and didn't know how to politely break it to the gift-givers without hurting their feelings.

"Open it," Mrs. Russell said, sounding like an eager girl at Christmas time.

I obeyed and scanned the first page. The words, 'First Edition', jumped out at me so fast, my head just about spun clean off my shoulders. "What? Where? How?" I couldn't frame a coherent sentence.

Everyone busted up laughing. "It was my mother's," Mrs. Russell explained. "I remembered how on your last visit to our house, you said Carolyn Keene was your hero, so I thought, 'What better way to reward you, than to give you a first edition of some of Carolyn Keene's work?'"

I couldn't accept this present. *Wouldn't Mrs. Russell want to keep it, for sentimental reasons? As a means to remember her mother?* As I looked up to object, her face was beaming with a happiness which made her look fifteen years younger. I got up and gave her a hug, and said in a choked voice, "Thanks a million, Mr. and Mrs. Russell."

"Would you like to stay for Crystal's party?" Emma asked them. "She's gonna' to have an ice cream cake, then there's the games and it's gonna' be loads and lots of fun."

"We wouldn't want to impose," Mr. Russell began.

"It wouldn't be imposing." Emma spoke the word slowly and carefully. "Please?"

"Please stay, Todd," Dad spoke up. "Unless your wife doesn't feel up to company, and would rather lay down to rest."

"I feel fine. We'd be honored to stay." Mrs. Russell smiled at my parents. "Thank you for asking."

"Are you hungry? We still have some left over waffles," Mom said.

The doorbell echoed throughout the house, and I looked at the clock hanging on the kitchen wall. *Why was everyone showing up, now? The party didn't start until eleven o' clock, and it was only nine o' clock.* "I'll get it," I said, hurrying to the door. I peeped through the peek hole in the door, and to my relief, it wasn't some pompous reporter, but Minx. I practically tore the door off its hinges as I flung it open. "Hey, Minx. You're here early."

"Yeah, I thought I could get here early and help with the decorations, since it seems like our detective is a little shorthanded." He playfully pinched the arm in the sling. "Or, is it short armed?"

"Oh, yeah?" I swung a punch at his head with my good hand, missing his hair by two inches.

"Hey, now!" He grabbed my arm and spun me around a little. He held out a present wrapped in Christmas paper. "I couldn't find any birthday wrapping paper, and decided this would have to do. I know jolly ol' Saint Nick usually don't come 'til Christmas, but he decided to come early this year, since you've been such a good girl."

I laughed, sounding like a giddy schoolgirl. "You can put the present over there." I motioned toward the coffee table, where the presents usually sat.

"But, I want you to open it now! I can't wait until everyone else gets here," Minx objected.

"It's only Granda, Terra, and a couple of aunts, uncles, and cousins coming, this year. I decided to have a big 'bash' with some classmates, later in the next week, or so. Come on into the kitchen."

We went into the kitchen and I made introductions. Minx had already met my family, but he hadn't met the Russells, yet. After the introductions were over, he again held out his present. "Would you please just open it, already?"

"It's not party time, yet," I told him.

"You opened our present to you, before it was party time," Mr. Russell spoke up, vigorously attacking his waffle. "One more, won't hurt."

"Yeah, c'mon, Crissy!" Emma coaxed.

My parents said I should open it up, as well. *What is this?* I thought, starting to rip Santa's face in half. *A conspiracy?* By the shape of the object, it looked like a book. I stopped and looked at Minx. "Is this another Carolyn Keene book?"

"Just open it," Dad urged me.

I complied, and what I saw caused me to squeal happily and throw my arms around Minx's neck. "Thank you! Thank you! Thank you!" I let him go and looked at the old movie in my hands. "I never knew they made a movie out of Carolyn Keene's second book, nor have I heard of Bonita Granville or John Litel." I looked at Dad. "Are they good actors?" The adults started laughing, and I wondered what was so funny.

"She asks if they're good actors, and the first person she looks at is you, Brian." Mr. Russell held his sides as he laughed.

"What cheek! She practically called me old, she did." Dad was laughing just as hard as Mr. Russell.

"This movie was made back in 1939," Mrs. Russell explained to me, in between chuckles. "It was made well before your dad was born."

"Oh." I felt myself blush. "I wasn't trying to call Dad old."

"We know you were, Crystal." Mom rubbed my arm, still laughing.

"Now, you know why I couldn't wait for you to open your present, with everyone else." Minx wore an ear-to-ear grin.

"Let's go watch it, Crystal!" Emma grabbed my arm and started tugging me to the den.

"I have to help get ready for the party." I tried in vain to jerk my arm free.

"Off with you, now." Dad waved me off. "Go have fun with your boyfriend, and be nice to your sister." He winked at me.

My heart was happy and light, as I raced to the den to turn the TV on. Minx helped me break the seal on the DVD case, and I popped the disc into the player. I fidgeted with impatience as the machine took its time in loading, and decided to grab some orange juice while waiting. As I went to the kitchen, I heard the grownups talking in low tones.

"Did they find it, yet?" It was Dad speaking.

"I don't know." Now, it was Mrs. Russell speaking, and her voice sounded puzzled. "It's been almost five years, and still no trace."

"The police have no leads, whatsoever?" Mom sounded dumbfounded.

"Nary a clue, and it don't look like they're even halfway interested," Mr. Russell drawled.

What were they talking about? I leaned closer to listen, without peeping around the doorframe to the kitchen.

"The only thing they have to go on, is a note crying out for help. Nothing else," Mrs. Russell sighed. "Part of me wants to give up. I just can't, because I know she's out there, somewhere. And I won't rest, until she's brought home safe."

"Maybe Crystal can help. She's good with those sorts of thin's," said Dad.

Good with what? And, what's going on, for heaven's sake? I thought impatiently.

"Crystal," Emma called, "the show's on."

Not wanting to be caught, I hurried back to the den. I settled down on the couch, and gave a sigh of pleasure. As the first few strains of music came from the television set, a shiver of excitement raced up my back. I could barely wait for the opening credits to end, and the picture to start rolling. I had taken my right arm out of the sling and found to my utmost delight, I could move it, somewhat. It still ached, but it felt great to get it out of the sling. Minx quietly plopped onto the couch beside me and placed a pillow between us, so I could keep my arm elevated during the show.

Dad came into the room with three plates of waffles. "At least finish your breakfast, while you watch the movie," he said, handing each of us a plate. The three of us thanked him, and after winking slyly in my direction, he disappeared in to the kitchen.

"You two look cute on the couch, there," Emma declared, stuffing a rather large piece of waffle in her mouth. She batted her eyes at me, while chewing her food. A sudden thought seemed to hit her, because she leaned forward and pointed her fork at Minx. "If you kiss her, Minxy, I'll sock you."

"Why, Emmy?" I cocked an eyebrow.

"'Cause, Daddy already kissed you today, and you can't be sweet sixteen and kissed twice!" she shot back.

Minx snorted a laugh and I rolled my eyes at my sister. As I watched the climax unfold in the movie, my mind was still pondering the events of the past thirty minutes.

Was this the happy ending that I'd been wanting for the past month? ...Or, was it the beginning to a whole new mystery?

The End

Excerpt:

Anything, But a Diamond

A Crystal O'Mally Mystery – Book 2

"Aw sheesh!" I blew out a frustrated breath. Night had fallen fast, and I couldn't see everything like I wanted to. Instead, I was limited to seeing whatever my sister aimed her beam of light at.

"What's wrong?" Emma shone the flashlight in my face.

"Don't do that." I angled the light away from me and on the ground, casting an annoyed glare at the half full moon. "The moon's not bright enough to where I can see where I'm going."

Emma aimed her flashlight at the moon.

"What are you doing?"

"Daddy said the moon reflects light, right?"

"Right." *Where was this going?*

"Well, I'm shining my light on the moon so it'll reflect the light, and it'll be brighter."

I bit back a laugh. "You're not close enough to the moon to make any difference."

"Hold this." She shoved the flashlight in my hands and before I could object, scampered up an oak tree standing right next to her. "I'll just shine the light from this tree."

"Emerald, come down here, right now," I ordered.

"Hey, Crystal, pass up the flashlight. I think I found something." Her voice was full of excitement.

I shone the light up in the leafy branches, until I caught sight of her holding something aloft. "Would you come down here, already?" I walked over and stood at the base of the tree.

"Catch!" She dropped whatever it was she was holding, and it hit me square in the face.

"Ugh!" I dropped the flashlight and jumped back, shaking the cold, wet object off myself. The flashlight lay on a root where it'd fallen, after taking its fall. Grumbling in disgust, I bent down to retrieve it, but stepped on something hard... and it crunched in a not so good way. It almost sounded like a fist getting broken. I snatched the flashlight, and bent down to find out what I was stepping on.

"Did you find it?" Emma asked, shimmying down the tree as fast as she could.

"Yeah. It's a soggy pouch." I turned it over and saw a broken zipper. I put my hand inside the bag and felt my eyes widen in surprise.

"What is it?" Emma thrust her hand inside as well, and withdrew a fistful of pearls. "Mrs. Lesler's necklaces!"

The tiger's eye I was holding, glittered like a cat's eye in the light. *Okay, Mrs. Lesler loses her jewels... and I find them... all in the same day? It's way too easy. And, God? About the little talk earlier... am I stuck solving stolen jewelry mysteries, for the rest of my career?*

A sudden, and loud, BOOM! exploded from the direction of the east pasture, followed by cows bellowing in fear, and the sound of a stampede.

I guess not!

Note from the author:

I hope you enjoyed 'The Diamond Caper '. Please visit me on Facebook at http://www.facebook.com/CrystalAndEmmasAdventures and at my blog, http://roseswritinggarden.blogspot.com/ for information on the release of 'Anything, But a Diamond', the second book in the Crystal O'Mally mystery series.

Leah Pugh

* * * *

Author Bio:

A graduate of the Institute for Childrens' Literature, and a current college student, Leah lives with her family in the rolling hills of Kentucky. When she's not working on homework, she's either playing with the family puppy or reading.

* * * *

Mystic Mustangs Publishing, LLC, provides a portion of proceeds to the Southwest Florida Rescue for Mustangs and horses that have been abandoned, neglected, or deemed untamable. Please visit http://www.swfl-rescue.com for more information on this humane non-profit organization and the publisher's website at http://www.mysticmustangsbooks.com.

Made in the USA
Charleston, SC
18 September 2013